# ON GOLDEN LAND

NAOMI P LANE

This is a work of fiction. Names, characters, places, and incidents are the product of the author's imagination or are used fictitiously. Any resemblance to actual persons, living or dead, events, or locales is entirely coincidental.


Cover design by Sophia J Mitchell

ISBN: (paperback) 978-1-7776602-0-8
ISBN: (eBook Edition) 978-1-7776602-1-5

*For my beautiful daughter and her crazy, adventurous life...*

# CONTENTS


PART I
Life Before Retirement

Chapter 1 — 3
*Andrea*

Chapter 2 — 6
*Paul and Jared*

Chapter 3 — 10
*Darlene and the Business*

Chapter 4 — 15
*Ryan and Talia*

Chapter 5 — 19
*Sonya and the Trip to Asia*

Chapter 6 — 25
*Retirement Beckons*

PART II
On Golden Land

Chapter 7 — 33
*Karl*

Chapter 8 — 37
*Building*

Chapter 9 — 42
*Completing Construction*

Chapter 10 — 47
*Finances*

Chapter 11 — 53
*Clay and Michelle*

Chapter 12 — 57
*Andrea's Health Crisis*

Chapter 13 — 61
*Troubles with Clay*

Chapter 14 — 66
*Christmas 2016*

Chapter 15 — 72
*Ryan Steps Out*

Chapter 16 77
*Paul's Father's Funeral*

Chapter 17 81
*Agricultural Production*

Chapter 18 86
*Clay's Wedding*

Chapter 19 90
*Talia's Yoga*

Chapter 20 94
*A Visit from Donovan*

Chapter 21 98
*Darlene's New Job*

Chapter 22 104
*Clay and Michelle Move Out*

Chapter 23 107
*The Pot Harvest*

Chapter 24 110
*Darlene's Troubles*

Chapter 25 114
*Pre-Xmas Ginger Harvest*

Chapter 26 120
*Jared's New Motorcycle*

Chapter 27 126
*Paul Volunteers*

Chapter 28 131
*Donovan Moves*

Chapter 29 135
*Talia and Jocelyn*

Chapter 30 139
*Marco Returns*

Chapter 31 145
*Ryan Exposed*

Chapter 32 150
*Talia's Love-life*

Chapter 33 155
*Accident at Paul's Shop Class*

Chapter 34 161
*Breaking the Silence*

Chapter 35 167
*Donovan's Wedding*

Chapter 36 173
*Karl's Health Crisis*

Chapter 37 178
*Ryan's Back*

Chapter 38 184
*Talia's Decision*

Chapter 39 188
*Karl's Recovery*

Chapter 40 193
*Less Ginger for Christmas*

Chapter 41 201
*Ryan and Talia Renew Their Vows*

Chapter 42 205
*Jared's Misadventure*

Chapter 43 211
*Andrea's Hunch*

Chapter 44 216
*The Trip*

Chapter 45 221
*Andrea Forgets*

Chapter 46 226
*Beginnings and Endings*

*About the Author* 233

# PART I

## LIFE BEFORE RETIREMENT

# CHAPTER 1
## ANDREA

Andrea Holbeck was a picture postcard California girl, with long blonde wispy hair, an athletic body, and tanned skin. She grew up in the suburbs in Torrance, L.A. in a white, middle class neighborhood, where her family lived in a mid-century modern stucco house with a single palm tree out front.

She had a little brother named Michael who died of leukemia when she was just six and he was four, so she had few memories of him. The first was a memory of pushing him on the little swing-set in the back yard and him yelling, "Up Rea, up Rea," when he wanted to go higher. The other memory was of him standing in her bedroom doorway just staring at her, dragging his blanket, as she played out a whole scene of Barbies with much animated dialogue. She hadn't even realized he was there watching her because he didn't say a word. This is how she usually pictured him in her mind, and he would continue to visit her, standing and staring like this, whenever she was in trouble throughout her life.

The first time she saw him, she was twelve. She got pummeled by a wave while surfing and felt herself pulled under. She had swallowed a mouthful of seawater and started to panic. Suddenly Michael was standing there calmly in front of her, and she relaxed and swam towards him. When she reached the surface, he was gone and she was choking and spluttering, but otherwise okay.

She struggled with whether or not to share this with her mother. Nor did she share with her friends; she feared their reaction and didn't want to be dubbed a freak. She was worried it might upset her mother and reopen the trauma of Michael's death. She would wait another ten years to share, when her mother was stronger, and she would take it as a happy sign that her son was okay and protecting his sister.

Because of her brother's passing and her mother's infinite sadness permeating her life, Andrea became somewhat of an empath and caregiver around women and children. She never understood why her mother didn't try to have another child and she never got up the nerve to ask. She just soldiered on, supporting her mother's fragile being as best she could.

She had always been creative in school and loved drawing, crafts and sewing and had a natural aptitude. As a kid, she could spend hours coloring or beading bracelets for her friends and was a contented soul.

She became more socially outgoing when she took up surfing in grade seven. After school, she would often head to the beach with her surfboard to catch a wave and hang with her friends. She had a calm aura about her, which drew people in and was always a good listener, so her friends valued her advice. Through her teen years, there were many bonfires on the beach, and she became more socially outgoing.

Boys were also drawn to her for her natural beauty. She had a few serious boyfriends but was never promiscuous. She always sought out a true friend and soulmate to connect with on a deeper level. She was just not a one-night-stand kind of girl and she had unintentionally broken a few hearts along the path to growing up.

When it came time for college, she chose to follow her creative passion and go into fashion design. She was drawn to creating lavish costume pieces, so by the time she graduated and went to their career placement fair, she had amassed a small collection of period pieces she had created around favorite historical book characters. One of the film studios took note and offered her a job. She was thrilled at first, but then realized that she really wanted to take some time off for herself after so many years of school. So, she politely declined the position and told them she would get back in touch in a year to see if they still had any openings.

She wanted to get out of her parents' house, so in 1984, she decided to head up to northern California to look for a job in the Emerald Triangle harvesting marijuana. Her parents weren't too thrilled, but she convinced them it was simply to get away from the city for a while and earn some rent to get her own place when she came back.

She packed up a giant back-pack full of clothes and toiletries and caught the Greyhound bus up north to Humboldt. It only took two days in a hostel to find work, as there were postings on a board in the local café asking for laborers. After making a few calls, and completing one telephone interview, she landed a starting position in a weed cutting room.

On the third morning she was picked up bright and early in a red Ford pick-up truck by an older woman named Jean, whose exuberant energy, sun-cracked skin and unruly hair, tied up in a bandana, was a testimonial to outdoor work. They wound their way up into the mountains on switchback roads for an hour and Jean talked her ear off explaining the shared accommodations, hourly pay rate and meal arrangement. Andrea was looking forward to getting her hands dirty and breathing the fresh air outside the city for a while.

# CHAPTER 2
## PAUL AND JARED

Paul Stevens and Jared Copeland met in high school in Sacramento California in 1980. They played on the senior soccer team together. They both came from idyllic middle-class suburban households in this paradisiacal city six hours inland from the Pacific Ocean. They bonded over girls and dirt bikes and hung out with the same group of friends.

Paul was the more outgoing of the two. He loved to play guitar and sing at parties and was naturally charming, with blonde surfer hair and blue eyes. Jared was darker, quieter and more introspective. He approached life cautiously and often deferred to Paul before joining into any adventure.

When high school ended, Paul went off to UCLA to study biosciences, while Jared joined the Army. Paul had tried desperately to talk him out of it, but Jared was determined to serve his country as his father had done before him. Paul was worried his friend would die overseas in some struggle that wasn't his. These fears seemed founded when Jared was sent to Bosnia as part of the peacekeeping force in 1995 after the war ended and the Dayton Accords were signed. Luckily his friend came home safely a year later, but not without seeing a lot of ugly shit.

When Jared returned stateside, Paul had just finished his degree.

They decided to head to the Emerald Triangle in Northwest California to try their hand at cultivating marijuana. They got hired on at a well-established farm and Paul helped improve their facilities and techniques with some modern horticulture methods he has learned in college. Jared was mostly working grunt labor, planting, harvesting and bagging product as well as maintaining buildings. He had a natural ability to fix and repair structures since his father had a large workshop, which he had grown up using.

There were about twenty people living on the farm and they really enjoyed this communal lifestyle. When a beautiful blonde girl from L.A. joined the group, Paul was instantly smitten. Her name was Andrea Holbeck, and her big brown eyes drew him in like pools of liquid gold. She had long straight hair that she tied back in a loose ponytail and lovely tanned skin that he longed to touch.

On the second day, the boss tasked Paul with showing Andrea the cutting room and getting her started. He was thrilled. He started joking immediately.

"So, you need to pull your chair up really close to me so you can see what I'm doing," he said, grabbing the arm of her chair and sliding her right beside him. He grinned at her like a puppy dog who had just been offered a treat. She started laughing.

"Okay so you get two sets of trimming shears, because they will get sticky with resin. Then put on these gloves, or if you hate the gloves, there's coconut oil here to rub on your hands so they will come clean afterwards. Now grab a tray and a branch. Hold the base of the branch and trim off all the fan leaves, like this. Then cut the bud off the branch. Now trim all these little crow's feet, we call these near the bottom and the tiny leaves working your way up. Also trim off these red pistils that don't have any trichomes on them. After you do five, walk over to this table and put them into the jars like this. Dump the scrap leaves from your tray into this bin. We use them for baking and making edibles. There's a washing station over here with alcohol wipes for cleaning your shears. Okay gorgeous? Any questions?"

Andrea blushed. "Yah, I think I got it. Are you staying here to help me?"

"Sure, I'll stay for a while until you get comfortable. Then there are five others coming who can help you too. I have to go back to irrigation in a bit. So, tell me Andrea, where are you from?"

"I grew up in LA, or in Torrance more specifically. My parents still live there."

"Cool, I come from Sacramento. So, we are both Cali kids. Nice. What brings you up here then?"

"Well, I just finished my degree in fashion design, and I even had a job offer in the film industry, but I wanted to take a year off before joining the rat race, so I decided to come up here."

"I totally get that," said Paul. "That's a lot of school. I'm doing the same thing, except this actually fits in with my degree in horticulture. I'm kind of a big deal around here you know," he smirked.

Andrea laughed. "You are a big deal in your own mind bro," she said.

She was determined not to get into a relationship but as soon as she met Paul, she knew she was in trouble. He was so hot, muscular, and blonde, with those blue eyes and outgoing personality. He would sing and play guitar every night after dinner and make everyone laugh. Her heart was doomed to fall for him in no time. They were simply relaxed and easy together and there was never any angst. It didn't take long before they were shacked up in one corner of the bunk house, away from all the others. Even without total privacy, their relationship blossomed, and they fell in love.

Andrea even felt safe enough with Paul to tell him about dead her brother's appearances in her life. Paul believed her and took it in stride, which further cemented their bond as a couple. After that, she knew she could share anything with him, and he would always be supportive.

A magical year of youth, sex, and sunshine passed quickly for Paul and Andrea, but Jared was getting restless. One night, he had a long talk with Andrea and Paul and the three of them decided to head back to L.A. together. Andrea's family would let them stay in the basement for a month to get settled and find work. She got in touch with her old contacts and started a job in costume design for a movie studio. Paul and Jared went into banging nails in construction. The three of them pooled their money to buy a used car so the boys could drop Andrea off at her transit hub every morning and then get to the job site. After a month, they rented a two-bedroom apartment and settled into their new adult lives.

# CHAPTER 3

## DARLENE AND THE BUSINESS

The construction company had an office where they would go pick up their paychecks every two weeks. The girl at reception was called Darlene and she had big brown eyes with long lashes, short spiky hair in a pixie cut, and very nice curves. Jared had been flirting with her for months. She reminded him of Betty Boop. Paul finally coerced him into asking her out. The next day, he brought her brought her a pastry for her coffee break and mustered the nerve.

"Say, Darlene, I was wondering if you might like to grab dinner with me one day after work?"

She kept her eyes on her paperwork and blushed. "Sure Jared, I think that sounds nice. What day did you have in mind?"

"I don't know, how about tomorrow? I could text you when we wrap things up at the job site?"

"Sure, that sounds fine. I'll see you tomorrow then."

They went to a casual steak house that was always busy and when they got their drink order, Jared began to pry.

"So, tell me about your background Darlene. Where are you from originally?"

"I grew up in Brooklyn and my folks and my younger brother Ryan are still there. I came to the west coast to go to business college. I stayed with my Aunt Liz, who lives in Mission Viejo. She is a super sweet and we are really close."

"Nice, well I guess you already know that Paul and I come from Sacramento, right?"

"Yah, I pretty much had to run background checks on you when you joined the company," she smiled, "so I know about your military service too. That must have been hard."

"Well, I saw some ugly shit, but it's what I signed up for so…"

"Well, I'm just glad you came home in one piece," said Darlene.

"Me too girl," he sighed and changed the subject. "Let's order, I'm starving!"

So began their relationship. As Jared got to know Darlene better, he fell in love with her generous heart. She was very gentle and sweet. She would always look out for other people's feelings, even strangers on the street. She would give money or food to panhandlers or ask old people if they needed help with their groceries. This was the kind of woman he wanted to be with.

Two months later, Darlene left her aunt's place and moved in with the three of them. They became a foursome that did everything together, from work to living together and socializing. They were remarkably compatible and there was usually consensus on most issues.

After six months of working for the construction firm, Jared was feeling disgruntled with the foreman, a big gruff man named Joe. He always nitpicked their work and gave them shit for having a beer on site after work. He was a rules guy and Jared was getting tired of being micro-managed every second. One day he'd made Jared stop installing sheets of drywall and redo a couple of floor joists that looked slightly crooked. That was the last straw for Jared.

When they got home that evening, Jared convinced Paul that they could start their own contracting business using Darlene's office management skills. They could hire their own crew and bid on their own contracts. They had learned enough to order supplies and subcontract out the plumbing and electrical. After a long discussion over many beers, they decided to quit and go out on their own.

They hired six guys to start, all with experience, and bought a single lot to develop with their savings plus a bank loan. Jared and Darlene got married, more to set up a family firm status for tax purposes than anything else. They did love each other to bits and their families were both thrilled, but they didn't really care about the piece of paper. The did the deed casually at City Hall with their parents as witnesses and had a barbeque party in the back courtyard of their building.

At work, Paul became the foreman who ordered the other guys around on site. After the first year of building and flipping single lots, they had made a healthy profit and decided to scale up and build multi-unit townhomes.

Then, Paul and Andrea got pregnant and also decided to get married. They welcomed a baby girl the following spring named April and moved into their own house. They were all living the good life and would hang out on weekends in Paul and Andrea's back yard with friends for dinners and drinks. Darlene wanted a child too, but unfortunately, she had three miscarriages before her doctor told her it would probably never happen due to chronic uterine cysts.

Instead, they decided to try foster parenting a young child. They took in a little Hispanic boy named Carlos who was five years old whose mother was a drug addict and whose father was nowhere to be found.

Jared loved having Carlos around the house as his new sidekick. He took him everywhere to see all the educational sites around the city like science exhibits, the aquarium and theme parks. They went to ball games and kids' movies and camped in a tent in the backyard. Jared was instantly a super-dad and Darlene found it so endearing to watch. Carlos gradually opened up and started to laugh more. He enjoyed kindergarten at their local school, and they began inviting kids from class over for playdates. Everything was going remarkably well.

Then came the shock they hadn't expected. Carlos' mother got herself clean and wanted him back. The social worker said she could start with supervised visits once a week and gradually increase her time with him. Darlene kept trying to cheer Jared up by saying the mother would probably relapse and be out of the picture again before too long, but she was wrong. Jared was devastated when Carlos was eventually returned to his mother's custody. The social worker arranged for Jared to spend time with the boy once a week as a transition period, but eventually the mother took him back to Guadalajara to be with her family.

Jared moped around for months, lamenting why they hadn't adopted him when they had the chance. Darlene couldn't seem to console him. It was a difficult time for their marriage, and she felt like a failure for not being able to have a child. They decided to go for counseling and made a joint decision to let the idea of adoption go, once and for all.

Jared and Paul's business continued to be successful now and they were making good money. Darlene was still their office manager and they had increased their staff to twenty people. Andrea had taken a few months of maternity leave with April and loved being a new mom.

In 1995, Paul wanted a change in the business structure so that he had full partnership status, instead of having Jared and Darlene on title as the owners. He had initially accepted his role; he was after all the highest paid employee as site foreman. But now it seemed unfair. Since he had started the business with Jared from the outset, he deserved to be an owner, especially if something happened and they needed to sell.

This became a bone of contention with Jared and Darlene for a while. They didn't want the hassle of changing the business structure on paper, with all its tax and legal implications. Tempers flared and it seemed like their friendship might implode under the pressure. Finally, they all agreed and hired a corporate lawyer to sort it all out. Jared became an owner and Darlene agreed to become an employee. Peace was restored and the business continued to thrive.

Paul and Andrea went on to have a son named Donovan. He was also a blonde-haired, blue-eyed baby like his father and Andrea and Paul were thrilled to have "one of each". Andrea once again took some time off work to raise the babies and often visited her parents, who naturally spoiled them to bits. Andrea started taking an interest in making her kids' baby clothes at this time. It was a hobby that would serve her well later in life.

In1993, Andrea and Paul left their two small children with

Andrea's parents for three weeks and together with Jared and Darlene, they went on a grand European tour. They lamented not doing this before having children, but were thrilled to be there, nonetheless. For this short period, they felt like teenagers again with no responsibilities. They ate and drank their way across Europe by rail and sunbathed naked on the Cote d'Azur. They visited the amazing galleries of Italy and rode mopeds in the crowded streets. They danced drunk on the tables in Greece. When they left, they all felt sad that their escape was over, and they had to return to the real life of business and kids.

# CHAPTER 4
## RYAN AND TALIA

Now Darlene's younger brother, Ryan, had just graduated college back in Brooklyn in electrical engineering and wanted to come out west and stay with her until he could find work and get set up. Paul and Jared liked the idea of hiring him as their own in-house electrician and he agreed. So, he stayed with his sister and Jared, sleeping in Paul and Andrea's old room for the first two months. When he had saved up enough for a damage deposit and first month's rent, got his own place. He was a quiet guy and very hard-working, so he fit right in. Darlene was thrilled to have her "little" brother living close by because they had always been close growing up.

Ryan had dark curly hair and green eyes and was of average height and build. The only striking thing about him was his smile. He had large teeth and his two eye teeth were prominent so that when he smiled, he appeared assertive and confident. This drew people in, and they often struck up conversations with him, even when he often wanted to be left alone. It was a strange combination. He was an introvert who looked like an extrovert and this challenged him his whole life.

One morning, Ryan was eating breakfast at the local diner when a woman sat down beside him at the counter and asked him to pass the sugar. She had striking deep set amber eyes and long curly auburn hair pulled back neatly from her face in a barrette which made it cascade down her back. She was slim and graceful with light brown skin. (He would later learn that she was bi-racial; her father was black, and her mother was white.) Ryan was fascinated by her raspy voice and take-charge demeanor; she wasn't shy about initiating conversation.

"So, I see you like doing crossword puzzles. I don't have the patience for that," she said.

"It's the only time I get to read," he said. "I work with my hands all day. I'm an electrician."

"Oh, that's a good job," she said, "you will always find work in that trade. Good for you."

"What do you get up to?" he asked.

"I'm a choreographer for music videos," she said.

"Wow, you must get to meet famous people?"

"Some," she said.

"Like who?" he asked.

"Well, I have to sign non-disclosure agreements before I can work with anyone big, you understand."

"Sure, sure, no problem," Ryan changed the subject. "Do you live around here?" he asked.

"Yah, right around the corner actually. Listen Ryan, it was great to meet you, but I've gotta fly. Work starts in thirty minutes downtown. If you feel like it, give me a call sometime."

She took out a pen from her purse, jotted a note, and slid him her business card: Talia Houser, professional choreographer, dancer, video and commercial production, Los Angeles. When he turned it over, her phone number was on the back.

"Sure, thanks. It was great meeting you too. Have a good day at work," and she was gone.

He told his sister about her that evening and she encouraged him to ask her out. They went on a few dates and really connected. After a few months of dating, he moved into her place. She made it clear to him that she never wanted to have children right from the start because she had a schizophrenic brother and was afraid this trait would be passed down to her children. She had seen her parents go through too much strife and didn't want any part of it. Ryan was not concerned. He loved her and that was all he cared about.

After a year together, Ryan proposed to Talia and they held a small wedding on the beach at sundown. Ryan and Darlenes' parents, flew out from Brooklyn to join them for a few days and then they took a quick honeymoon in Cabo.

Because children were not an option for Talia, they settled on a big German shepherd called Mojo as a suitable replacement. Mojo followed Ryan everywhere and became a fixture on the jobsite.

Then there came another major setback. When Ryan was thirty-two years old, he was driving to a job site one morning along the Santa-Monica highway, when the unthinkable happened. A five-ton rental truck with an inexperienced driver pulled out of a rest area without giving himself enough leeway to get up to speed. He cut Ryan off as he came around the bend doing the speed limit and couldn't hit the brakes fast enough. He smashed right into the back of the truck. His car was totaled, and he was taken by ambulance to the nearby hospital.

His injuries were severe. He had a broken right leg, a fractured pelvis, three cracked ribs and spinal compression in his lower four disks. Luckily, there was no head trauma. Talia came as fast as she could and then Paul, Andrea, Darlene and Jared joined her. They waited through a lengthy surgery on the leg to reset his tibia and fibula correctly and put pins in. When he came out, the doctor explained that his pain level would be severe for months and they would have to manage it carefully to avoid addiction to opioids.

Talia was understandably a wreck and Darlene went to stay with her for the first week to take care of Mojo while she was at the hospital. Two weeks later, the doctor has a hospital bed delivered to their home and Ryan was released to recuperate with a nurse visiting for a while to make sure he was coping with self-care routines, like using a walker to get to the bathroom and self-dosing the pain meds carefully. It was an incredibly stressful time.

Darlene, being Ryan's brother, wanted to be included in his recovery plan. She had attended several meetings with Talia at the doctor's office, so she knew what to do to spell her off for a break. Talia really appreciated all Darlene's love and support, otherwise she would have lost her mind. However, things got tense when the two women disagreed on care options. Darlene believed whole-heartedly in traditional medicine, whereas Talia was more open to trying New Age treatments. She wanted to rent a barometric chamber to speed up his healing process. Darlene thought that was ridiculous. She wanted to try an electro-stim machine to stimulate his muscles, but Darlene thought the physio exercises were sufficient. Talia wanted to try CBD oil as a pain therapy, but Darlene worried that this would interact dangerously with his pills. The two women almost came to blows one day as this bickering reached a boiling point. Jared had to intervene and tell his sister to back off. After all, technically his wife was his legal representative in these matters anyhow. His sister needed to let go of the reigns.

It took a full year before Ryan could work again. He did gain back good mobility, but he would never run or play sports again. Luckily, Paul and Jared had set up a good medical insurance plan for their employees, but Ryan was deemed at fault for rear-ending the truck, so there was no settlement coming his way. They had survived on Talia's income and the insurance and had used up whatever nest egg of savings they had in the bank. Their friends continually offered to help them out with money, but they always refused. They did not want to feel indebted to anyone.

So, the six friends were now three connected couples now living in L.A. in the early nineteen-nineties. Life went back to normal, and their careers were going very well and the future looked bright.

# CHAPTER 5

## SONYA AND THE TRIP TO ASIA

Talia met a feisty new co-worker on the set of a commercial shoot. Her name was Sonya, and she was a tiny spitfire of energy with curly brown hair, beady sharp brown eyes and a petite muscular build. She was an actress and stand-up comedienne who also moonlighted as a waitress in a bar and did some freelance comedy writing. Talia immediately liked her, and they ended up becoming besties and hanging out a lot. Ryan liked her too and they would often go see her perform at local comedy clubs after work. Sonya soon became part of their inner circle.

Sonya liked to have a few cocktails after her comedy set, but a few started turning into five or six highballs every night and Talia grew concerned about her friend's drinking. Eventually, she got up the nerve to confront her about it one Saturday morning over coffee.

"So, I want to talk to you about something, but it's a little touchy," said Talia.

"Okay, well I have a pretty thick skin so fire away," said Sonya.

"Well, I have noticed that you have been drinking quite a bit lately?" Talia said.

"Yah so, what's the harm? Everyone likes to have a good time once in a while, right?"

"Sure, but not every night. You have been hitting it pretty hard for the past month or so, don't you think? What if you can't go without it?"

"I'm not an addict, Talia. I can stop any time I like," Sonya said.

"Okay, prove it. I'll bet you can't go one week without booze."

"Screw you, Talia. You're not my mother. I'll do whatever I damn well please!" She got up and left the café.

Sonya refused to see Talia for the next month. Finally, they reconciled after Sonya woke up in a strange bed with a guy from the club who she didn't know and couldn't remember how she got there. She reached out to Talia and admitted that she had a problem. Talia dragged her to an AA meeting and made sure she got a sponsor. Sonya even took a time out from comedy gigs to work on her sobriety and focused more on her writing and acting.

Talia really wanted to travel, especially to Asia to visit all the various temples of the Far East. She was interested in Buddhism and was drawn to its various permutations across different countries. However, her husband Ryan could not get on board with this plan, as work was really busy, and he didn't want to let Paul and Jared down. So, it was a happy coincidence that hey decided she might have to go with a female friend, which was perfect timing for Sonya's sobriety.

So, in late 2005, the two women decided to go to Asia together. Sonya had remained sober since she started attending AA meetings. It was the perfect opportunity for her to get away from her present surroundings and clear her head. She was also a hilarious travel companion and Talia felt lucky to bring her along.

Talia and Sonya were both frugal, so they planned to travel cheaply. In November, they flew into Hong Kong and then transferred planes to Phnom Penh, Cambodia. It was a grueling flight and they arrived exhausted with sore backs from sitting too long.

Pushing out of the busy airport into the crowded heat of midday, they were hit with all the colors and smells of the open-air markets and restaurants. Each pulling a compact wheelie suitcase behind them, they used their GPS to locate the address of the Airbnb they had booked. It was a ten-minute walk, but they were already sweating by the time they arrived.

They rang the bell to what looked more like a small office block, but nobody responded. A pretty young girl of about ten was playing pick-up-sticks with a friend in the alley. She looked up from her game and came running over. In broken English she said, "You lady Sonya? Come, come."

She pulled a key from her dress pocket, unlocked the door, and led them up two flights of stairs. They passed a nail studio in the hallway and she unlocked the door at the end to reveal a barren-looking room with a counter, a sink, a two-burner hot plate and kettle, a small table with two chairs, and two twin beds. It was as basic as could be but would serve their needs. At least there was an air conditioning unit stuck in the window that kept it cool. Then she led them across the hall to a washroom with a separate WC and shower. It was very minimalist, but clean. They wondered how many other people might be sharing this but didn't have the language to ask. Sonya offered the girl eight US dollars for the first night, but she refused to take it. They assumed her mother or father would deal with the account later on. She gave them the key and left.

After a shower and a nap, Talia and Sonya went out to find food. They exchanged some American dollars for riel at a window that looked reasonable and then found something that looked like rice noodles with vegetables and sauce. They ordered two plates and some coconut water. It was delicious and not too spicy. Then they walked through the closest market and bought some snacks, drinks and instant coffee, and coconut milk. They located a tuk-tuk stand around the corner and sat on a patio going through their list of which temples they wanted to visit here in the city. They planned to stay here for a week and then catch a one-hour flight east to Ho Chi Minh City for five days, then back to Siem Reap airport to visit Angkor Wat for two days and finally head west on to Bangkok for the last week. They already had the airline tickets.

After sleeping like logs and drinking a Nescafé with some biscuits and fruit, they caught a tuk-tuk to see Ounalom Pagoda and the nearby Royal Palace. The pagoda temple was bright with its yellow walls and orange rooves. Talia and Sonya knew to dress respectfully, so had switched their tank tops for loose fitting cotton dresses that covered below the knee. They removed their shoes and sun hats and entered by stepping with their left foot first, as custom dictated. Inside the temple was a giant marble Buddha in the center surrounded by flowers, fruit, and burning incense. They bowed with their palms facing inward as two monks in orange robes passed by smiling at them. Then they sat with other visitors on a small carpet and took in the scene in silence for about twenty minutes. Talia felt for the first time that she had truly arrived and was fulfilling a lifelong dream. She breathed deeply and tried to appreciate her feeling of gratitude in that moment.

After finding some lunch, they hopped over to the Royal Palace to see the emerald Buddha under its golden canopy. Never had they seen such a beautiful piece of stone. Sonya pulled her along to find a cold drink outside the temple because the afternoon heat was stifling. Sonya wrote in her journal, keeping up a daily travel log as they sipped their mango-coconut smoothies in the shade. Then they headed back to their cool room for a nap. The little girl, whose name was Botum, came back with her mother Chenda to collect the week's rent. She wanted cash only, apparently not having a credit card machine, so Sonya ran across the street to the currency exchange and brought back the full amount, along with a bag of candy for Botum.

The next day they visited Wat Langka, with its intricate marble carvings in all the walls and golden sleeping buddha. This time they brought oranges to place on the altar, being careful to use only their right hand. A group of school children in uniform came through and Talia remarked on how beautiful they were, with their shiny black hair, brown skin and white smiles. For a moment she felt sad that she never had children.

Sonya wanted to explore the market next and dared Talia to try some strange foods, like crickets and raw gooey duck (giant clam). They plugged their noses and washed it down quickly with a Coke, grimacing in disgust. Then they found something more palatable for a late lunch, tried on a few dresses and went back to their cool room to journal about their trip thus far and take a nap. That night they danced in a nearby club that was filled with ex-pats. Sonya wanted to bring an Australian guy back to their place, but Talia told her to grow up and keep it in her pants. She was fifty-three, but still a wild woman.

The fourth day they visited Wat Phnom with its two giant lion statues out front and magnificent gardens. Talia told Sonya that she would like to spend the afternoon alone in meditation before they left. Sonya was fine with that because she wanted to go shopping for a dress and some souvenir gifts, so they split up.

Sonya bought a cheap bamboo mat and headed back to the gardens, which were shady and beautiful. She found a comfortable cross-legged position and sat for two hours in contemplation near a pond. She let her mind float away into stillness and had an epiphany. She realized that her life was in transition and she was entering a new chapter. She felt an immense love for Ryan and gratitude that he had encouraged her to travel and spend this time alone in self-discovery. She felt more certain than ever that she wanted to grow old with him. Then she focused on the lotus flowers in the pond and tried to clear her mind of all thought, until she felt only calm and in peace.

The next day, it was time to catch their flight to Ho Chi Minh City. This time their accommodations were a lot nicer. The Airbnb was a real apartment with a couch and tv and its own bathroom. They were thrilled. The food was delicious, and everything was so cheap. They spent five days exploring this Vietnamese city and took a short trip to the oceanside port of Vung Tao to spend a day at the ocean. The natural surroundings were incredibly beautiful, and the ocean looked bright green. The Vietnamese people were so friendly, and they met a couple of women from Tulsa who invited them to spend an evening dancing at a local disco. Talia checked in with Sonya first that she would be okay to go to a nightclub and not drink alcohol. She was fine with it and just ordered virgin drinks all night. The next day, they were sad to leave but had a flight to catch back to Siem Reap.

Angkor Wat was amazing, and two days was barely enough time to explore its many nooks and crannies. They paid a very polite young Cambodian man to be their tour guide because he knew so much about the history and culture and they didn't want to miss anything important. This twelfth century temple was built by the King of the Khmer Empire and was originally a Hindu temple honoring Vishnu, but later on became a Buddhist site. The sandstone was gradually eroding over time, which was sad considering the beauty of its intricate carvings. The giant fig trees encircled the temple and seemed to be creeping their way inside the structures, as if the passage of time were strangling the past.

After two days, they left to catch their flight to Bangkok, feeling overwhelmed by the beauty they had witnessed. Their final destination offered a lovely shared mini hotel with eight rooms. Their hosts were ex-pat Brits, so there was no language barrier. They really enjoyed the shared kitchen and dining room because they met other travelers from Sweden, Spain and Canada to share their meals and chat with. Sonya spent the night in one of the Swedish fellow's rooms after they went out dancing with him and his friend. Talia made it clear from the start that she was happily married to avoid any uncomfortable situations. The two women enjoyed delicious food, a Thai massage and a traditional dance show while they were there.

They left Thailand after a week feeling happy and fulfilled. It had been a wonderful trip that had met all Talia's hopes and expectations. On the flight back home, she realized how lucky she was to have a friend like Sonya. They were so compatible and comfortable with each other after many years. After their extremely long journey home, she fell into Ryan's arms at LAX and wept. He panicked and thought there was something wrong, but they were tears of joy.

# CHAPTER 6

## RETIREMENT BECKONS

The years between 2005 and 2015 were the busy child rearing years for Paul and Andrea. April and Donovan consumed all their time outside of work. They were a typical loving California family with all the usual moments of joy and stress.

Both their children were born blonde and blue-eyed like Paul, but Donovan's hair had turned sandy- colored and thick, whereas April's stayed straight and wispy. They were both athletic and popular, with many friends, but April was more reserved and thoughtful than her brother, who tended to dive in without thinking sometimes. They were two years apart and very close. They looked out for each other at school and in social circles.

When April got her tonsils out in grade two, Donovan took all the money out of his piggy bank and bought her a hamster. Paul and Andrea were touched by this and April named it Pika, after Pikachu, and adored her pet. When it died a year later, Donovan helped her bury it in the back yard, complete with a shoebox coffin, buttercups, and a solemn poem. Paul and Andrea took a video for posterity.

The family had a crisis when Donovan got acute appendicitis in grade seven. Paul and Andrea were called and came running when he collapsed in pain on the soccer field. His sister was crying in the waiting room while he had surgery that night. Andrea comforted her in the waiting room and she finally fell asleep on her mother's shoulder. Andrea saw her dead brother Michael staring at her from the corner of the waiting room for a few brief seconds and jolted awake as the doctor came to tell them Donovan's surgery was successful.

April waited on her brother hand and foot for the first couple of days, making him toast and chocolate milk and changing his CD's for him. It was quite adorable. He was feeling better in a week and went back to school.

Things got a little more serious in their teens. April became interested in a senior in grade nine and Andrea and Paul had to step in and send him packing. They did not approve of a sexually active fourteen-year-old and reminded this boyfriend that he was bordering on statutory rape because he would be turning eighteen soon. They told him to let her down easy and move on. She was naturally heartbroken, but never figured out that her parents had interfered.

Then Donovan started using drugs in grade eleven and things got ugly with his parents. The third time they found ecstasy in his bedroom, they kicked him out of the house and Paul asked Jared and Darlene to offer him their spare room for a while. This lasted three months and with some careful mediation by Jared, Donovan agreed to stop using drugs in exchange for a promise to let him go to college out of state. Donovan had always wanted to go to New York and Darlene said her parents would let him stay with them for the summer after he graduated until his dorm room was ready. He could find a part-time job and get settled. Paul and Andrea had their son back for his final year of high school and he was excited about the future. He wanted to study kinesiology and become a physiotherapist.

Before the kids left home to pursue further education, Andrea decided to share with them her secret about her brother Michael's "appearances". She was worried about how they would react, but they were very open-minded and supportive of their mom. They admonished her for not telling them sooner, like there was a part of their mother's life they had missed out on. Andrea hugged them close and told them she had been scared that she would come off as a flake.

Donovan left for college and settled into life in New York quite easily. He was very social, like his father, so he had no trouble making friends. He worked as a bike courier two days a week while attending college and was doing well in his program. He lived in the dorms the first year, but then rented a tiny apartment with two friends. Life was fun and exciting.

Meanwhile, April had already started a computer programming degree at UCLA. She had a natural aptitude for math and tech and was doing well in her coursework. She would eventually graduate with honors and get a job in Silicon Valley.

Paul and Andrea were in their mid-fifties now and couldn't believe their kids were grown. Their daughter April met an Indian colleague named Sim, short for Simarjeet, and they had fallen in love. They were married in a lavish Indian ceremony and soon thereafter, became parents to a lovely little girl named Krishna. Paul and Andrea were suddenly grandparents, and they were over the moon.

Unfortunately, the next few years brought much sadness to Andrea and Paul and their four best friends, as their elderly parents began needing care. Paul and Jared had to make frequent trips to Sacramento to empty their family homes, deal with their financial and legal matters, and move their parents into care homes.

Andrea's father got bladder cancer and she was often leaving work to take him to chemo over the course of two years. Her brother Michael appeared several times while she was at the hospital visiting her dad. She had never told her father about these sightings; her mother had asked her not to because he was a fairly conservative guy who probably wouldn't accept the idea that his dead son was still hanging around. He finally succumbed and she regretted not sharing this with him. Andrea had to help her mother adjust to living alone and eventually, sell the family home and downsize into assisted living.

In 2014, Ryan and Darlene had to fly home suddenly to New York after their father had a heart attack. He died shortly thereafter, and they invited their mother out to California to live with Darlene and Jared. The adjustment was hard, but she was a sweet lady who was easy to live with. She helped around the house and walked the dog when they were working. Unfortunately, two years later she had a stroke and also went into a care home. When she died, Darlene and her brother, Ryan, held a moving tribute in their backyard with some old friends from New York in attendance.

Talia's father had already died some years earlier, but her mother developed MS and became quite impaired in her mobility. Talia and Ryan took her in for a year, but eventually she also needed more complex care. She died in 2015.

It was a decade of tremendous loss for all of them. As they approached retirement age, they began to consider selling the business and what their life might look like when they stopped working. They all still felt healthy and active and had enough energy for some kind of exciting change.

The three couples got together for dinner one night to discuss in earnest their dream scenarios of what retirement could bring. Paul and Jared proposed a big idea. They wanted to move some place quieter, having tired of the rat-race of Los Angeles. They suggested New Mexico as their ideal location, preferably somewhere around Taos in the North. There they could take advantage of winter skiing and hiking in the mountains.

Ryan also liked this idea, but he took it one step further. What if they bought a piece of land where all six of them could live and build their own place with several outbuildings to accommodate the three couples and a few guests? It would be like communal living, but with them each having their separate quarters for privacy. They could even take in a couple of other residents if they wanted to. They might need someone to help with the manual labor of building the place, hooking up the well water, and other routine maintenance. They were all handy, but it would be a big property with plenty to do.

Darlene liked her brother's ambitious idea. She had longed for a quieter life for some time now. Running a busy construction company office for thirty years had worn her down. She wanted to plant a big garden, grow herbs and generally relax. She was fully on board with leaving California and she knew that Paul, Ryan and Jared needed a project to keep them busy and inspired and this sounded perfect.

Talia also thought it was a cool idea. They could get way more bang for their buck in New Mexico. She dreamt of having them build her very own little Buddhist meditation space. She longed to recapture the quiet, peaceful setting of the Cambodian temples.

It suddenly dawned on her that she would miss Sonya terribly. She wanted to invite her to come live on the property in Taos with the six of them. Perhaps they could divide up one of the smaller outbuildings into two suites and let her have one of them. Then there would still be room for guests on the other side. She shared this idea with the group and after much discussion, they all agreed to her proposal. Talia phoned Sonya that night to give her the news and Sonya was thrilled to be included.

The only person who was not keen on moving was Andrea. She wanted to spend more time with her granddaughter Krishna, who lived in Silicon Valley, and also visit her mother in assisted living. That would mean staying in California. She also wanted to start her own boutique online, a home business designing and sewing baby clothes, but that could be done anywhere. Paul and Jared had to convince her that the incredibly artistic local community in Taos would be a great place for Andrea to sell her baby clothes and they could fly out April, Sim and Krishna to visit as often as she liked. Finally, Andrea threw in the towel and reluctantly agreed because she was outnumbered five to one.

So, the plan was made. The next six months were a flurry of wrapping up and selling their business and everyone put in for retirement basically at the same time. Talia had already shifted from dancing to teaching in a studio a while back, since the aches and pains of a lifetime of dance had taken a toll on her body. Andrea sold her costumes off to one of her colleagues and said goodbye to her film studio friends. It was a fast transition, but they were ready for it. They had all worked hard for many years and needed to move on.

They took a trip to New Mexico to scout out properties around Taos. It didn't take long before they had picked out a lovely five acres piece of land near the town of Talpa, just to the south of Taos. It already had a small serviceable house on it which could act as home base for them to stay in while they customized and built three more smaller homes. The well needed work, so they would use a rainwater collection tank temporarily, but there was a lovely view of the Sangre de Cristo mountains. They could envision what they wanted to create and were excited to get started.

They drove into Taos to the Planning Department at City Hall and asked for recommendations on who to get locally to draw up the plans and how long the permit process would take. They met with a local German architect named Lars and invited him out to the property. After two more meetings, they felt confident that Lars understood what they wanted and could act on their behalf once they flew back to California. The ball was rolling, and they were all excited.

# PART II

## ON GOLDEN LAND

# CHAPTER 7
## KARL

One of the first people Jared and Paul met when they started drawing up plans for Taos with the architect was Karl. They needed a plumber, especially since they were unfamiliar with bringing well water to a house. He came recommended by the architect, Lars, who had lived in Taos for years.

The other five were back in LA. Ryan and Darlene were trying to sell the business. The three couples had to put their homes on the market and Sonya had to give notice on her rental apartment for three months hence. They all began packing and tying up loose ends. Andrea was spending as much time as she could with her grandkids in Silicon Valley before they moved.

Paul and Jared arranged to meet Karl in a coffee shop in Taos. In strolled this tall lanky fellow with a grey ponytail, big moustache, goatee and work boots. He shook their hands, ordered a coffee and sat down. He was cool as a cucumber and reminded them of every laid-back California grease-monkey they had ever met. However, as it would turn out, he was a voracious reader and extremely knowledge-able on all manner of subjects.

Karl explained to them that he was currently managing a small apartment building and working the odd plumbing job on the side.

They explained their plans to him and asked if he would be interested. He agreed to their terms and they loosely talked about dates and duration of the job. Karl said he wanted to see the site so that he could order whatever materials he needed to get the job done so they arranged to meet the following morning at the property.

Karl arrived the next morning in the requisite beat-up old pick-up truck. They walked the property for over an hour and looked closely at the well. Karl even surprised them by producing a water quality test kit and taking a sample at the source. He said he would call them with results in a couple of days.

As they walked, they got Karl's backstory. He was divorced with one grown daughter named Roxanne who had walked a hard road in her life and was now clean and sober and living in Santa Fe. She was mother to his one grandson named Clay, who was nineteen and lived with him. He explained that Clay often helped him as a laborer, and would they mind that? They said it was fine, as long as they didn't have to pay him directly. Karl said he would look after Clay's compensation, since he was basically a trainee earning his room and board anyhow. Karl agreed to the job and said he would start with the well and running pipe up to the property. He knew a good excavator who happened to live just down their road. Then he would come in intermittently as each of their four planned buildings started to get framed in and do all the interior pipes and hookups. They were happy to have such a pleasant and seemingly competent guy on board for the project.

Meanwhile Lars was preparing their permit application, and everything was moving ahead according to plan. They left him a big cheque to move things along as they headed back to LA to help pack up and sell their homes and close up shop. Darlene already had a buyer lined up for their construction business. They were just doing their due diligence with their lawyers to make the sale happen. Paul and Jared were impressed with Ryan and Darlene for putting this deal together so quickly while they were away. They took them out for a fancy dinner with champagne to celebrate the sale once the cheque was handed over.

As the project permits progressed, Karl spoke more and more often with Paul and Jared by phone and the well-water passed inspection and contained no harsh minerals, other than a little iron, which was normal in New Mexico and not harmful. He would simply install a filter on their taps. A month later, they flew out a second time with Ryan for the ground-breaking. Karl had recommended a local excavator to clear the land and dig out the foundations. Ryan was super impressed with Karl. He said they couldn't have hired a better guy. He was so likeable and handy. In fact, when Ryan learned that Karl was renting a shitty apartment in town with his grandson, he came up with a better idea. What if Karl and Clay lived in the other side of Sonya's building in the second suite? Wouldn't it be amazing to have access to his expertise twenty-four-seven? The other guys liked the idea but weren't sure how their wives and Sonya would react. They had never even met Karl.

Paul face-timed with Andrea that night to run it by her. She was not keen because that suite was supposed to be for their daughter and her family to come visit regularly. Paul knew this would be the sticking point, so he offered to build another suite as an addition on the back of their building to accommodate April and Sim and the grandkids or their son Donovan whenever he came out from New York. Andrea liked that idea but wondered if it would delay the project. Paul asked her to meet with the three other women to get their approval and then call him back. Then he would go to city hall while he was out there and get the plans changed for the extra suite.

Andrea arranged to meet Talia, Sonya and Darlene for coffee the next morning at their favorite local cafe. She treated them, naturally, to sweeten the mood. She really wanted to come through for her husband because she could hear in his voice how important this guy Karl was to him. When she explained the proposal to the other women, they were a bit reticent, especially Sonya, being the only single woman on site. How did she know he wasn't a creep who would hit on her? Andrea said that Paul and Jared were better at judging someone's character than that and she should trust them after all these years. They would kick his ass out if he tried anything weird. Besides, he had been married for a long time and was taking care of his grandson. That proved he was a good guy. Sonya acquiesced and Darlene and Talia were also on board. Andrea phoned Paul as soon as she left to tell him the good news. He was thrilled. Karl had become a good bro by this time. Now he just had to ask Karl if he was even interested in living with them.

So, Paul, Jared and Ryan invited Karl and Clay out for a nice dinner one evening. They figured the nineteen-year-old might weigh in favorably, since he had been spending quite a bit of time on the property lately and seemed to enjoy hanging out and working with all of them. Maybe he could influence Karl into liking the idea. After Paul made the invitation, Karl took a deep breath and a long sip of his beer in reflection. He said he would have to give his building owner two-months-notice to find a replacement manager. He asked if they were fine with him working other jobs and keeping his own business going. He asked if they could create a separate bedroom for Clay. Then finally, he smiled a big smile and said he was in. They bought a round of whiskeys and toasted to their new living arrangements. Paul phoned Andrea before bed and told her to let the other women know that Karl was all in. Andrea was pleased that she had helped pull this off.

In the spring of 2016, the plan came together. Two by two they all drove halfway across the country with their moving trucks soon following. Sonya put her belongings in Talia and Ryan's truck and flew out. They had all reduced their worldly possessions by about half in order to scale down their footprint. They were leaving LA permanently for the first time in their lives. They wanted to live a simpler, cleaner life with less baggage. This communal living situation seemed like a dream come true.

# CHAPTER 8
## BUILDING

In the spring of 2016, they began building their houses. They also discovered that their property was covered in tiny yellow flowers. The neighbor walking her dog told them they were bladderwort mustard flowers. Their front grass looked like a meadow from The Sound of Music. It was so pretty they decided to call their property The Golden Land.

The living arrangements were very tight during the first couple of months at the site. There were mattresses on the floor in every corner of the main house and nobody was getting any privacy. They had to decide who was preparing meals because they couldn't fit more than three people in the kitchen at once, so they made a schedule with one cook and one cleaner per meal. If the men were all building, then the women volunteered to cook and clean. Often one or more of the women wanted to be a laborer too, so then they would get out of kitchen duty and Clay was called upon to help with dishes. Everyone was busy and happy to contribute.

When Sonya was first introduced to Karl, she thought he was handsome and there seemed to be a mutual twinkle in his eye. She quickly volunteered to help him with whatever building project he was working on. She loved banging nails and laying floors and was pretty handy herself. They got into great debates about whatever music was playing and which were the greatest bands of each decade. They were at odds about whether the Rolling Stones were greater than Led Zeppelin, but they could agree on The Clash as being amazing.

One evening Sonya casually announced that Karl was taking her to his favorite pub for dinner. Clay had already taken off with friends for the night. She hopped into Karl's old pick-up truck, plunked in a Steely Dan CD, and headed off into Taos for a beer and a burger at the Shady Grove bar.

When they were seated with a cold drink, Sonya asked if he was willing to share the story of how he came to be raising his grandson Clay.

"Well, my daughter Roxanne was always a handful, even as a toddler. She had ADD and a learning disability, so she struggled all through school. She dropped out in grade eleven and started waitressing in bars. Then she got involved with an older biker named George who was a terrible influence. First, he got her pregnant and she had Clay. Then he got her hooked on coke and I managed to drag her out of there when Clay was a toddler and I put her in rehab. She got her shit together for about a year after that and things looked promising."

"Where was your ex-wife in all this? Didn't she care about her own daughter?"

"Shawna had already moved to California when Roxanne dropped out of high school. She was at her wit's end. She had tried everything with that girl and couldn't handle her anymore. She called me up and said she was leaving town and I would have to keep my eye on her. I really couldn't blame her, you know. Roxanne had put her mother through the wringer."

"So, what happened after rehab?"

"Well, like I said, Roxanne kept it together for a year living at my place, but then one night, after her shift at work, she went back home with George and all my hard work was instantly undone. She started using again. I told her she would not be caring for Clay in that state and she told me I could keep him then, in an angry huff. She only wanted to party. I went to the social worker and made my case to become his legal guardian. Of course, she has come around begging for custody again in brief periods of sobriety and remorse, but I never gave in. She could visit him whenever she wanted at my place, so they kept a fairly good relationship. Now that Clay is full-grown, he fully understands everything that happened, and he can decide when he wants to see his mother."

"What about George," Sonya asked.

"Oh, Clay knows all about his father. George moved to Santa Fe when Clay was twelve and he hasn't seen much of him since. They talk on the phone once in a while and he occasionally sends him a birthday card, but that's about it."

"Well Clay was damned lucky to have you as his grandfather," Sonya said. "Without you, I'm sure he would have turned out a lot different. You have turned him into a polite, hardworking young man."

"Well thanks, but polite is a bit of a stretch. I'd love to see him pick up his dishes at home like he does for you guys," said Karl.

"You are his safe place to be a teenager. All teenagers are bums. He will grow out of it."

"Yah, I guess you're right," said Karl.

Their burgers arrived and they started eating.

After dinner, Karl asked Sonya," So what about you? You haven't told me anything about your life?"

"Well, to be honest, I can relate to Roxanne's struggles a little bit. I used to have a drinking problem. It was Talia who dragged my ass to AA and got me straightened out. I really owe it to her for turning my life around. She has been a true friend through thick and thin."

"Ah, I wondered about the iced tea," Karl said, "that makes sense now."

"Yah, I never touch the stuff," Sonya admitted, "but I still like to smoke weed. That's my only vice."

"Well, I'm pretty sure I'll find at least a couple more vices," Karl winked at her, "at least I'm hoping to." He reached over and squeezed her hand gently. She loved the feel of his warm, rough skin.

"Well why don't we go back to your place and find out?" Sonya was not shy.

"Check please!" He raised his hand in the air to get the waitress' attention.

Needless to say, Sonya never came home that night. She texted Talia so they wouldn't worry. They had a cozy night of delicious sex and cuddling, and she fell asleep with her head on his chest. It had been a long time since either of them had been with anyone.

Clay looked a little surprised when she emerged from Karl's bedroom wearing one of his oversized t-shirts the next morning. She greeted him cheerfully.

"Good morning sunshine. Got any coffee started?"

"Uh no, that's grandpa's job."

"Well, you're old enough to make a freakin' pot of coffee my dear. Get over here and I'll teach you how."

Clay dragged himself off the couch with a little grumbling. She ruffled his hair and showed him how to grind the beans, measure out a scoop, add the water and turn it on. Karl appeared from the bedroom and smiled.

"Woah, am I seeing straight? Is that my boy making coffee? Damn woman, you can come over here whenever you want. At least he listens to you!"

They all laughed.

When they showed up back at the land at 9:30 a.m. everyone was teasing them. Paul, Jared and Ryan chastised Karl saying he was late for work and winked at him. Talia grabbed Sonya and wanted all the juicy details, like they were suddenly teenagers again. Andrea coolly shot her a congratulatory smile and Darlene teased her by slipping a bottle of massage oil in her pocket at lunch. They were all really happy for them to have found each other.

Practically speaking, they also realized that this could potentially free up half a house if they decided to live together. Clay would eventually take advantage of this to ask for his own place, but Karl put him in check saying he would have to pay rent. Clay quickly backed down, realizing that free room and board was a much better option. They would end up combining Sonya and Karl's suites into one house instead, with an extra bedroom for Clay.

In the meantime, Sonya figured out that she much preferred staying at Karl's apartment in Taos to sleeping on the floor in a cramped house with three other couples. She didn't have to wait her turn every morning for a shower either. Besides, he had good weed, good coffee and a lovely dog. Clay had his own bedroom, so it was fairly private, especially because he always had music on or played noisy video games like Grand Theft Auto.

Thus began the relationship between Karl and Sonya. They were both smitten. It remained to be seen whether it could last, and they could all cohabit in harmony.

# CHAPTER 9
## COMPLETING CONSTRUCTION

The construction process was going full steam ahead starting from the spring of 2016. Their goal was to have the 3 homes ready to inhabit before winter. Jared drove into Taos some mornings to hire a few casual day laborers just to bang nails and clean up the jobsite. Paul and Andrea agreed to stay in the older house and the addition for the guest suite began taking shape at the back. Even young Clay was really pulling his weight and Karl was proud of his grandson for being a quick learner.

Sharing close quarters in the original house was becoming stressful at times. Andrea and Talia started locking horns on meal planning and who was in charge of the kitchen roster. Ryan could tell that his wife was about to lose it on Andrea, so he pulled Talia aside one morning after breakfast and gave her a bear hug.

"Look, my love, I can see that you're just about ready to kill Andrea," he began.

"She's driving me fucking nuts!" Talia growled, venting her anger.

"I know, I know. I can see it. Can I offer you some loving advice?"

"Okay fine," Talia sounded resigned.

"Why don't you step back entirely from the kitchen and offer to do the house cleaning, like sweeping, bathrooms and laundry instead? That way you can get out of her space completely."

"But I like to cook. It lets me prepare my vegetarian dishes the way I want to."

"I know honey, but it's just not worth damaging your friendship over. Just take a break to get some breathing room. You can always come back to it later."

"Okay, you're right. I will talk to Andrea when I've calmed down. Right now I'm going to bang some nails to get this out of my system."

"Perfect. I love you," Ryan said.

"I love you too," Talia squeezed him hard.

Andrea appreciated the gesture and saw it for what it was: a truce. She took over the cooking with Darlene, Sonya and Clay taking turns on clean-up. Everyone could feel the mood immediately begin to lighten and felt relieved.

After Karl and Clay completed the initial well connection to the houses, Paul and Jared would start framing with the day laborers and then Ryan would do the electrical. Talia and Darlene got really proficient at drywalling and laying floors. Darlene also managed their finances and banking and kept them on budget with the project. Sonya was a floater and would do whatever odd jobs they asked of her. She often had to run into town to get building supplies. Andrea did all food shopping, and cooking, which was a big job with nine residents plus the day laborers. They became a high functioning team which was generally very harmonious. They were all motivated by the common goal of getting their own privacy and creature comforts back.

In May 2016, Sonya was busy writing in her journal when she got a call out of the blue. It was Kindred Hospital in L.A. calling to tell her that her father, Gary, had a stroke and would need care. Sonya felt conflicted because he had abandoned her when she was eight years old and left her alcoholic mother to raise her. Life had not been easy, and her mother had died ten years previous from pancreatic cancer. Sonya had taken care of her in her final months and now she did not wish to care for this man she hardly knew. They had met up only three times for a meal in the last ten years.

She decided to call his current wife, Gina, who told Sonya she needed money if she was going to care for him at home. His state pension from driving the airport shuttle bus for years and her old age security barely met their needs, and he would need nursing support at home. Sonya quickly put the kibosh on her money grubbing by saying she didn't have anything to give. She did agree to fly out there and help her organize his affairs and apply for whatever state subsidies for in-home care were available. She was motivated by the fact that some of her mother's belongings, such as her childhood photo albums, were still with Gary, so perhaps she could retrieve them at the same time.

Karl put his arms around her after she got off the phone.

"He doesn't deserve you," Karl said.

"You're damn right he doesn't!" she agreed. "He has never done shit for me my whole life. He didn't even come to my high school graduation. He said he had to work. What an asshole!"

"Well, you will sleep easier knowing you did the right thing, but I will miss you. The bed will be a lot colder at night while you're away."

"Aww, that's so sweet. I'll miss you too baby." Sonya drew him closer and kissed him deeply.

"Gross," Clay was walking past with an armload of bathroom tile. "Get a room you two!"

They laughed and Sonya left to book her plane ticket online. She decided four days would be plenty to get the ball rolling on his home care and just about all the time she could handle with Gina, who was nice enough, but a little condescending. She never understood how her father could have abandoned her as a child and how deep those wounds still run. Gary had probably glossed over the whole situation and told Gina what a great dad he had been and what a bitch his ex-wife was, preventing him from seeing his child. The truth was that despite her drinking problem, Sonya's mother had always worked two jobs to support them and had a heart of gold.

While Sonya was in California, Karl realized how attached he had grown to her. His place seemed so quiet and empty without her infectious laugh. Even Clay commented that he missed her chatting up a storm every morning while they had coffee. Karl figured out that perhaps his grandson enjoyed having a solid mother figure around, which he had never experienced. Karl felt happy that they would all be moving into a new place together once it was built. It would be an exciting new chapter for both of them. Even Mojo was sulking because Sonya often kept doggy treats in her pocket for him at the jobsite.

When she returned, Karl picked her up at the airport and wrapped his arms around her.

"I missed you so much," he said. "How did it go out there?"

"I missed you too Babe. It was okay, but Gina never stopped trying to get me to tell her how much money I have in the bank. I finally got mad and told her to drop it. We found him a room in a state care facility that his pension and old age security will cover. Gina is going to move into a cheaper place next month. I helped her pack some boxes and wished her well. I even scored Mom's old photo albums and a few pieces of her jewelry."

"That's great sweetheart. Well done. Now let's get you home. Clay and Mojo are dying to see you."

Back at the property, the heat of summer was a difficult slog for the builders. They were not young anymore and were really feeling the temperature at midday to be overwhelming. They would often knock off between two and four o'clock for a siesta and then worked in the evenings when it was cool. They made a tarped temporary shelter with hammocks for the casual workers to rest in the shade with a sprinkler to cool down and a cooler full of sodas. In July, Jared pulled a muscle in his back and had to take a week off on muscle relaxants, which slowed things down. They were worried the homes would not be ready by their deadline of October.

All through August and September they were finishing the interiors, laying floors, installing windows and doors and fixtures. They were getting closer and it was exciting to watch their new homes take shape. The women started ordering furniture, appliances, blinds, bedding etc. They were each given an equal fixed budget by Darlene to ensure fairness. Their tastes were very different. Talia was still an old hippy at heart, so she went with soft lavender paint, grass mats, rustic wooden furniture, beaded curtains and lots of cushions on the floor for her meditation space. Darlene had a modern esthetic, so minimalist clean lines, grey tones, leather couch and chrome accents were her style. Andrea was more traditional and therefore opted for floral impressionist prints, soft pastel colors and a creamy fabric sofa. She also ordered enough for her guest suite in the same style but darker colors. Sonya loved the cowboy-chic esthetic, so her furniture had that distressed farmhouse feel with horse blankets on the bed and nature themed artwork. They had a lot of fun with this stage of designing their new spaces, with just a little input from the men. Happy wife, happy life.

When the new housewares started arriving in the fall, it was like Christmas had come early. The excitement was tangible every time a delivery truck pulled into the long gravel driveway. They all wondered whose stuff was coming today. They would gather round and examine the labels and carry off their treasures to unpack. Every day after dinner would be a show-and-tell of what had been installed in each small new home. This went on for about a month until they were all settled in. They had met their October first deadline and felt a huge collective sense of accomplishment. It was decided they should go out for a celebration dinner.

That Saturday night at dinner, Jared proposed a toast to their new lifestyle.

"May we all live long and happy lives together in peace and harmony and take care of each other as we grow old!"

Everyone raised a glass of champagne, even Clay, who was still underage. They ate a marvelous meal and went home exhausted but satisfied.

# CHAPTER 10

## FINANCES

That first fall was blissful. They were so content with their new homes and finally had the separation and privacy they had sacrificed for the past six months of building. Everyone was more relaxed in their own space, preparing their own meals and having way more sex. They had found a healthy balance between spending time as couples and socializing with the larger group. They often gathered outside after dinner around the new fire pit Paul had built, which became their communal space, weather permitting.

Their first real group challenge was to create a budget that worked for everyone without making anyone feel inferior. They didn't have a mortgage, but they did owe some money from the build and furniture expenses. Darlene was in charge of finances, so she brought this up gently after dinner one night.

"Okay guys, I know y'all are just getting used to receiving your old age security checks, and you know that only Talia and Andrea have pensions from the film industry, and we have already talked about our individual 401K's and set up monthly withdrawals from those. I have totaled up our bills and what everyone gets, and we are looking pretty good. Our debt from the build is only $28,000 and with my calculations, we should be able to pay this off gradually over five years. We have pooled our funds into the communal account, and I am deducting a small amount from each household monthly before I transfer your remaining funds into your own bank accounts. Karl is keeping his money separate, but he is contributing to paying off the debt and he is acting as our caretaker and also supporting Clay on his own dime. So, I need feedback from y'all at the end of each month about how you are managing day-to-day and if anyone is falling short on what they need. I can make some adjustments if necessary, but it will all be out in the open. Is everyone cool with that so far?"

There was a chorus of yups.

"Do you have any questions?" she asked.

"How do we go about making a will?" Andrea asked. "I'm the only one with kids and a granddaughter, so what happens if Paul and I both die in a freak car accident. I feel like I need to provide for the group, but also protect my own kids."

Paul looked surprised, like they had never discussed this.

Darlene responded, "Well that is a great question Andrea. Honestly, I really hadn't thought that far ahead. Let me mull it over and get back to you real soon okay?"

"Sure, thanks for considering our unique situation everyone. I know it puts a burden on the group," Andrea said.

"Hell no," Jared spoke up," your kids are part of this big family we've created. They need to be included in this equation."

Paul chimed in, "Thanks buddy. Love you bro."

"Of course. We all love April, Sim and little Krishna. Dom is a pain in the ass though."

They all laughed because Paul and Andrea's son was actually a lovely guy. He had completed college in New York and was still living there and working as a physiotherapist. He had visited them briefly in the springtime, right before they moved to Taos.

A week later, Darlene spoke to Andrea and Paul privately and recommended that they leave half of their estate to the group and half to their kids. Paul and Andrea were fine with the idea.

Darlene explained the situation to the group that evening at the firepit and suggested that everyone should make a will and leave their estate to the group in the form of their partner as first beneficiary and then two of the others as second and third beneficiaries. She also advised that they each appoint a secondary medical representative from the group, in case of illness or accident. It all sounded very sensible and practical, so they all agreed to see a lawyer and draw these up as soon as possible.

However, the conversation was a little awkward for Sonya and Karl, who had only been together for a few months. They weren't necessarily ready to make this kind of commitment, even though they were already living together. They were unusually quiet for the rest of the night and neither of them broached the obvious elephant in the room.

Darlene sensed this unease at the firepit and knocked on their door the next morning.

"Listen guys, I know that conversation last night was a bit weird for you two because you are just starting out. I don't want you to feel pressured. I also know that you have a strained relationship with your daughter, Karl, and any will that you make must include Clay as a beneficiary. So, take whatever time you need to sort this out okay? Sonya, you need to leave the bulk of your assets to the group please, but Karl can do as he pleases. Karl, it would be nice if you contributed something to the kitty, but ultimately, it's your decision. We are treating you as an independent entity okay?"

"Thank you, Darlene," Sonya breathed a sigh of relief. "I didn't even know how to hash this out, but it all makes sense how you put it. We are so lucky to have you guiding us in these matters." She gave Darlene a big hug as she said goodbye to them.

Karl also looked visibly relieved. "Thank god she came over to clear the air. I was scared to say anything in case I offended you." They hugged it out.

"I know Clay needs you," Sonya said, "I know he comes first."

"But he's almost a man now too Sonya. Pretty soon he'll be able to fend for himself."

"Yah, I guess that's true. He will definitely make a good plumber once he gets his ticket."

"He will get his trade license next year once he finishes the apprenticeship training hours, the coursework and the online worksite safety exam. I'm actually proud of him. He's turning out pretty great."

"That's because of you, my darling. He has a great role model."

"Can I borrow your truck Grandpa?" the apprentice burst into the house.

"Where are you going?"

"I want to go into town and get a fancy coffee at Baxter's Grill."

"Oh Yah, you wanna see that pretty girl who works there; the one with the purple hair. What's her name?" Karl teased.

"Michelle, and so what if I do? I want to invite her to a party on Friday night at Doug's place. Please Grandpa?"

"Okay kid. I couldn't stand in the way of true love." He threw Clay the keys.

"You're the best Grandpa." He bolted out the door smiling with excitement.

"That's so cute," Sonya said. "Remember when we got that excited over meeting someone?"

"Yes, I do," Karl said, and gave her a big squeeze, "it was only a few months ago."

"Aw, you are adorable." She pulled him into the bedroom for some spontaneous morning sex and shut the door.

Everyone seemed fine with the financial arrangement and drawing up of wills until Jared spoke to Darlene the following night. He reminded her that Paul and Andrea's daughter April and her husband Sim were making more money than god and probably had more savings at thirty years old than any of them had earned in a lifetime. Jared didn't think it was fair that their inheritance should rob the group of much needed funds, but he didn't want to rock the boat.

"I know that if they disinherit their own daughter, it might seem terrible, but the truth is, she doesn't need the money."

Darlene tried to calm him down. "I know you're right sweetheart, but it's really up to them to see this and make the right decision. She's their daughter so she has every right to be included."

"Can't you say something to Andrea? I know she respects you so much in these matters."

"I will try, if a moment arises where I feel there's a window of opportunity. I'm not going to come at her like a ton of bricks."

"Okay Dar, thanks. You are the glue, I mean it. Without you, we would be at each other's throats, I have no doubt. Talking about money is way more challenging than I ever imagined."

A few days later, Darlene and Andrea were out in the greenhouse harvesting the last of the season's lettuce, tomatoes, and beans for dinner. They were laughing about how they caught Talia sunbathing naked on her porch that morning and sprayed water on her with the hose. Darlene felt the window of opportunity opening that she was looking for.

"You know Andrea, I was thinking more about the issue of making our wills the other day and I realized that April and Sim are actually pretty wealthy, wouldn't you say?"

"Well, yah for sure. They both have huge paychecks compared to what we ever earned. Their house is already paid off and they both drive luxury cars, so I'd say their careers have worked out just fine. What are you getting at?"

"Well do you think it might be possible for you to talk to April about your estate planning and the financial needs of the group? Do you think she would understand if she got less than say, her brother?"

"Oh wow, I never considered that as an option. Paul and I have always tried to treat them equally. "

"I know. I get how important that is when you're raising kids, I really do, but they are adults now. Maybe she can see that she is set for life and would realize that she doesn't need any money from you guys. Do you think that's a possibility?"

"I will run it by Paul and see what he thinks. Let me get back to you."

"Sure, of course, no pressure. I'm just trying to consider what's best for everyone," Darlene said, quickly changing the subject. "Now let's wash up these veggies and split them up for the four houses before the others start making their dinner plans."

Everything was in place with the group's estate planning and April had agreed to forego her rightful inheritance in favor of the group. They were all content with the arrangements and enjoying their new homes and lifestyle. They had even built an enclosure to house the well and keep the pump warm and dry over the winter so they could do any required maintenance easily. Talia and Darlene had also worked hard to cover the garden with some posts and plastic tarps to protect it from snow, knowing that Taos was a ski town and could get some real cold snaps. They were all set for winter.

# CHAPTER 11
## CLAY AND MICHELLE

Karl's grandson Clay had taken up with Michelle, the server from Baxter's Grill. She had even started sleeping over at their place occasionally, after an awkward discussion with grandpa about safe sex. Karl had thrown a box of condoms at him and told him to "bag it" or face eighteen years of child support payments. Then he sat him down and went over the list of STDs he could get if he didn't and basically scared him into thinking that his dick might fall off if he didn't listen.

Michelle seemed like a lovely girl. She was a quarter Pueblo on her grandmother's side and half German on her father's, so she had thick dark hair and light blue eyes, which made her very striking. Clay worshipped the ground she walked on because she was basically his first real girlfriend and regular sex seemed like the greatest thing on earth for any young man. They both had a large circle of friends and usually had parties to go to on the weekends.

One morning, over coffee, Sonya asked Michelle about her Puebla roots.

"So, tell me about your grandma Michelle. Where did she grow up?"

"She has lived in Jemez, northwest of Albuquerque, her whole life. She had four brothers and sisters and they had a hobby farm and raised and sold chickens or traded with other families for corn flour or other stuff they needed. Two of the brothers drove into Albuquerque for work every day. They brought in enough money to take care of the family. She has had a pretty tough life, but she's always cheerful."

"She sounds wonderful. Do you go visit her?"

"Yah, I usually go there every school holiday, but now that I'm working it might be harder. I'd love to take Clay to meet her soon."

"You definitely should. He needs a little more culture in his life."

"We can go to the hot springs there too. He would love that."

"That sounds amazing. Well, there's a long weekend coming up at Thanksgiving. Why don't you get Clay to ask Karl if you can use the truck? I'll put in a good word for you guys."

"Would you really? Oh, thank you so much Sonya!" She gave her a hug and left for her shift at the diner.

The two young lovers went on their weekend trip and had a wonderful time. On the way back, Clay told Michelle he needed to stop in and visit his cousin Marco in Santa Fe. They got some lunch at a burger stand and pulled into Marco's place. It was a run-down adobe house that he shared with three other guys. It had a messy back yard piled with used car parts, a rusty old swing-set and various other junk.

Marco was a little older than Clay, probably almost thirty Michelle thought. They looked like family, with the same shaggy brown hair, deep-set brown eyes and ski-jump nose, but Marco was taller and thinner than Clay. He offered them a beer and they sat on a rickety picnic table in the back yard.

"So, I'm glad you came through." Marco gently swatted his cousin across the head, knocking off his ball cap.

"Yah, I thought about it and I think it sounds like a good opportunity," Clay said.

"What opportunity?" Michelle asked.

"I'll explain later," Clay cut her off.

"Come inside cuz," Marco invited Clay. "Michelle, you wait here a sec okay?" Clay looked serious. "I'll be right back."

Michelle stroked a brown tabby that had jumped onto the picnic table and wondered what Clay was up to. The afternoon sun made her squint and she was hot and tired. She wanted to get going so she could have a second Thanksgiving dinner with her parents, like she promised.

Clay came back soon carrying a plastic grocery bag and gave his cousin a lean-in bro handshake, shoulder bump and back slap.

"See you in a couple of weeks Marco. Thanks for hooking me up."

"Nice to meet you Michelle. Take care of this little man okay," Marco smiled.

"Okay sure. Bye," Michelle sounded skeptical.

When they got back into the truck and on the road again, Michelle asked Marco what was in the bag.

"Oh, just a little weed. I'm gonna sell it for Marco around Taos. He's gonna cut me in for 10% so I can make a little extra money."

"What?" Michelle was not happy. "That's a terrible idea. Why didn't you tell me before we came here?"

"Well, it's my family and my decision babe. It doesn't really affect you. I didn't think you would care this much honestly."

"Of course I care!" Michelle was pissed. "You're my boyfriend. I don't want you doing illegal shit. What if you get caught? Then you've fucked up your life and mine too!"

"I'm not gonna get caught. I'm only gonna sell to friends I trust. That way nobody will rat me out."

"Oh, perfect plan, but what if a cop sees you or happens to notice you exchanging money for baggies in public?"

"I would never do that in public. I'm not that stupid babe. Relax, you're getting all worked up about nothing."

The rest of the ride home got quiet and when they reached her family home, Michelle grabbed her bag, slammed the door and left with no kiss goodbye. Clay was taken aback.

When he walked into his grandpa's house, Sonya greeted him.

"Hey kiddo, how was your weekend?"

"Um, great." Clay sounded distracted and unenthused.

"It doesn't sound like you're feeling great," Sonya said.

"Oh what? I'm just tired from all that driving. I'm gonna crash for a while." He headed for his room.

"Well, I'll leave you a plate of dinner on the stove and you can nuke it when you wake up."

"Okay, thanks." He shut the bedroom door.

Karl came in from outside, unlaced his work boots, grabbed a beer and flopped onto the couch.

"I saw the truck. Where's my boy?"

"He just went to bed. He said he's tired from the long drive but I'm not buying it. He sounded miserable. Maybe there's trouble in paradise?" Sonya said.

"Ah well, young love," Karl replied, "you know how fickle that can be. Hey, is it okay if we eat on the couch and watch the news? I'm too bagged to move right now."

"Sure, my love, of course. I'll fix us a couple of plates."

"Thank you my darling. I don't know what I did to deserve you," said Karl.

"Me either," Sonya teased, "you must have been a really good dude in your past lives I guess."

Meanwhile Clay slipped his half pound of pot under his coveralls in the bottom drawer of the dresser. Tomorrow he would make things right with Michelle. Maybe if he told her he was saving up for them to get their own place, she would stop being mad at him? He thought about buying baggies to portion out the weed and who he would sell it to and soon fell fast asleep.

# CHAPTER 12
## ANDREA'S HEALTH CRISIS

As winter came to Taos, tourists began to arrive in town for the ski season. Only Ryan, Darlene and Jared had ever skied before, so the rest of the group wasn't terribly interested. The three skiers persisted, telling them that they were never too old to try something new and they didn't know what they were missing. Finally, Talia and Andrea acquiesced, with saying they would get snowshoes from the local Army surplus store and go for a hike instead.

They took two vehicles and drove the half hour route north to Ski Valley Resort. The scenery was breathtaking, especially after being in the dry valley all year. They had not explored the mountains and were surprised to see bigger trees and different plants growing up there. It was a completely different biosphere.

After they all got rental equipment and arranged to meet at the chalet for lunch, Andrea and Talia set off for their hike. They loved the quiet sparkling snow and could hear nothing but the birds and the crunching of their feet on the snowpack. It took them about ten minutes to get the hang of it, but then they felt comfortable in this new footgear. However, they were surprised how tiring it was.

After about twenty minutes of walking, Andrea suddenly doubled over and moaned in pain.

"What's wrong?" Talia rushed to her side.

"I don't know. I have this terrible pressure in my abdomen. It feels like heavy period cramps, but we both know I haven't had a period in years."

"Shoot, well sit down for a minute." Talia rummaged through her backpack and found her light rain jacket. She slid it under Andrea's bum so she wouldn't get soaked. She looked at her cell phone and realized they had no reception up there. She pulled out her water bottle and two Tylenol.

"Here, take these for the pain. Can you stick your hand down your pants and see if you're bleeding?" Talia suggested.

Andrea did this and looked at her fingers and there was no blood.

"Ok that's one good thing. I'm going to go get help. You rest here and don't get up."

"No problem, I don't think I could even if I wanted to," Andrea said.

Talia took off as fast as she could on those awkward snowshoes. When she got to the lodge, she grabbed the first ski patroller she could find.

"My friend needs a lift back from the green hiking trail. She's having a lot of abdominal pain and can't walk."

"Ok, I'll get the skidoo sled over there. You can ride along. Come with me."

He radioed for the sled and the driver let Talia hop on the seat behind him.

"Hold on around my waist," he directed.

As Andrea lay in the snow, she saw her baby brother Michael standing in the snow staring at her, still dragging his blanket. This mysteriously gave her comfort, and the pain subsided a little and she breathed easier. When she looked again, he was gone.

After a quick skidoo ride, they loaded Andrea onto the sled gently. She was still moaning in pain. They took her to the medical station and called for an ambulance.

"I don't need an ambulance," Andrea was embarrassed.

"It's better this way," Talia said. "I need to stay and meet the others and tell them what's going on. Then we will come down to the hospital and get you."

"Okay, okay, if you insist," Andrea gave in, "but can you please just phone Paul and he will come get me and you guys can carry on with your day?"

Okay, I will call him as soon as you've gone."

The ambulance left and Talia reached Paul on the clinic's landline.

"What's wrong with her?" Paul sounded understandably worried.

"I don't know, she just has terrible abdominal pain. Can you meet her at the hospital in town? She'll be there in twenty minutes."

"Sure of course. I'm leaving right now."

Talia met the others for lunch and explained what had happened. After much debate, they decided to ski a few more runs and then stop by the hospital on the way back.

When they arrived, Paul was sitting in the reception waiting area. He explained what was going on.

"She has a prolapsed uterus. She already got an ultrasound and the doctor discussed it with us. They are prepping her for surgery. She's getting a hysterectomy. I'm freaking out! This is all happening so fast, but the doctor told me it is common among women her age and it's a fairly routine surgery."

"Jesus, we're so sorry," Darlene spoke for the group. "When will she be released?"

"In a couple of days, but she can't do much of anything for six weeks."

"You will have to wait on her hand and foot," Jared teased him. "That's good, it will make you a better husband."

"No seriously guys," Sonya spoke up, "he's probably scared right now. Go easy on him. Paul, do you want one of us to stay here with you?"

"No, no, go home. I'll be fine, but it might be a long wait."

"Can we at least bring you some dinner before we go?"

"Yah, that would be nice. Go get me a take-out burger and fries from Baxter's. Say hi to Michelle if she's working."

"Ok, we're on it. Promise you'll phone us as soon as she gets out of surgery okay?"

"For sure. Thanks guys. Think positive thoughts please. I hate hospitals. They make me nervous," Paul said.

Andrea's surgery went well but she was still pretty out of it when they let Paul in to see her. He took her hand and kissed her forehead.

"Hey there sweetheart, you gave me a scare you know?"

"Yah, I'm sorry honey," she said weakly.

"Don't apologize my love. I'm just so glad you weren't alone when this happened, and everything worked out okay. Now you rest and I'll come see you first thing in the morning. I'll bring you your cell phone and charger and a change of clothes and a toothbrush." He kissed her again and left, exhausted.

Andrea lay there recuperating and thought of her mother who had died two years earlier of Alzheimer's. It had been a long gradual demise where she finally couldn't remember how to swallow and had to be tube fed. Andrea had made the excruciating decision to end her life with dignity, which had just become legal in California. Now, in this hospital bed, she imagined what all those months of care must have been like. She wondered if her brother Michael had watched over her mom too.

It had been a very long day, but Paul felt so relieved. Andrea's collapse had scared him. He couldn't imagine life without his wife after thirty-five years. He started to choke back a tear and quickly pushed that thought away as he drove home.

# CHAPTER 13

## TROUBLES WITH CLAY

As Christmas approached, Andrea was on the mend and able to resume light activities. Everyone was busy decorating and making or buying small gifts for their gift exchange. Karl wanted to cook Christmas dinner for them as a way of saying thank you for welcoming him into their living community over the past year. Sonya said it would be tight with everyone crammed into their dining room, but they all wanted to be together.

Clay had begun selling his baggies of weed around town to friends only, to avoid any trust issues. When Michelle saw how much money he was making, she stopped complaining and told him she just didn't want to be a part of it. He would deposit ninety percent of the money every month into his cousin's account and keep his own ten percent. His cousin had a buddy named Phil who worked in Taos regularly so he would drop off a fresh supply to Clay whenever he ran out. The whole plan was working great for all parties involved. Clay had even managed to buy himself an old Toyota Rav-4 with the proceeds, which surprised his grandpa.

"Where'd you get the money for that?" he asked. "I must be paying you too much if you can afford a car."

"I'm just very frugal," Clay said, "I've been saving every penny since I started working for you Grandpa."

"Wow, I had no idea! Well good for you son. I'm impressed. I thought most of it went on beer and food at Michelle's diner."

"Nah, she feeds me for free with her employee discount," Clay lied.

"Excellent," said Karl, "that's a good girlfriend you got there."

"I know right?" Clay walked away feeling chuffed, but slightly guilty for lying.

One Tuesday morning in mid-December, Clay drove out to meet Phil for his monthly supply. They normally went to the laundromat, each carrying a black garbage bag which looked perfectly normal. Phil would throw some old rags into the machine that he had no intention of ever retrieving and then pretend to use the washroom. He would stash a package of a pound of weed in the small cupboard, which contained only toilet paper and leave. Then Clay would go into the washroom, add Phil's package of pot to his fake laundry bag, and leave a few minutes later.

Clay saw Phil's old Camaro parked in front of the laundromat. He pulled in a few stalls over, grabbed his bag and went in. The only other person in there was a young guy with shoulder length hair near the front of the place who was folding his clothes. He was wearing a t-shirt, jeans and a ball cap and wasn't paying them any attention. Perfect. Phil came out of the washroom and gave him a nod as he passed by on out the front door. Clay casually fished in his pocket counting his quarters for the machine, swearing audibly as if he needed to get more change. Then he went into the bathroom and shut the door. He opened the cupboard and retrieved the small parcel wrapped in brown butcher paper as per usual. He flushed the toilet and turned on the water for a few seconds to mimic washing his hands. Then he walked towards the door. The young man folding his laundry suddenly spoke to him.

"Hey, I saw you needed more quarters. If you want, I can make change for a dollar?"

"Nah thanks, but I need smokes anyways. I'll just run across to the corner store."

"Not so fast buddy. Police. You're under arrest for drug dealing. Put your hands behind your back."

Clay's mouth hung open as this scruffy character pulled a gun on him and grabbed his wrists. Clay couldn't even move. He was frozen with fear. As the undercover cop pushed him out the door, he saw Phil standing beside his car with another cop holding him too, also in handcuffs.

"Shit," Phil said. "What have you done?" he snarled at Clay.

"Me? Nothing!" Clay replied.

"Shut up, the pair of you," the cop ordered. "Move over here and stand here silently until my back-up arrives to take you in."

A black and white patrol car with lights flashing pulled up fast and the cop pushed Clay into the back seat. Then he pulled up a few yards and the other plain-clothes cop pushed Phil in beside him.

They rode in silence to the station. Clay had never been so scared in his life. What would his grandpa say? What would Michelle say? Would he have to go to jail? How long do you get for a first offense anyhow? His mind was racing.

Clay was taken to an interview room as Phil was separated from him in another direction down a hallway. An officer in uniform came in with a clipboard, unfastened his handcuffs and turned on a recording device.

"I'm detective Ramirez from the drug squad. You're being charged with possession of an amount under one pound with the intent to sell. Have you been read your rights?"

"Um, I'm not sure," Clay was stunned.

"Well, you have the right to remain silent and anything you say could be used against you in a court of law. You have the right to an attorney and if you cannot afford one, a legal aid attorney will be provided for you. Do you understand?"

"Yes." Clay had watched enough crime shows on tv to know the basics. "Can I make a phone call?"

"After we're done here, yes. You'll be allowed one call after bail has been set."

"Okay, I want an attorney," Clay remembered this was important from tv.

"Okay, I'll be back. He shut off the recording device. Do you want something to drink? Coffee, tea, water or pop. That's all we have."

"I'll take a Coke please."

Another officer brought him a can of Coke. He took a long drink and realized his hands were shaking. He quickly hid them under the table as the door opened and an attractive woman in a dress suit came in.

"I'm your lawyer, Stephanie Caldwell. Whatever you say to me is in the strictest confidence and cannot be used against you. Do you understand?"

"Yes," Clay nodded.

"So, tell me what happened and be honest. I can't help you unless you tell me the whole truth. How old are you, by the way?"

"Twenty."

She started writing things down as he talked. He told the story of how he met Phil every month to get the package of weed and then sold it around town. Then she asked the question he was dreading.

"Okay, do you know who Phil gets the package from?"

Clay pictured his cousin Marco in his backyard with his Andrea cat on his lap smoking a cigarette. Their mothers were half-sisters through Grandpa Karl's ex-wife's previous marriage. His aunt was born five years before Karl and Grandma had Roxanne, but since Clay rarely saw his mother, he hadn't seen his auntie Janice in years. Marco would be furious if Clay ratted him out and who knows what kind of trouble Marco had seen previously. If he had priors, he would get a jail term for sure. Clay started sweating.

"Look," Stephanie said, "I can tell by the look on your face that you know. You really need to tell me now. This information might save your ass from any jail time and, if you're really lucky, the judge might decide that you were simply an informant and leave your record clean with a warning, since it's your first offense."

"Okay, okay. Crap, it's my cousin Marco," Clay hung his head in dismay.

"Last name?"

"Jeffries. He lives in Santa Fe near that big railway crossing in the center of town. I forget the street name."

"How old is Marco?"

"Twenty-eight."

"Tell me the details of how you got involved in this."

Clay spilled his guts to the lawyer and eventually found out that the cops had been watching Phil for some time and knew that Phil was connected to somebody above him. They wanted Marco and whoever was above Marco in the supply chain. They knew Clay was just a small fish in the pond. They set bail at five hundred dollars and told him he could make that phone call.

"Hello Grandpa? Is that you?"

"Well, yah. Who the hell else is it going to be son? And why do you sound so weird? Are you okay?"

"No, I'm not okay." There was a long uncomfortable pause. "I'm in jail. Can you come and get me?"

"What? In jail! What the hell for?"

"I've been selling pot. I'm really sorry Grandpa. It was Marco's idea. I'm never going to do it again. I'm sorry."

"Marco. That little shit. I knew nothing good could become of him. His mother was just as useless as Roxanne, no offense. All right, stay put, I'm coming now. Jesus Christ kid. You're making me old before my time."

"Thanks Grandpa. Wait. There's one more thing. It's going to cost $500 bail to get me out. I'll pay you back as soon as I can. I promise."

"Shit kid, you're damn straight you will. I'll stop at the bank on my way in. See you in about half an hour."

"Thanks Grandpa. I'm so sorry," Clay hung up, dejected.

He sat in a cell with three other men and waited, grateful that Phil was nowhere to be seen. When Karl arrived, Clay was handed a document asking him to appear before a judge at the end of January. They told him that Miss Caldwell, the lawyer, would be in touch before then. When they got in the truck, Clay burst into tears and Karl let him cry it out. They took a long quiet ride home and Clay went straight to his room, closed the door and slept for twelve hours straight.

# CHAPTER 14
## CHRISTMAS 2016

On Christmas Eve they all gathered around the fire pit with some mulled wine and Paul pulled out his guitar to lead some carols. Mojo the dog had died some years back, but Ryan had replaced his beloved pal with a German Shepherd named Lucy, who Clay threw sticks for as they sang. It was a cold clear night with twinkling stars, and everyone was in good spirits.

Nobody knew about Clay's recent troubles other than Karl and Sonya. When Clay had looked glum in the days following his arrest, Karl told the others he was having relationship woes with Michelle, which everyone believed without hesitation. In fact, it was true, Michelle had been keeping her distance as she re-evaluated whether she wanted to be with Clay anymore. Karl told Sonya to keep the arrest a secret because he didn't want Clay to be seen as a pariah or worse, a risk to their cohesive community. He told Clay not to share his personal plight with anyone because it would tarnish their view of him irreparably. Clay was all too happy to oblige.

Andrea and Paul's son, Donovan, had flown in from New York to be with them for Christmas week. He had cut his thick sandy brown locks so short that he looked older and more professional now. His physiotherapist career was going well, and he was made partner in the clinic. His girlfriend, Shawna, was staying with her own family, so they would have to wait until spring to meet her, but he was clearly smitten. They had been dating for seven months and Paul and Andrea thought there might be an engagement soon because he hinted that he might like to have a wedding one day here on their land, if that was okay. They were thrilled and dying to meet Shawna. Andrea couldn't stop pressuring him all week to have babies soon because she wanted more grandkids. He kept telling his mom to slow down. There would be plenty of time for that, but Andrea was thrilled her son had found "the one".

Christmas morning was lovely. They all exchanged little gifts and Clay even received a couple of plumbing tools he needed from Karl. Sonya had knitted him a beautiful dark green sweater. He was humbled by the love and support of his surrogate parents after the trouble he had caused. Afterwards they all enjoyed a big brunch at Jared and Darlene's house. There were pancakes, scrambled eggs, bacon, fresh baked scones, coffee and mimosas.

Their daughter April, Sim and Krishna would be arriving on Boxing Day. April would see her brother for two days before he flew back to New York. Andrea and Sonya were cleaning the guest suite for them and making up the beds. Andrea was hiding gifts around the place as a treasure hunt for her granddaughter, who was now six.

"Do you think she will find this if I put it behind the wood stove, or do you think she'd be scared to look there?" Andrea asked.

"No, I think it would be fine. Her parents will tell her it's not hot," Sonya replied.

"That sweater you knit for Clay was gorgeous. I think he was really touched."

"Yah it seemed to fit him perfectly. I was really pleased," Sonya said.

"So how come Michelle never came by for brunch yesterday? We haven't seen her for a while. Have they had a falling out?"

"Yah, ever since the incident she has been keeping her distance," Sonya let it slip.

"What incident?" Andrea asked.

"Oh shit," Sonya tried to backpedal, "Clay kind of made out with another girl at a party," she chose to lie.

"The little bugger," Andrea said, "I never thought he would be that stupid. He obviously loves her. I'm going to have a talk with that young man."

"Oh no, please don't. He needs to figure this out on his own," Sonya sounded serious.

"Well okay, I will try to stay out of it, but I don't see why a little motherly advice couldn't help him."

"Please Andrea, just give him some space right now. He's already hurting enough," Sonya insisted.

They hung a few sparkly decorations in the suite, turned off the lights and shut the door.

Unfortunately, Andrea couldn't leave it alone. Every time she saw Clay, she'd ask him how Michelle was doing or say that she missed having Michelle around. Clay just kept telling her that Michelle was working a lot more because the diner was really busy with out-of-town guests for the holidays and ski season. Finally, one day he cracked.

"Look Andrea, could you please stop asking about Michelle? She doesn't want to see me right now."

"Why not," Andrea played dumb, hoping to engage him in a conversation.

"Because I fucked up, okay, now please leave it alone," Clay sounded exasperated.

"Look, making out with another girl is not that big a deal if it was only a kiss. I know you really love each other," Andrea said.

"What? No! I never made out with another girl. Who told you that?"

"Sonya did."

"No, I got arrested for selling weed," Clay blurted out.

"What? When? What the hell Clay? How could you do something so stupid? You've almost finished your training for a great job. After that, you'll have enough money to do whatever you want."

"I know, I know. I fucked up. My stupid cousin talked me into it. It's over now. It will never happen again."

"Well good because we don't want any criminal activity around here, do you understand me?" Andrea was taking a more serious tone now. "We all trusted you to live here with us and you've broken that trust now. Jesus Clay, now I'm going to have to tell the others."

"Please don't, I'm begging you. There's no reason to tell them. I've cleaned up my act. You can totally trust me, I promise."

"Hmm, well I can't keep a secret from Paul. He's my husband. I will let him decide if the other should know or not."

"God damn it, Sonya and her big mouth." Clay sounded mad.

"Don't blame Sonya for your troubles Clay. You brought this upon yourself," Andrea said.

"I know, I know. I'm leaving now." Clay stormed off all gloomy. He marched straight home and confronted Sonya.

"Why can't you keep your big mouth shut?" He burst into the kitchen.

"What? I covered for you. I only said Michelle wasn't around because you made out with another girl at a party."

"Yah, but then she got the truth out of me didn't she and now everyone will know. She is telling Paul as we speak."

"Shit Clay, I'm so sorry. Don't worry, your grandpa and I will vouch for you. This will all blow over, I promise."

Clay slammed his bedroom door and turned his music on loud.

"God damn it," Sonya muttered to herself as she wiped the counter, wondering how this story could have spun out of control so fast.

The next day April, Sim, and Krishna arrived, and the mood was bright again. There were hugs all around and Sim passed out small gifts from his family to each of them. Krishna was delighted to meet Lucy the dog and wanted to take her back to their guest suite, but Ryan had to refuse by gently promising her she could walk Lucy later on. Andrea took them on a grand tour of the place and then Krishna did her treasure hunt with squeals of delight as she found each present. After lunch they all needed a nap.

Clay was nowhere to be seen. Sonya told Karl what had happened, and he got really quiet. Karl seemed worried that his grandson would not feel welcome there anymore. Sonya felt terrible, but he hugged her and reassured her that this wasn't her fault.

Meanwhile, Clay had decided to try harder to win back Michelle. He had bought her a ring for Christmas. It wasn't an engagement ring, but it was a promise ring of gold with a small blue sapphire and two tiny diamonds. He bought six pink roses and walked into the cafe.

She saw him coming out of the corner of her eye as she served three burgers to some hungry tourists. She decided to let it happen because there was no way to avoid it in this public setting.

"Hi," he greeted her.

"Hi," Michelle said.

"I came here to say I'm sorry and I love you and to give you your Christmas present," Clay said matter-of-factly.

"Not here." She grabbed his arm and pulled him into the back storage room.

"Well open it." She unwrapped the little box and opened the ring case.

"It's beautiful. I love it. Thank you," she said as she slid it on her right-hand ring finger.

"I miss you Miche. Can you please stop freezing me out?"

"I miss you too," she admitted. "Why don't you pick me up at five when I'm done with my shift and we can talk."

"Thank you," he said, smiling, and gave her a quick hug. "See you at five."

They patched things up that night and got back together. Clay went for his court appearance the following week and the judge let him off with just a warning for cooperating. Clay got a nasty call from his cousin Marco's mother. She called him a no-good rat and told him that Marco would see at least two years jail time because of a prior arrest. Then she ended the call by saying Clay was dead to her, just like his mother. Apparently, there was no love lost between his mother Roxanne and her sister. Clay had no idea why. He only cared that he had Michelle back in his life.

Karl told Paul and the others around the fire pit one night that Clay would not have a criminal record and that he would be keeping his nose clean from now on. He made Clay apologize to the group for breaking their trust. They accepted his apology and forgave him. They admitted they had all made mistakes in their young lives and said he had learned a good lesson. They told him they were thrilled to see Michelle back around the place because she was a lovely girl and she made Clay so happy. The balance had been restored.

# CHAPTER 15
## RYAN STEPS OUT

It was January 2019, and Ryan was out running some errands in Taos. He had gone to the post office, bank and vitamin store and was getting hungry. He stopped in at his favorite deli called The Hungry Moose. He had noticed the woman behind the counter many times. Her name was Jocelyn, and she was about forty-five and gorgeous. Her long black hair was woven into braids and she looked part native American, part something else he couldn't quite put a finger on. She had striking green eyes and the whitest teeth he had ever seen.

There had been a subtle flirtation going between them for some months now, although he wasn't fully admitting this to himself. He still truly believed he was there for the delicious sandwiches. As he approached the counter, she smiled at him coyly, as she always did.

"Howdy stranger. What can I get you today? Is it corned beef on rye with extra hot mustard again?" she asked.

"Nope, I think I will break the mold and have the turkey and Havarti on a Kaiser bun this time and a coffee please."

"Alrighty then, just help yourself to the coffee and I'll bring your sandwich out. You know the drill," she winked at him.

He sat at the table closest to where she was working and couldn't help stealing glances at her taught body. He loved Talia, but it didn't hurt to look. He wasn't dead after all. She brought him the sandwich and also put down a small bowl of coleslaw with a napkin tucked underneath.

"This is our new slaw, on the house. We want to get feedback from our customers to see if we should add it as a side or stick to green salad. "

"Great thanks," Ryan started eating and she went back to her work.

As he picked up the bowl of slaw, he noticed something written on the napkin underneath. It was a phone number and the name Jocelyn. He was shocked and didn't know how to react. Didn't she know he was married? He had a wedding band on after all. Hadn't Talia ever come in here with him? He couldn't recall. He started chewing slower to give himself time to think. He would have to say something on his way out the door, but what?

Luckily the deli got busier just as he was finishing his lunch. He quickly made an escape while she was taking orders to avoid saying anything. He did, however, grab the napkin with her phone number and shove it deep into his jeans pocket, making a mental note to get rid of it before throwing them into the laundry basket. He felt guilty already, even though he had not done anything wrong, yet.

Over the course of the next week, he kept on staring at Talia, taking assessment of her looks and their relationship. She was still slim and beautiful, with the dancer's body she always had. Sure, she had gained a few pounds in retirement, but they all had, himself included. He squeezed the little paunch above his belt and knew he wasn't as young or as virile as he used to be. He imagined himself with Jocelyn, who was fifteen years his junior. Would he even be able to perform as she expected? Surely, she had been with much younger men who could satisfy her better than he could. He was lost in a reverie when Talia suddenly spoke.

"Where are you right now?" she asked. "You look like you're off in la-la land and this is not the first time. You have been distant all week. What is going on with you?"

"I don't know. Nothing. Maybe I'm just getting old and doddery, or maybe I'm a creative genius and I'm working on my next big idea."

"Oh yah, that's got to be it," Talia laughed, "except I've never seen you create anything in your life other than building beautiful houses."

"Well, you'd be surprised. I might just patent the greatest new invention and make us rich one of these days."

"Great! I'm looking forward to it," Talia said.

Ryan walked away to take a shower and realized that he'd better stop dreaming about Jocelyn when Talia was in the room.

Three days later, Ryan was in town picking up a parcel when he decided to pull the trigger. He pulled over and called Jocelyn's number and she answered right away.

"Hi, it's Ryan."

"Who?" she asked.

"Ryan; corned beef on rye with extra hot mustard. You gave me your number last time I came in for lunch."

"Oh yah, sorry, I just couldn't put the name to the face. How are you?"

"I'm great. Are you free for dinner in the next hour?"

"Yah sure, I'm just getting off work now. I just need to go home and take a shower and then we could grab a bite. You can meet me at my place in half an hour if you want? It's at 583 Sumpter Way. It's a green four-plex and I'm in the lower left-side unit. Just walk through the gate and then knock on door A."

"Ok, I'll see you soon."

"Sounds good, bye for now."

Ryan quickly called Talia and told her he was famished and was just going to grab a burger in town instead of having dinner at home. She didn't even blink. She was going to watch a movie with Darlene and Sonya after supper.

When he got to Jocelyn's place, the door was cracked ajar for him. He walked in and found her towel drying her hair in a pink terry-cloth bathrobe. She was drinking a beer and offered him one. She went over to her docking station and put on some acoustic guitar music.

"So where do you want to eat?" Ryan asked innocently.

"Well, to tell you the truth, I'm not really hungry yet." she replied, walking closer. "Why don't you help me work up an appetite?"

She let the belt of her robe loosen to reveal her naked body underneath. She was tanned, with full, soft-looking round breasts and wore pink lacy thong underwear. Her boldness took his breath away for a second.

"Oh wow, okay, you really aren't wasting any time."

"We are too old to play games, don't you think? I gave you my number and you called me, so why be coy about it. You're obviously attracted to me and I'm attracted to you."

"I didn't even bring a condom because I never imagined this would be happening so fast." Ryan looked embarrassed.

"That's okay. My tubes are tied, and I've just been tested so I know I'm clean, if you are?"

"Are you kidding? I've only had one partner for the last thirty years!"

"Well great, then we can skip the condom."

She took his hand and led him into her bedroom. He was moving, but felt like he was in a dream, out of control of his own mind and body. She took the lead and started kissing him deeply, undoing his jeans. Before he even had time to think, she was on top of him licking his chest and taking him into her mouth. The pleasure was intense, and he let himself give in to her powerful seduction. She slid his shaft into her body and rose up and down rhythmically on it until they were both moaning. Ten minutes later, they were both spent.

Lying there, Ryan began to feel the magnitude of what had just happened. A wave of fear swept over him. Had he just ruined his marriage of thirty-five years for one instant of intense pleasure? Would he lose his new house, his community of treasured friends, his share of the group's savings, his reputation as a solid guy, and perhaps even his dog because of this? Selfishly, he was worried about how this would affect him. Then his thoughts turned to Talia. She would be devastated if she found out. He imagined her in tears being consoled by his sister Darlene, who would be furious with him. Suddenly it all seemed like a huge mistake.

"I have to go home," he blurted out, getting up and pulling his jeans on.

"What about dinner?" Talia said, "I'm really hungry now. You're not going to make me eat alone are you?"

"I'm afraid so. I'm sorry Jocelyn, but this was a huge mistake. I can't do this. I'm really sorry. I love my wife. I can't see you anymore. Please don't tell anyone about this."

"Oh jeez, are you having a crisis of conscience now? Well, it's a little late for that. You called me, remember?"

"I know. I'm sorry. You are so beautiful, and you will make some guy really happy. It just can't be me." He sounded pitiful.

"Oh alright, don't worry, I won't tell anyone. I never wanted a relationship anyhow. It was just sex. Don't get your panties in a bunch."

"Thank you for understanding Jocelyn. You're an awesome lady."

"Don't call me a lady. It makes me sound old. Just go home to your wife and do me a favor; don't come into the deli for at least three months. I don't want to see your face for a while."

"No problem." And he left.

He drove home slowly, to give himself more time to think. He poured his water bottle onto a napkin and wiped his face and neck to make sure he didn't smell like her when he greeted Talia. Then he realized she would be at Darlene's so he could jump in the shower. Thank god! He threw Jocelyn's phone number out the window. He felt like a fool for letting this physical attraction to her get the better of him. Now he would always have to worry about Talia finding out.

For the next few weeks, Ryan was especially loving and affectionate with Talia. She didn't know what hit him, but she was happy to have her former lover back. Just like when he was courting her, he brought her flowers, made her breakfast and massaged her tired shoulders. They made love more frequently and he told her he loved her repeatedly. It was like a second honeymoon, but for all the wrong reasons. She had no idea.

# CHAPTER 16
## PAUL'S FATHER'S FUNERAL

In February 2019, Paul got a call from the hospital in Sacramento. His mother had already passed three years earlier of heath failure, after several angioplasties. Now his father had had a stroke, and the prognosis was bad. He was told he should come right away if he wanted to say his good-byes. Paul was shocked. He had just called his dad the week before and scolded him for climbing a ladder by himself to take down the Christmas lights. At eighty-six, he was still the tough, stubborn old man he had always been.

Andrea insisted on driving to the airport, in case Paul was too emotional to focus on traffic. They flew to LAX and deplaned. Checking their messages, they saw a voicemail from the hospital saying they were sorry, but Paul's father had just passed. He had missed him by just two hours. Paul sat down heavily and put his head between his hands and pushed back the tears as best he could, since they were in such a busy public space. Andrea rubbed his back and kept quiet so he could gather his composure.

They trudged on to get their connection to Sacramento. Sim picked them and offered his condolences to Paul with a hug. He drove them home in a very quiet car to their daughter's place. Andrea scooped little Krishna up in their arms and gave her too many kisses. April gave her dad a long hug.

"Hey Dad. I'm so sorry about Grandpa. He was a great man."

"Thanks honey. Yah, he was. He was a stubborn old fool, but he was as solid as they come."

"Come in and have a cup of tea and something to eat."

"I'd rather have a stiff drink if you have anything?"

"Sure Dad, we got a bottle of scotch for Christmas. We will open it for this special occasion and have a toast."

So, they ended up planning a funeral and stayed for five days. Many people came to pay their respects, including some old friends from his work in the agricultural machinery business. Paul had to give a speech, since he was an only child, which was terribly difficult. He broke down three times in the process and had to gather himself. Afterwards, they milled about at the reception, eating sandwiches and chatting with the attendees.

When they got back to April's, he crashed right away, completely spent. Andrea helped her daughter prepare dinner while Krishna played ball with Sim in the back yard. She had been sitting still far too long for a small child and needed to run around.

"Mom, can you pass me that olive oil please?"

"Sure honey, but I can fix the salad dressing if you want?"

"That's okay. I make it a little different than you do, but at least Krishna likes it, so I'm sticking to my recipe."

"Listen honey, I don't want to step on any toes, but am I sensing a little tension between you and Sim since we got here? Is everything alright?"

"God, I can't hide anything from you can I Mom?" she sighed. "No everything is not alright. We have been bickering for months and I'm afraid I might need to do something more drastic, or I'll go out of my mind soon!" She dropped the knife she was holding and started to cry.

"Come and sit down, sweetheart." Her mother led her to the nook. "Have you guys tried counseling?"

"Yah, we did it for two months, but we weren't getting anywhere. He just doesn't feel things on a deeper level like I do. He misses all my cues when I'm upset or want to try a different approach with Krishna. He's just so inflexible!"

"I'm sorry honey but promise me you won't do anything rash without consulting a lawyer. You two have a lot of assets and somebody needs to represent your best interests."

"Yah, I know Mom, I won't just storm out of here and give up my house or anything stupid. Besides, Krishna loves her school and her playmates, so he would have to move, not me."

"Well, that's very sensible. Does his mother know about the troubles you've been having?"

"Oh, hell yah! She is part of the problem. He can't even blink without his mother's approval. Since his father died, we are her only source of entertainment. That's another thing that's driving me nuts! She wants to have Krishna over every Sunday like she always has, but Krishna's getting older and wants to see her friends on the weekend. Sim is just too spineless to tell his mother that. I swear he worships the ground she walks on."

"Okay, I get that. Mother-in-laws can be challenging. It's probably a cultural difference as well you know. He is probably expected to respect his mother's wishes more than us Americans do, which is not necessarily a bad thing," she teased Andrea to make her smile.

"Well, here they come for dinner, so please don't say anything Mom, I'm begging you."

"I promise, I will stay right out of it, but please keep me posted. I care about you both, obviously."

April quickly splashed a little cold water on her face to hide the redness from crying and they all sat down for a nice meal. Everyone made light conversation as if nothing was wrong. After dinner, Andrea played barbies with Krishna in her bedroom, got her ready for bed, and read her a bedtime story to give her daughter a break. Then she took out her laptop to show her daughter the baby clothes she was designing. Sim was doing some work on the computer in his office.

"This looks great Mom. You have four different patterns ready to go, but how will you produce enough to sell online?"

"Well, I met a Mexican woman in Taos who does beautiful sewing. She already sells a few items in a local shop. She said she would be willing to sew with me two days a week for twenty dollars an hour. I've done the math and can turn a decent profit if I sell at least twenty outfits a month. I've been invited to put them in two shops in town and also, I'm doing the Sunday artisans' street market once the weather gets warm. Then I need a website. I was wondering if you could help me with that?"

"Sure Mom, no problem. This is really cool. I'm proud of you for starting a cottage industry in your retirement. Most people just get lazy and watch game shows or soaps all day."

"Thank you dear, I knew you would approve." She leaned against her daughter and whispered into her ear, "What you told me earlier, it's not about another man is it?"

Andrea pulled away and looked at her mother with wide eyes.

"No Mom, but you are scarily perceptive. There's a guy I met at a tech conference last November who has been messaging me pretty steadily ever since. He must know I'm married because of the ring, but I'm sensing the interest is more than professional."

"Well take it slow, whatever you decide to do. You need to put Krishna first. She has to feel stable before anyone new enters the picture, right?"

"Of course, Mom! I wouldn't dream of exposing her to another guy until all the kinks are ironed out. She is my priority, you know that."

"Yes, yes, of course I do. You're the best mother in the world. I didn't mean to offend you. Sorry sweetheart."

The next day, Paul and Andrea packed their bags for the flights home. Andrea decided she would fill her husband in on her daughter's marital problems once they got on the plane. They hugged their daughter's little family good-bye and set off back to Taos.

# CHAPTER 17
## AGRICULTURAL PRODUCTION

In spring, they felt a sense of contentment in their newly established homes. The first golden bladderwort mustard flowers peeked through the snow, ushering in the spring equinox and beckoning every living creature into a hum of activity.

When Andrea and Paul returned from California, Darlene called everyone together one night after dinner at her place. Jared served some coffee and cake while Darlene passed out an information sheet and set up a rolling whiteboard from her office. She began speaking to the group. It seemed that life was not as perfect as they thought. She had reviewed their annual budget and discovered that, at the rate they were spending, their retirement savings would run out in ten years. Therefore, in short, they needed to generate a new income stream. Darlene had burst their dreamy bubble, and everyone was a little shocked.

So began a brainstorming session. Karl and Clay offered to take on more plumbing jobs around town. Right now, he was only taking odd jobs by word of mouth. He could advertise in the local paper and online. Clay was still doing his practicum, but once he was done, he would probably move into town and start his own life with Michelle. They were very happy and wanted to move in together.

Andrea offered to hire another seamstress to help produce more baby clothes, at least for the summer market season to see how much revenue she could generate in her first year. Her Mexican employee, Carmen, had a cousin named Marisol, who had already asked if she could sew three days a week. Both women had their own sewing machines so this would save Andrea the cost of buying new ones.

Now Paul chimed in. With his degree in bioscience and experience on the marijuana farm in California, he suggested they start a small grow-op to produce medicinal marijuana, which was already legal in New Mexico. He had visited the medical dispensary in town and talked to the owner about the possibility of distributing through them. Jared and Ryan could help build a large greenhouse in the front field to house the operation and together they could all help plant and harvest the crop.

Talia chimed in. What if they diversified and grew a second medicinal crop, like ginger? They would already need to purchase an industrial dehydrator for the pot, so this would be no additional cost, other than a capsule filling machine. They could market their locally grown high quality ginger capsules to all the Whole Foods and vitamin stores in town. Since ginger is harvested in the winter, they could focus their efforts on the two crops at different times so they wouldn't be spread too thin. She and Sonya offered to do all the research and report back to the group, but Paul would need to share the greenhouse space with them.

Everyone liked this idea. Darlene would help crunch the numbers on production and sales projected revenues before they committed to this plan, but it seemed plausible. In the meantime, Jared, Paul and Ryan would begin construction on the greenhouse. Karl and Clay would install the irrigation lines. Andrea would be free to continue her own business endeavor.

Everyone was buzzing with excitement. Thankfully, they were still strong and healthy enough in their early sixties to undertake such a project and they really loved collaborating as a team. With forty years of friendship, they all knew each other's strengths and weaknesses and who to call on for a particular task. If they needed more help, they could hire a couple of day laborers in town, without divulging what they were growing. Darlene would work on the state and city business permits to keep it all legal.

In late March, Darlene gave the go-ahead, with positive revenue projections. Over the next few weeks, there was a hum of activity as lumber got trucked in and hammering started on the greenhouse. Rolls of clear polyethylene plastic sheeting were laid and nailed tightly over the frame. Karl and Clay waited a bit longer for the ground to thaw before bringing irrigation lines up from the well. This required renting a Bobcat and hiring day laborers to dig the required narrow trenches. Ryan's electrical skills became invaluable in hooking up lighting so they could work in the evening at harvest time and also an alarm system. He installed a heater just in case they got an unexpected cold snap so they wouldn't lose their crops.

Then the growing troughs were built and installed on top of the cheapest sturdy tables they could find, and the soil was trucked in. They spent two days shoving sphagnum peat moss into the troughs for the ginger. Then they shoveled a more expensive, specialized soil into the marijuana containers. It contained other organic elements, such as bat guano, earthworm castings and forest humus. Talia, Sonya and Darlene all helped with the planting and were taught by Paul about ideal spacing and proper care of the plants. He also worked with Ryan to set up a timer on the irrigation lines for regular watering.

By mid-April, they were all tired but satisfied with their new greenhouse. When the first green shoots appeared a few weeks later, they were overjoyed. Clay was given strict instructions not to tell any of his friends about their marijuana crop. He promised to keep their secret, if he could just tell Michelle. They brought Michelle over one day to explain to her the importance of discretion and she agreed to keep their secret from her family. They were worried that if word got out, their plants would be stolen. They told the day laborers who came earlier that they were growing tomatoes, so that would not be an issue.

Every day, they all had specific tasks to perform. Paul would check the crop first thing every morning. Then he would meet Jared, Sonya, Talia and Darlene every other morning at nine o'clock to give specific instructions on trimming the plants. Darlene would bring them coffee and baked goods at ten-thirty. Then they would all work a little longer and break for lunch. Andrea usually made them all sandwiches and they would eat with her, Carmen, and Marisol. It was a chance for them to all report-back on their daily progress and socialize. Carmen and Marisol had been brought into their inner circle and were asked to sign non-disclosure agreements about their crops. They were lovely women, who Andrea adored, and they were now treated as part of the family. They were also very knowledgeable about plant life in the area and had some good insights about the soil conditions and local plants. Paul especially enjoyed sharing this with them, as did Talia and Sonya, who took care of their small flower gardens at the front of each house.

Talia and Sonya worked hard to go out in the afternoons and find a market for their ginger. They obtained a written agreement from five stores in town to carry their capsules when they were ready. They researched pricing and learned online how to use the dehydrator and capsule filling machines. They purchased bottles and capsules in bulk and practiced with the color label-maker they had bought. Andrea, being the most artistic, helped to design a logo for their products. They decided to call their brand "Golden Land" for both crops, in dedication to their communal property. Andrea drew out a simple sunrise between mountains logo and Talia used Photoshop to design the label. Everything was coming together nicely.

One day Clay and Michelle appeared at lunchtime and looked very excited.

"We came to make an announcement," Clay began. "Michelle and I are engaged, and she is pregnant!"

Everyone cheered, then hugged and congratulated them. Michelle showed off her small solitaire diamond engagement ring and told them her mother was over the moon with excitement about the coming baby. They asked if they could get married on their property and the answer was a resounding yes. They planned for the month of June, before it got too hot to be outside. Then suddenly, Clay looked alarmed.

"What about the secret crop? If we invite friends to the wedding, they will probably find out?"

"Right," Paul spoke for the group. "Well maybe we can set up down below, closer to the gate so people won't be coming up here.

Either that or we can tarp over the greenhouse for one day and make it look like a construction site. That might be better, because we will need the kitchens and bathrooms for your guests. We will work out the details later," he said.

"Thank you, guys. This means so much to us," Clay said.

Michelle echoed his sentiment, "Yes, thank you. This will save us so much money because we won't have to rent a hall for the reception. I have a large family, as you all know. Some cousins and aunties and uncles will be coming up from Albuquerque and Santa Fe as well. We want to have about fifty people. Is that okay?"

"Sure, sure," Andrea spoke. "We will make it work for you, don't worry. It might not be super fancy, but we can all pitch in and make your day really special. You and I can sit down and plan the food, music, decorations and seating plan. It will be fun."

Michelle gave Andrea a big hug.

Then Karl asked, "What about your mother Clay? Roxanne will want to be there for your wedding you know. Even though she's been a crappy mom, she should probably be invited."

"Oh yah, I didn't even think about that," Clay said. "Maybe you and I can talk about this later?"

"Sure, sure, we will figure it out. I will have to insist that she stay clean and sober for the occasion. I'm not going to let her put on a show and ruin your wedding. We will need to set some ground rules."

"Good idea," Clay said. "Thanks Grandpa, for always having my back."

"Of course, kid. She is my daughter after all. I know what she's like, trust me."

"I do trust you, Grandpa."

They said good-bye to the group and left. It was going to be a busy summer with a wedding and two new business ventures. They all felt motivated and happy with their busy, fulfilling lives.

# CHAPTER 18
## CLAY'S WEDDING

After a very busy spring of budgeting, building, buying supplies, and planting, the wedding date in June crept up on them quickly. Andrea had collaborated with Michelle's mother as the main organizers. They would sage and bless the altar and then a local shaman would perform a traditional Pueblo wedding vase ceremony. Then they would bring out the food for the reception.

A rental company had set up one giant tent with long tables and chairs and a microphone for speeches. Talia and Sonya had gathered yellow wildflowers for the tables and hung curly red streamers. Michelle's aunties had taken over Andrea's kitchen all day to prepare a mountain of food. They were also using Talia and Darlene's kitchens for roasting meat and making soft corn tortillas on a griddle. All three houses smelled wonderful and there was lots of laughter and harmless bickering over family recipes.

Karl had invited his daughter Roxanne to the wedding and greeted her at the gate to make sure she was clean and sober and in a good headspace to be on her best behavior for her son. Karl was pleasantly surprised that she looked healthy and composed. Her wispy brown hair was pulled up neatly into a bun, her skin looked smooth, and her dark blue eyes were clear. She wore a pretty green dress and actually seemed humbled to be included. She told Karl that she wanted to be a part of this new baby's life after it was born and so she planned to keep on attending her regular Narcotics Anonymous meetings. Karl led her up to Talia's house to see her son and daughter-in-law, who she had only met twice at Baker's Grill in town.

At the start of the ceremony, a handbell was rung by her maid of honor and six men with blankets draped over one shoulder came to be seated in the front row. These were elders from Michelle's grandmother's community in Jemez. Then, after everyone was seated, Clay walked down the grass from Talia's house in a navy suit, followed by Michelle and her father. She looked absolutely stunning with her long black hair tied in braids swooping down around her face and a long white, frilly, beaded dress. The officiant took a long, beaded sash and draped it over the shoulders of the couple so that they were bound together by it.

Three weeks before the ceremony, Karl had been asked to meet with Michelle's parents at the river near Michelle's grandmother's home in Jemez to gather soft clay from the riverbank. Together they made a two-spouted vessel that would be fired in a kiln. Now the shaman filled it with herbal tea, offering it first to the groom, who offered the bride a drink from one spout. Then she turned the wedding vase clockwise and offered the groom a drink from the other side. Finally, they both drank from the wedding vase together. The Pueblo tradition says that if they can do this without spilling a drop, they will always have a strong, cooperative relationship. Michelle and Clay did this successfully and they looked relieved. After the vows and rings were exchanged, the men came up and gave their brightly colored traditional blankets to the bride and groom.

Gifts from her Pueblo relatives had been placed on the table in bright red baskets with yellow flowers placed among a nest of red paper. Her grandmother's gift contained sweets and bread, salt, jalapeño peppers, mesquite honey, and a bottle of champagne, symbolic of a life full of sweetness, spice, and happiness. Then there were other American style gifts in more glossy wrapping paper.

Clay's friend had recorded a mixture of cheerful Mexican American and pop music on his iPod for the dinner, which was served buffet-style. The food was delicious, and everyone ate their fill. Then Michelle danced with Clay for the first dance and then with her father, a tall German man who was beaming with pride. Her Pueblo mother looked tiny beside him, but everyone could see how much they loved each other. After the first dance, everyone else joined in for a fun evening of partying. There were little children running around gleefully now, who had been sitting far too long. Even Lucy the dog got in on the action.

The greenhouses had been tarped over with black tarps for the day to avoid any issues. It was only Roxanne who asked Karl about the apparent building site.

"What are you guys building under the tarps?"

"Oh, we are planning to grow vegetables so we're building a greenhouse."

"Great idea," said Roxanne innocently," can I take a peek?"

"No, there's loose lumber everywhere and I don't want anything falling on you," Karl lied.

"Hmm, okay then, another time then." She dropped it, but seemed curious, nonetheless. Karl was wondering if Clay had inadvertently said something he shouldn't have, but when would he have seen his mother? As far as he knew, they barely spoke.

"Is it okay if I come by here to visit Carl now and then? He asked if I could help him find a place in town to rent and help him with sewing curtains and decorating it, since Michelle is really tired these days after work. You know I am good at that sort of thing," Roxanne asked.

"Well, I will leave that up to Clay, as long as you give us a heads-up before you drop by. Our place is small for the three of us and I don't want Sonya's nose getting out of joint."

"Sure, sure, no problem. Thanks for this, by the way Dad, it means a lot."

"No problem Roxanne, it's good to see you looking so healthy. I'm proud of you for getting your shit together and going to meetings. I hope it works out for you and you can stay the course this time." He gave his daughter a hug.

They went back to the party. Jared had been tasked with taking photographs and he ran around with his camera catching everyone in the moment. It was a lovely wedding and they saw the bride and groom off to spend the night in a hotel room in town and bid farewell to their guests. Exhausted, they put the leftover food in the fridge, leaving the rest of the clean-up 'til morning, and collapsed into bed.

# CHAPTER 19
## TALIA'S YOGA

In July, the marijuana plants were getting quite tall, and they were clipping them daily to produce the best ratio of buds and leaves. They had worked out a good routine to harvest their crop in the fall. They planned on drying the product in the dehydrator and selling it all in bulk to the local dispensary for an agreed upon price. They had already taken in a sample to have it tested and graded and the dispensary was satisfied with the quality and potency of their weed. It would be labeled as Golden Land Sativa.

Meanwhile, Talia had a new idea for generating some income. Since she had ended her dancing career, she had suffered from aches and pains in her joints. She had remedied this through daily yoga. She did a routine every morning by following online tutorials and now she felt quite proficient. She asked the group if she could run a yoga class in the guest suite twice a week and they all agreed it was a great idea. If she got eight participants at ten dollars per session, that would bring in six-hundred and forty dollars a month. She would just have to move the living room furniture into the dining area and set up mats in its place.

She practiced teaching her routine several times to Darlene, Sonja and Andrea until she became fluid in her instructions. She recorded an hour of Zen music to run during her sessions.

They complimented her on her relaxing approach and said it would be perfect for all ages and ability levels, even beginners or seniors, like themselves. Talia hated being called a senior, so she changed the flyer to include people with joint pain. She stuck them to cork boards around Taos, in the cafes, artisan shops and the seniors' center. She posted a start date of the last week in July running until Labor Day.

Jared and Paul insisted she direct them with a sign to take the gravel ring-road to the park at the back of their property so they wouldn't see the greenhouse, which was fine. The response was good, and seven people showed up, all women. They ranged in age from thirty-five to seventy-two. Talia was really pleased to meet some new like-minded women and she often stayed and chatted with them afterwards. She really liked one woman in particular who seemed to share her love of travel and dance. Her name was Jocelyn. She worked in the deli in town where they made those great fresh sandwiches.

Of course, Ryan was nowhere near the yoga class, so he had no idea who his wife was getting friendly with. One morning, he was over in the greenhouse fixing the irrigation pump. When he went in for lunch, Talia was prepping a big tuna salad for both of them. He nuzzled up to her back and wrapped his arms around her.

"Hmm, that looks yummy. Is it almost ready? I'm starving!"

"Yah, if you could just butter those two rolls and pour us some juice, I will bring you a bowl."

"How was your yoga class today?"

"Awesome. I'm really liking these women. I talked to one of them today for a while after class. It turns out she used to be a dancer as well. She ran a small studio in Albuquerque for many years."

"That's cool. I'm glad you're enjoying it honey and making some new friends. I get how living here can be isolating at times; that's why I'm going to join a pool league in September at the pub in town on Tuesday nights."

"That's a great idea. You love playing pool. It will be good for you to get out once in a while," Talia said.

After lunch, they had a nap and then decided to fix up the signage for her parking area to make it brighter and easier for new guests to see. This could be used for anyone coming to visit, not just the yoga patrons, and would avoid their worry about the greenhouse drawing attention. They spray painted some boards with neon yellow lettering and arrows and hammered them in several places, starting at the gate and moving to the left along the property line to the back.

"We should bring in a backhoe and dig out the grass here for easier parking," Ryan said.

"Wouldn't it just keep growing back?" Talia asked.

"Not if we place rocks around the perimeter and Weed-Whack it once in a while. We could mark off eight spots with the rocks as well."

"Great idea. Let's call that guy down the road tomorrow morning to dig it up. He was really reasonable last time he dug out the greenhouse site," said Talia.

So, the project began a couple of days later and was ready by her next yoga session on Friday. Ryan wanted to watch the women arrive and park their cars to get some feedback on how the rocks were placed. He stood there with his travel mug of coffee and his furry sidekick Lucy smiling and greeting each participant as they arrived.

The last one to arrive pulled up in a green Jeep. She looked familiar, but Ryan couldn't see her clearly until she stepped out of the vehicle. He was shocked and scared.

"What are you doing here?" he approached and spoke in a hushed voice, sounding alarmed.

"What do you mean? I'm here for the yoga class. What are you doing here?"

"I live here!" he said defensively. "Talia is my wife!"

"Jesus Christ," said Jocelyn, "I had no frickin' idea. I just saw the ad at the coffee shop and signed up. Your wife is awesome by the way." She reached down to scratch the scruff of Lucy's neck.

"I know she's awesome. So, what do we do now?" he was freaking out.

"Nothing," she said, "we just act normal and carry on with our day. I won't say anything if you don't."

"Okay, well that's good. Of course, I won't say anything. It would kill her. Please don't get too friendly with Talia. She likes to make new friends and I cannot have you two getting all chummy."

"Well, you're a bit late for that," Jocelyn said. "We already chatted about dance for like thirty minutes last session and she said she wanted to watch some of my old performance videos."

"Shit, that was you? God, this is the worst. What am I going to do?"

"Just cool it. If she never found out four months ago, she's not going to find out now. Just chill bro."

"Okay, I will try, but if you can avoid spending time with her, that would be best. Make up some excuse if you have to."

Suddenly they heard Talia's voice calling.

"Hey, you two. What's the hold up? We are ready to get started Jocelyn, if you're done chatting? I see you met Ryan."

"Yah, he was just admiring my Jeep and asked me how much I paid for it. I'm coming now. Sorry to keep you all waiting." She left Ryan standing in the dirt field looking lost as the two former dancers hugged and went inside.

"Fuck my life," he said out loud and ambled off in a daze to refill his coffee with Lucy following behind him.

# CHAPTER 20
## A VISIT FROM DONOVAN

Two weeks later, Donovan came out with his fiancé, Shawna. They had just got engaged and he was excited to introduce her to his parents. He also wanted to show her the land to see if she would agree to holding their wedding there the following year. Talia and Ryan had moved back all the living room furniture and Andrea explained to Donovan that they would have to vacate the suite for an hour on Friday for Talia's yoga class. This was no big deal, since they could just go over to his parents' place ten feet away for coffee.

Paul and Andrea were thrilled to meet Shawna. Andrea threw her arms around her at the airport.

"Look at you, with that flaming red hair and those blue eyes and freckles. Imagine the adorable freckled, ginger grandbabies the two of you are going to have!"

"Settle down Mom," warned Donovan, "you're freaking her out. We aren't even married yet!"

"I'm sorry sweetheart, she is just so beautiful!" Shawna was blushing.

On the car ride home, they learned that Shawna got her red hair from her father's Irish side of the family. She worked full-time as a bank teller in Brooklyn and she and Ryan were saving up to buy a condo. They had met at a Christmas party last year at a local bar and hit it off right away. She had moved in with him four months later, partly to save them from paying two expensive rents.

Andrea tried to be more discrete, but couldn't help asking Shawna, while they were cleaning up dinner, if she wanted to have children. Shawna said yes, and the sooner the better, because they weren't getting any younger. This was music to Andrea's ears, and she relayed it to Paul during their bedtime pillow-talk that night.

Shawna loved the property and agreed it would be perfect for their wedding, but she warned them that she had a big family who would all want to fly out next summer. Paul suggested a budget motel in Taos where they could book a bunch of rooms at a discount because he knew the owners through their architect Lars. He drove them to check it out and they thought it was suitable, so they picked a date of July twelfth the following year and pre-booked ten rooms.

Andrea sat with Shawna and made up the guest list and seating chart and they agreed to use the same set-up that Clay and Michelle had, with a giant tent outdoors and rental furniture. However, this time the family would not be cooking. Paul and Andrea offered to pay for caterers to come in and they agreed on a local company and a menu based around roast beef, with one vegetarian option for her cousins. They booked the caterers a year ahead, just to be sure.

"Would you like to wear my wedding dress?" Andrea offered. "Before you say no, let me show it to you. It's pretty spectacular and I am a seamstress, so I can tailor it to fit you perfectly."

"Wow, that's very sweet. Well sure, let's take a look at it. This could save us a lot of money too."

Andrea loved how pragmatic this girl was. She went to her closet and brought the dress out. Shawna loved it, but asked if she could remove the shoulder pads, since it wasn't the 80's anymore. Andrea got her to try it on and marveled at how gorgeous she looked. It was a real bonding moment for the two women. Andrea would cinch in the waist an inch or so and shorten the sleeves and hem.

The only difficult decision seemed to be who would marry them? Shawna's parents were Protestant, but she hadn't been to church since she was little and no longer believed. After calling her mother and talking for quite a while, they decided on a Justice of the Peace in Taos who had good reviews online and booked her too. Apparently, her parents weren't as hard-set on a religious wedding as she had feared. Shawna was relieved.

After two days of planning, they just wanted to enjoy the local scenery, so Paul and Andrea drove them up to the local mountains for a day hike. They marveled at the gorgeous scenery, with its colorful layered rock formations and higher altitude conifers and could imagine themselves leaving the big apple for a quieter life. Paul and Andrea encouraged them to seriously think about it. They would love to have any future grandkids close by and Donovan's physiotherapy skills would be easily transferable to Taos, especially with all the ski injuries in winter and extreme cycling injuries in summer. Perhaps Shawna could get a transfer to work in a bank in town? She agreed to look into it. After their hike, they drove back into town for a pub lunch.

Over dinner, Donovan filled his parents in on his sister's divorce action.

"You know she's going ahead with it, right?"

"Yah, she sounded pretty determined last time she called," said Paul.

"Well, she has just served Sim with the legal papers last month and he was apparently an emotional wreck. He even booked time off work to deal with the shock and find himself a lawyer," explained Donovan.

Andrea and Paul couldn't help feeling sorry for Sim. He was such a jovial guy normally and April had really taken him by surprise. How could he not have seen their marriage unraveling? Was he so in denial?

"Sim's parents are furious with April and won't even speak to her," said Donovan, reaching across the table for the Caesar salad. "April's lawyer is insisting that she keep the house, for Krishna's sake, but Sim hasn't moved out yet. They are still living under one roof until the end of the month, and it sounds really awkward. I think he is going to take an apartment close by. April is dreading the talk they need to have very soon with Krishna about why daddy will be moving out."

"How awful," said Andrea. "It breaks my heart that Krishna has to go through this. I will call April in a couple of days to see how she's holding up, poor girl."

The next day they drove Donovan and Shawna to the airport and hugged them good-bye. Two months later they got a call early one morning. It was Donovan announcing that Shawna was already pregnant. They had also decided that while she was on maternity leave next year, they would move out to Taos. Paul and Andrea were elated.

# CHAPTER 21
## DARLENE'S NEW JOB

The group now had money coming in from multiple sources. There were Andrea's baby clothes sales, which were steadily improving, Karl's odd plumbing jobs, Talia's yoga, and the pot and ginger crops, which were still growing.

Darlene decided she had better step up her game and contribute something as well. She heard from her hairdresser in town that they needed a bookkeeper, so she offered her services. Then she saw an ad in the local paper asking for a small business accountant. The ad specified:

"Accountant wanted - person of discretion."

Darlene thought, "Well duh, it kind of comes with the territory," and called them up. She found out it was the gaming arcade in Taos where all the teenagers hung out and played games after school. She arranged to meet the manager, a guy named Joe, the following day.

Joe was a slovenly looking fellow in an old white t-shirt with a beer belly who sounded like he came from Eastern Europe somewhere. He showed her his disheveled office and the filing cabinet drawer with all his bills and receipts. This was going to be a challenge. He had not filed taxes for two years and she would have to go through his mess and come up with something coherent. She told him it wouldn't be cheap because she would bill him by the hour, but he agreed. She said she would come in on Tuesday mornings and he agreed to let her use the office for three hours each time.

Joe turned out to be a really nice man with a warped sense of humor she enjoyed. She thought it was odd that he still used a pager. She didn't even know you could still buy those. He said he preferred it because he could feel the vibration on his hip even though the games were loud in the arcade. She was told to buzz him whenever she had a question, and he would come back to the office.

Darlene made piles of bills and organized them neatly into folders by month for the first hour. Then she needed a coffee. There was a small concession stand in the arcade that served hotdogs and nacho chips with that fake disgusting hot liquid cheese that kids love. Darlene decided to risk it and try their coffee. To her amazement, it was actually pretty good. Standing at the concession counter, she noticed a door to the left that said "private" and wondered if Joe had living quarters on site.

She asked him about it.

"No, no I don't live here. We play cards. Come, I show you."

He led her through the door into a barren concrete room with posters and flags of Serbia plastered on the walls and a TV mounted on the wall blaring European football (aka soccer). Ah, the accent was Serbian, she realized. There were four burly guys sitting around a card table, smoking and playing poker. Joe introduced her.

"Guys, this is my accountant, Darlene. She's a great lady. You make her feel welcome."

They all said hello and gave her a wave, never relinquishing their hand of cards. Darlene noticed a small pile of money in the middle of the table, but decided she'd better not say anything about the legalities of gambling. She had enough to do just figuring out his taxes.

"Nice to meet you," she said and walked out of the smoke pit to go back to the paperwork.

On her way out she heard one man at the table say," Hey Joe, give me fifty on Arsenal to win."

At that moment she realized that not only were they playing cash poker, but he was a bookie as well. Hmm, this was getting a little more sketchy than she cared for, but hell, it was a paycheck. She would just pretend she never heard or saw any of that. She pushed it out of her mind and went back into the office. At the end of her three-hour shift, Joe handed her cash payment for her time.

"Oh no Joe, I can't accept cash like this. I have to keep my business above board and bill you for my time. Otherwise, I cannot submit my work to the IRS to file your taxes. I have to give you my official receipts as well. You can pay me at the end of each month."

"Really?" He was taken aback by her forthrightness. "Okay, okay, you the boss." He spread his arms in a gesture of "hands up" to capitulate to her demands.

"See you next Tuesday Joe," Darlene walked out.

That night in bed, Darlene told Jared about Joe and his business. Jared was a little concerned.

"Are you sure you want to work for this guy? He sounds pretty shady to me."

"Yah, he's harmless. He's just a fat old Serbian teddy bear. I think I've got a good read on him," Darlene tried to reassure him.

"Ok then honey, but the minute you feel compromised in any way, you walk outta there. Promise me that."

"Sure honey, I promise. I'm not going to damage my name as a professional for this guy. Don't worry."

As the weeks went on, Darlene became more and more curious about how much money Joe was making on the down low. There seemed to be different guys coming and going all the time and there were even a few bikers, which made her uneasy.

She decided to do a little snooping around in his office one day, so she casually pushed the button in on the doorknob to lock the door. She had seen him many times go into the bottom drawer of his desk to grab some cash. He told her it was to make change for the arcade machines, but that made no sense because a lot of it was bills, not coins. She pulled open the drawer to find a bright red metal cash box inside. There were wads of bills spilling out the sides, mostly hundreds. She lifted the lid and did a quick count of what was there. It was over four thousand dollars. This was a lot more than petty cash. She had seen him wrap up these wads into a tight roll and stuff them into his pocket several times already. If he was banking over $4000 a week in bets, this was serious tax evasion. She had a lot to think about. She quickly put the money back, messed it all up as it was before and unlocked the door.

On her way home, she decided not to tell Jared anything about this because he would make her quit instantly and she wasn't sure what to do yet. Should she report him to the cops or to the IRS? Should she confront him? Should she turn a blind eye? She had trouble sleeping that night and woke up visibly tired the next morning. Jared noticed.

"What's going on with you Dar? You were tossing and turning all night and you look like you haven't slept?"

"Yah, I think it's these damn hot flashes," she lied. "I need to put the fan beside the bed tonight, if that's okay with you?"

"Sure, sure, whatever you need sweetheart. Why don't you go for a nap this afternoon to catch up?"

"Good idea," she said, and they carried on with their day.

The following week, Darlene decided to confront Joe with her concerns. She figured the direct approach was best because she liked him and, somewhat naively, she didn't want to see him go to jail.

"Joe, can I talk to you for a second in your office?"

"Sure Darlene, whatever you need."

"Listen Joe, I couldn't help noticing the big wads of cash you are taking out of your poker room. I know those guys are placing bets with you and that makes you a bookie. You know this kind of gambling is illegal right?"

"I'm not hurting anybody," Joe was quick. "It's just a little innocent fun between friends."

"It's a little more than that Joe, and you know it. I've seen all sorts of guys coming in here to see you who don't look like friends. I'm worried about you. You are putting yourself at risk. I don't want you to go to jail." She was really trying to sound like she was on his side.

"I'm not worried. I trust these guys. They know me. Why you gotta worry your pretty head about this? I just want you to do my arcade taxes. Please Darlene."

"Well, you're putting me in a difficult position Joe. I'm a professional who is supposed to uphold ethical standards. If anyone knew that I was associated with this gambling, my career would be finished."

"Nobody will find out. I promise. You just do arcade. We keep it all above board, professional, I promise," he looked like a sad puppy dog.

"Ok Joe, let me think about it. I will keep your secret for now, but I'm not feeling great about it, if I'm honest. It's a good thing I like you Joe."

"I like you too Darlene, you the best accountant I ever seen. Thank you for working so hard for me." She could tell he was really trying to butter her up.

"Sure Joe, well I gotta go. See you next Tuesday." She left feeling a little greasy.

The following week, things got worse. Joe pulled her into his office and spoke to her in a more serious, quiet voice.

"Listen Darlene, I know you thinking about my cash game and you worried. I come up with a solution I think you gonna like. How 'bout I cut you in for three percent of the weekly take and then we all good. Nobody needs to know. I pay you all cash. "

"What? No Joe, that is not an option for me. Like I told you, my reputation is at stake here. I can't do something like that."

"Look Darlene, you don't work much anymore. You practically retired. It don't matter what anyone think because they never know. Just think about it. Take your time. You let me know next week."

"Joe, you are really making this difficult for me. I really want to finish your taxes now that I've got all the files organized, so please, just let me do my job."

"Of course. Sorry, sorry. Can I bring you a coffee and a muffin at least? You like two creams, one sugar, right?"

"Sure Joe, that would be great," and he waddled off.

For the next week, she couldn't help thinking about his offer. Three percent of four thousand would be almost five hundred a month free money for doing nothing. It was really tempting. Joe was right that she was practically retired already. She wouldn't need to sell herself based on her reputation to find work much longer, maybe never again. As long as she didn't tell Jared, she could keep the money in their community account for rainy days and nobody would be the wiser. She was shocked at herself for even considering it, but also felt a small rush of excitement.

She decided to accept his offer. She knew it was essentially hush money, but she couldn't help herself. She loved the idea of supporting their community with extra funds. When she told Joe the news, he was elated.

"Wow, you like the daughter I never had." He gave her a big hug. Then he went to his desk drawer and counted out five hundred-dollar bills and stuffed them into her coat pocket. "Now you part of the family." He was beaming ear to ear.

Darlene felt happy to be appreciated, but slightly ashamed of herself at the same time. She tucked the cash into the back of her wallet and carried on with her work. She wondered what would happen when she finished his taxes.

# CHAPTER 22

## CLAY AND MICHELLE MOVE OUT

In mid-October, Michelle was four months pregnant and starting to show. Michelle had been staying with her new husband at Karl and Sonya's place since the wedding, but they were dying to get their own place. They had both been working and saving money for rent and a damage deposit. Clay had been searching around town for an apartment, with the help of his mom, who had learned what to look for from Karl. Roxanne suggested a townhouse in a strata-complex he knew that had aged well and had a decent manager who was also a friend of hers. They went to meet him and take a look.

Clay really liked the place, and it was affordable, so they called Karl to discuss it and signed a one-year lease for November first. Karl told him to take some pictures and they measured the rooms so he'd know what furniture would fit. Clay had his queen-sized bed and dresser, and Michelle had a couch from her parent's basement rec room, but they really needed a dining room set. Roxanne offered to buy them one as a house-warming gift, so they stopped in at a consignment store on the way back and found a plain white dinette set. They drove back and dropped it off in the place because it was currently empty. Clay was super excited to have his own place for the first time.

The Golden Land friends gathered some extra kitchen ware and bed linens for the young couple. Michelle's parents and siblings also donated lamps, throw pillows, plants and two old recliners that still looked reasonably nice. It was all coming together. On November first, everyone pitched in to help them move. Michelle just watched and gave directions on where to put the furniture. Then she helped unpack the lighter stuff into the kitchen and bathroom cupboards.

They ordered in Chinese food for lunch and all sat around eating together.

"So, this is a big day for you two," said Karl. "You are finally starting your adult lives together as a married couple."

"It's about time," said Clay. "We have been living under your roof for far too long. No offense, we love you guys," he quickly added.

"None taken," said Sonya, "of course you need your own space and privacy. My god, you are having a baby! You need some time for nesting and getting cozy here together. I always loved settling into a new home."

"I am really excited," said Michelle, "and grateful to all of you for supporting us this whole time. We couldn't have done it without you guys."

"That's what family is for," said Talia. "I remember when I first left home, I was terrified. I remember calling my mom to ask her how to cook rice. I was totally useless in the kitchen. Just call us if you need anything and don't be shy."

"Thank you," said Michelle. "My mom and dad will be dropping by later and bringing us some dinner. She is making enough to put in the freezer for a few more meals so we can relax and set up house. My cousin Linda is dropping off her old TV for us as well."

"Perfect, well it sounds like you have loads of support. Will you keep working at the restaurant until the baby comes?" asked Darlene.

"I will work as long as I can because we need the money. Then I will probably take a few months off on maternity benefits. My parents offered to help out if we can't make rent during my time off. They are the best."

After lunch they all hugged the couple good-bye and told them to take a nap, for the baby's sake, and not to overdo it. They all drove back to the land for a nap of their own. They had all worked very hard that morning.

On the drive home, Sonya said to Karl, "Well honey, we've finally got the place to ourselves. I'm so happy!"

"Yah, but I'll miss the little punk too," said Karl, "he's been part of my life for so long, he's like my own kid. I am way closer to Clay than to my own daughter."

"Yah, I know, he is a sweetheart, but you will still see him at work, right?"

"Yah, but pretty soon he will start taking on jobs on his own. He will be finished his apprenticeship and ready to start his own business. Darlene already offered to help him with the bookkeeping. He already chose a company name. He wants to be called Clay's Plumbing. He had already designed a logo and ordered business cards."

"How original," Sonya laughed. "What does the logo look like?"

"Well, he wanted to use the poo emoji, but I told him that was too gross and would turn off some customers. He finally agreed and he's using a pipe with water running through the letters of his name. It's actually pretty clever."

"Hmmm, smart kid. I hope he figures it all out. Now let's go home and have loud sex for the first time," said Sonya with a big smile.

Karl shot her a sideways look with one raised eyebrow.

"You have no idea how loud I can get," she said and they both burst out laughing.

# CHAPTER 23
## THE POT HARVEST

Over the summer, Paul, Jared, Ryan and Karl had built a drying shed for the marijuana. Ryan installed a cooling dehumidifier to keep the room at optimal temperature for drying and cutting their product. He also installed proper ventilation to avoid alerting the visitors to the smell of weed.

In October of that year, after carefully checking the color of the white trichomes, reddish pistils and yellow base leaves, Paul announced that it was time. The four women canceled their other commitments for those days because it was all-hands-on-deck for the harvest. They had watched videos together to learn proper drying, cutting and bagging technique and felt as ready as they could be.

They removed the plants from their pots in the greenhouse, gently brushed off all the excess soil around the base and hung them upside down in the cool shed from the hanging bars Jared had built. They carefully checked the thermostat to make sure it stayed at sixty-eight degrees Fahrenheit and shut off all the lights. Then they spent a couple of days cleaning out the greenhouse for next year's planting.

In two-weeks' time, they were ready for the cutting, which would take a whole day. They gathered the seven most comfortable chairs from their homes and formed a line in the cool shed. They set up folding tables in a long row along the wall and set to work. They decided to keep the leaves for their own personal use, since they couldn't sell them to the medical dispensary anyhow. Only the precious buds could be weighed and counted. Paul had deliberately chosen the Blue Dream big bud strain to try and eke out the highest yield possible from their twenty plants.

The cutting was tedious, and everyone complained of their sore scissor fingers and backs. They got up to stretch and take coffee and meal breaks throughout the day, but it was hard work. Each plant was supposed to yield seventeen precious ounces of bud, but of course they lost a little bit through human error and one bud had to be disposed of quickly because of mildew. After carefully sealing the bags, they ended up with fifteen pounds of sellable product. They were thrilled because this would net them over fifty thousand dollars at the going rate. After carefully locking the shed, they decided to celebrate by going into town for dinner.

As they toasted to a job well done, Talia reminded them of what lay ahead.

"Remember you guys, we will be doing this again in December with our ginger crop and we need everyone to pitch in."

"Right, I forgot when that was happening," said Paul. "Do we need to watch some videos to get prepared for that too?"

"Well, we all know how to peel a ginger root right? That will be the most labor-intensive part," said Talia.

"Yah, you think your hands are aching from all this cutting. I think all that peeling will be even worse," said Sonya.

"As long as you two have researched how to do the dehydrating and fill the capsules, we should be okay right?"

"Yah, we are on top of it," said Sonya, but we don't know how to use the food processor. That will be Andrea's department."

"I have a food processor too," said Darlene, "so I can help with that part."

"Excellent. We will really need two of those to keep a good flow going," said Talia.

"Ok we will be your slaves," said Jared. "You can boss us around all you want when the time comes."

"Yay!" said Darlene to her husband, "can I get that in writing?"

They all laughed and tucked into their meals with a hearty appetite. It had been an exhausting but rewarding day.

The next morning, Jared, Paul and Darlene loaded the harvested Ziplock bags of pot into their truck and drove into town to meet with the dispensary buyer. After showing their permit to the manager, two young, bearded men in white lab gear took their product into the back room for weighing and grading. They came back and slid a piece of paper to their manager at the desk.

"Okay, this looks like some nice quality product. You will receive the state mandated rate of $227 per ounce for 14.9 pounds for a total of $54,117. Take this downstairs to the cashier and she will issue a company cheque in that amount. The three of them high-fived each other, shook the manager's hand, and went downstairs to collect their earnings. They texted their friends back at home, who were all thrilled. They planned on repeating the whole process the following year.

# CHAPTER 24
## DARLENE'S TROUBLES

Darlene went into the arcade for her regular Tuesday shift early in December. She was making good progress on Joe's taxes and was wrapping up the previous year's paperwork. She thought she could file on schedule for his two years of arrears by the spring filing season. Then he would be caught up and she'd have a system in place for keeping him up to date.

After she arrived, she had a coffee and a chat with Joe at the arcade concession counter. While they were standing there, three burly men walked by and headed into the poker room, saying hello to them as they passed. Joe said he'd be with them in a minute. Darlene brought him up to speed on her progress and Joe said she was doing great work. He slipped her five hundred- dollar bills and said this was her agreed upon share of the betting take for the month. She thanked him and placed the money neatly in the back of her wallet. Then she left to settle into his office and begin her paperwork.

A half hour went by and suddenly she heard a lot of commotion. She got up and poked her head outside the door. There were four uniformed cops walking the three men and Joe out briskly in handcuffs. Joe flashed her a downtrodden look that seemed to be somehow apologetic. Then one of the cops yelled at her.

"You! Don't go anywhere. We will be right back for you."

She froze in shock thinking, "Holy shit, what is happening right now? Am I going to be arrested too?"

They loaded the four men into police cars and the one who had shouted at her came back.

"Put your hands behind you back. You are under arrest for fraud. You have a right to remain silent and anything you say could be used against you in a court of law. You have the right to an attorney…"

Darlene was unceremoniously loaded into a different police car from the men and taken to the Taos police station. She was led into a room by a female police officer and sat at a table. They took off her handcuffs and closed the door.

Darlene was in total shock. "What the hell is happening?" she wondered. "Why am I being treated like a common criminal when I am just an accountant?" Then she thought of the cash in her purse and started to panic. "But how would they even know it was given to me by Joe?"

The policewoman came back in with another male officer. He sat down and explained what was happening.

"You are being charged with fraud in connection with the off-site betting parlor run by Joe Stankovic. After searching the arcade, we have retrieved your purse and are holding it as evidence. We have yet to determine the amount of money you have accumulated with respect to this charge or how exactly you are involved, but we will get to the bottom of it, whether you explain it to us or not. You have the right to legal representation and if you cannot afford a lawyer, one will be provided for you should you choose. So, tell us Miss Roberts, what is your involvement in all this?"

Darlene was so nervous, she immediately started spilling her guts. She totally forgot about asking for a lawyer. She even forgot about the hush money Joe had been paying her in cash. She told them she was just his accountant and was working on his taxes every Tuesday. She said that she had seen a lot of shady-looking characters coming and going but wasn't really sure what they were up to.

"So why did we find five crisp hundred-dollar bills in your wallet that match in sequence numbers with the bills from the gaming room?"

Darlene suddenly realized her incriminating omission and clammed up.

"I want a lawyer," she said.

They broke off for thirty minutes until a court-appointed lawyer came into the room. She was a large black woman in a grey skirt and blazer with a green-striped blouse. She introduced herself as Aurelia Banks and told Darlene to tell her the whole truth about what was going on.

Darlene started to cry and told her everything. Ms. Banks explained that the key to lessening her charge would be to keep it at $500 as a regular hush money payment. If she cooperated with police and gave up everything that she knew about Joe's gambling set-up, she could probably get a plea deal of full misdemeanor fraud under $500 with one year probation and a one-year commuted sentence with no time served. Darlene agreed to tell them everything.

They took a break and brought her a dry ham and cheese sandwich and a coffee and let her use the washroom with the policewoman as an escort. Then they got her full statement, and the lawyer offered the idea of a plea deal, which was agreed upon by the cops. After the interview was over, they allowed her to make one phone call. She called Jared and he picked up after two rings.

"Hello?"

"Hi honey," Darlene started crying again.

"What's wrong? Are you okay?"

"I'm at the police station. I've been arrested."

"Arrested? What the hell for?" Jared sounded amazed.

"I'll explain it all later. Can you just come and get me and bring $500 bail?"

"Bail? Why do you need bail?" Jared was freaking out.

"Just go to our bank and I'll explain it all after you pick me up, please Jared."

"Okay, I'm coming right now. My god, Darlene, what kind of mess have you got yourself into? I told you this job wasn't worth it. I know this Joe character was no good. God-damn it, I'll be there in half an hour."

"Thank you." She hung up and stood there for a long minute with her head hanging down, trying to gather her composure.

"When Jared arrived and paid the bail money, she was released and fell into his arms sobbing.

"I'm so sorry honey. I should have listened to you. Now, I've ruined everything. My career is over."

"It's okay, it's okay. Everything will be fine. You don't need to work anymore. We have enough money. It's time for you to retire anyhow. Just explain to me what happened please."

On the way home, Darlene told him everything from the beginning. He listened without criticizing her and said he was happy that she got a decent lawyer. She would have to appear in court in January and testify against Joe as part of the deal. It would be stressful, but it was her only option. She would have to report to a probation officer for a year and would not be allowed to do business with anyone outside her family during that time. She knew her accounting license would be revoked permanently.

When they got home, Jared made her some soup and toast and then she collapsed into bed and slept until dinner time. When she woke up, she made Jared promise not to tell the others. She would tell them herself when she was ready. She just needed some time to feel normal again and wash away the shame that she felt. It had been one of the worst days of her life.

# CHAPTER 25
## PRE-XMAS GINGER HARVEST

When Darlene got the courage up to talk to the group three days later, the only one who was angry about her arrest was her brother, Ryan. His whole perfect image of his big sister crumbled in that moment and he lashed out, asking how she could do such an irresponsible thing and furthermore, how could their little community trust her with their own money? Darlene started to cry, and her husband stepped in to smooth things over. Jared reminded Ryan that Darlene had been doing an excellent job of managing their money for decades and then he promised he would act as a second pair of eyes over their accounts and investments. Ryan simmered down and everything went back to normal.

A few weeks later, it was time to harvest the ginger, before Christmas was upon them. The plants had finished flowering and the leaves were drying up and turning yellow and the stems were starting to droop. Everyone came together for this event and Talia and Sonya gave the orders.

First, they cut off the precious roots and washed them in warm water. They were patted dry with paper towels and laid out on the tables in the harvesting shed to dry completely with the humidifier on.

This took most the whole morning. They congratulated themselves for completing stage one and broke it off for the day.

They came back the next morning, ready to begin peeling. This was a painstaking process. They all sat in a row in comfortable chairs with paring knives and sliced off the peel, saving as much of the rhizome as possible. Three hours later, their hands were all cramping, but it was done. They broke for lunch and came back to prepare the capsules. One by one they ground the ginger roots in the food processor and smoothed out the pulp onto the racks in the industrial dehydrator. After dehydration, they poured the dried powdery ginger into the capsule stuffing machine, which made batches of one hundred at sixty grams each. The first batch was spoiled because they calibrated the machine for the wrong sized capsules, and they got mangled. There was much swearing and panicking at this juncture. After recalibrating the machine, they got it running smoothly and into an assembly line groove. By the end of the night, they had a huge tub full of capsules and they were all exhausted.

The third day was for bottling and labeling the product. Talia and Sonya had premade all the labels to save time. They used large plastic funnels to fill the plastic bottles with sixty capsules each and ended up with almost a thousand bottles. Sonya carefully stuck the labels on, and they boxed the bottles for delivery. Golden Land Ginger was ready to be shipped out to the three stores who had agreed to carry it on a trial basis. They calculated that if each bottle sold for sixteen dollars, and markup was typically forty percent, they would end up making a profit of roughly nine thousand dollars. They were thrilled with their efforts and hoped everything went according to plan.

The following day, Sonya and Talia drove the product to the one grocery and two health food stores. They met with each manager to suggest their retail price, but ultimately it was up to each store. The product was well received, and they promised to mark it as local organic ginger on the shelves. They hoped that this would entice more customers to choose their brand. They came home feeling relieved and celebrated by buying the group a bottle of champagne on the way home to share a toast after dinner. They were all tired and happy with the end result and decided they would repeat it the following year, provided sales panned out.

Now the group was freed up to plan for Christmas. April would be flying out with Krishna for a week, having now separated from Sim, who had moved into his own place. Krishna had adjusted to the routine of staying with her dad on the weekends, after some initial bumps in the road and many tears and arguments between her parents. The divorce would soon be finalized, and they were both financially independent with great jobs, so that wasn't an issue. April had begun dating the fellow she met at the tech conference the year before and was taking things slow. Sim's parents were still mad at her but were putting on a good face for their granddaughter.

Christmas was Andrea's favorite time of year and her enthusiasm rubbed off on everyone. She loved all the baking, decorating, planning the gift exchange and stocking stuffers and especially shopping for her granddaughter. She also sent a baby gift package out to New York for her soon-to-be second grandchild. She commandeered Paul to help her find and book a horse-drawn sleigh ride for Krishna up at the local ski hill, so he used this as a good excuse to go skiing for a day with Ryan and Jared. The women wanted to stay home and have a wrapping, baking, and tree decorating day at Andrea's. They put on Christmas music and got quite drunk on rum and eggnog while they wrapped all Krishna's gifts and hid them at Talia's house. When the guys got home in the afternoon, their wives were all passed out on the couches at Andrea's in front of a sparkly tree with racks of warm, fresh cookies on the counter they had to steal. Even Lucy the dog was fast asleep. It was pretty adorable.

On December 23rd, Paul and Andrea drove to the airport to pick up April and Krishna. To their surprise, April had cut off her long hair and now wore a spiky blonde pixie-cut. Krishna was taller now, at age seven, and her baby face had turned into a girl face, with thinner cheeks and a more confident air. She wanted to tell her grandma and grandpa everything she knew about everything and had become very talkative. She had even looked at a real map of Taos with her mom and was proud to tell them that she knew about the Sangre de Cristo Mountains. Paul and Andrea praised her for being such a smart girl and promised to show her the town. She even made a pronouncement in the car.

"My daddy has a new house."

Andrea didn't hesitate. "Yes sweetheart, your mommy told us that you even have your own bedroom. Is it nice?"

"Yes, I even have my very own wallpaper. It's got dolphins splashing in the waves!" she said proudly.

"Oh, how wonderful. You're a lucky girl!" Andrea egged her on. "What else is in your bedroom. Let me guess? Is there a bed?"

"Yes, I have a big girl bed with two pillows and a blue quilt with more dolphins on it."

"Do you have a dresser?" Andrea continued.

"Yes, I have a white dresser and a bookshelf with all the books you sent me."

"Fantastic!" This game went on for a while as they drove home. Paul started making silly guesses to make her laugh.

"Is there a toaster?"

"No silly, that goes in the kitchen!"

"Is there a roller coaster? Is there a bubble bath? Is there a horse?"

"Grandpa, you're crazy!" She was laughing now.

"You're right Krishna, I am crazy." They arrived at the house.

The following day they drove up to the ski hill for the sleigh ride and Krishna marveled at all the snow. She had only ever seen snow at Mount Shasta before, but she was too little to remember that trip. After their sleigh ride, she wanted to roll in it, make a snow angel and build a snowman.

Then they went into the ski lodge for lunch and hot chocolate. They took lots of photos for posterity.

That night was Christmas Eve. As Andrea was tucking Krishna in and reading her a bedtime story, Krishna began to cry.

"What's wrong sweetheart?"

"I just realized my daddy won't be here on Christmas morning. He will be all alone."

"Oh, darling, he won't be alone, he will be with his family and you will be flying home to see him three days after that and he promised to open presents with you again when you get to his house, right?"

"Oh yah, I forgot. I guess my other grandpa and grandma will give him presents. Ok, can you finish the story now?"

"Of course, dear." Andrea hugged her closer and finished reading "The Night Before Christmas". She kissed her and turned on the night-light.

April and Paul had their feet up and were drinking a glass of wine in the kitchen.

"Poor thing, she was worried about her dad being alone on Christmas morning."

"Aw, that's sweet," said April, "we tried to make it as smooth as possible for her and I promised he could have her on Christmas morning next year, but you know how it is. Everything is a negotiation."

Paul asked her, "So tell us about this new man in your life. Is it something serious?"

"I'm not sure yet. His name is Nick, and he is also divorced. He has a little boy Taylor, who is five. Krishna has met them twice and they played together quite happily for a couple of hours, so that was promising. Nick works at Intel and has a really nice house only ten minutes from us."

"What does he look like?" Andrea asked.

"Oh Mom, he's a tall drink of water, let me tell you," she said, pulling out her phone to show them pics. He was classically handsome, tall with dark hair, a neatly trimmed goatee and blue eyes."

"Hubba-hubba," said her mom. "You weren't kidding. He looks really fit too."

"Yah, he is seriously into cycling. He rides for like four hours every Saturday morning with a group of guys. They go all over the valley."

"Well do you think he is looking for a serious relationship?" Paul asked.

"Yah, I think so. He actually has a good working relationship with his ex-wife, and he has his son during the week, so we are both free on the weekends, which worked out perfectly."

"Well, if things do progress with him, you are welcome to invite him out here with you next time you come."

"Thanks Mom. Krishna's probably asleep now so we should go get the presents from Talia's house and put them under the tree."

"Right, right. Can you and your dad do that please? I want to finish cleaning up the kitchen and somebody needs to stay with Krishna."

"Sure, Mom, let's go Dad. Bring your Santa sack. If I know Mom, I'm sure she has spoiled Krishna rotten."

The next morning, everyone came to Andrea's for breakfast. Sonya offered to cook so that Andrea could watch Krishna open everything and take pictures. Then the grown-ups did their gift exchange and Talia was thrilled because April, being well-off and getting discounts through work, bought her a tablet computer. Everyone else got little things like socks and hand lotion.

Ryan complained.

"No fair! Next year, I want April as a partner. She gets all the best swag!"

"Hey," said Paul, "quit complaining. I hunted all over town to get you that foot massager buddy."

"Ok thank you, man. It is something I definitely need. "

They all grabbed a plate of pancakes with warm sliced peaches on top and sat wherever a seat was available. Then most of the adults went back to bed and April and Andrea stayed up with Krishna, as she played with her new toys.

Two days later, as they drove to the airport, Andrea felt sad that her daughter and granddaughter were leaving. She reminded April that her brother was planning to move to Taos with his wife and new baby the following year to see what her reaction would be.

"That's great Mom, but you know my career is in Silicon Valley and besides, I could never move Krishna away from her dad. That would just be cruel."

"Okay, you're right of course, but I had to try. I just love having you guys around."

"We love you too Grandma!" said Krishna from the back seat.

# CHAPTER 26

## JARED'S NEW MOTORCYCLE

In the new year, things were quiet around the property. Talia went back to her yoga classes and Andrea, to her baby clothes production. Darlene had to make up an excuse to leave the bookkeeping job at the hair salon because of her probation, so she said she had to care for a sick mother-in-law who didn't really exist. She handed over the file with the work she had already completed and recommended another accountant she had met in town.

As Jared got older, he started to look a bit like Harrison Ford, with that same well-worn and hard-scrabble manly exterior. He also shared the same broodiness of the Indiana Jones character, so Darlene sometimes called him "Indy". He was the kind of guy who always liked to be busy, and right now he was bored and needed a new hobby. He had tried out many things unsuccessfully, like building and flying model airplanes, taking guitar lessons from Paul and listening to podcasts about ancient history. Nothing seemed to quite catch his interest and stick.

Suddenly one day he walked into the kitchen and made an announcement. "I'm buying a motorcycle."

"What?" Darlene was shocked, "that's too expensive."

"It's not expensive. This guy in town came into the coffee shop and put up a flyer. He's only asking three thousand dollars for an old Honda Goldwing he can't use anymore because of his arthritis. I went over and talked to him and we drove over to his place. It's in really good shape and I want to buy it. I can use the money I made helping the neighbors build their barn last summer."

"Great, now I have to worry about you falling off the damn thing and injuring yourself," Darlene could already see he had made his mind up so there was no point even discussing it further. Jared was as stubborn as his military father before him. When he said he wanted something, it was going to happen, regardless of her opinion.

So, the next day he rode up on the thing wearing a free helmet the guy had thrown in with the deal. Paul and Ryan were immediately jealous.

"I want one too," said Ryan, like a kid who sees his older brother with a new toy.

"Well, if you can find one as cheap as this, then I'm all for it. I would love to have someone to go on rides with," said Jared.

Talia just shrugged her shoulders. She was a free spirit, so she was happy to support whatever made Ryan happy. Andrea did not feel the same way. She cut Paul off at the knees before he could even chime in.

"Don't even think about it, my love. You have a new grandchild coming in a month and he or she wants to meet you all in one piece."

"Jeez Andrea, you're such a ball-breaker."

"I just love you too much to let you do something that stupid, no offense Jared."

"None taken. I already knew Paul was whipped. That was obvious years ago," he teased.

"Fuck you buddy," said Paul to his best friend. "I know who you're going to be calling to come scrape your ass off the highway in the middle of the night, so you'd better be nicer to me."

Jared threw a tarp over his new toy and walked up to Ryan.

"The guy I bought it off has a riding buddy with another bike for sale that's also three-grand. It's an older Yamaha Virago, but he said it still runs great. I was already thinking of you when I got this. I knew you'd want to come on short trips with me."

"Awesome, let's go take a look at it," Ryan said.

Talia spoke up." It's your birthday next month. I'll give you my yoga money to pay for half," she offered.

"Wow babe, thanks a lot." He gave her a big hug. "You're the best wife a guy could ever have, you know that?"

"Yah, I know," said Talia.

"I'm too tired to go look at it right now," said Jared, but I'll give him a call and tell him we'll come by in the morning."

"Sounds great. I'm excited," said Ryan. "Just text me the time you want to leave."

So, the next morning they drove back into town to check out the Virago. It was a dark blue 750CC with a V-twin engine. It started right up, and he took it for a spin. He came back and paid the guy on the spot with a cheque. He also got a free helmet thrown in and a pair of leather riding gloves. Jared bought a second pair of gloves off him for ten dollars.

It was unseasonably warm that day, so Ryan rode it home, with Jared driving behind him in the truck. He rode up the driveway beeping the horn to get everyone's attention and they came out to see.

"So, looks like you're all set," said Talia. "I'm happy for you guys. Now you can take me for a ride on the back."

"I have to get you a helmet first," he said.

"No, you don't," said Sonya. "We have one of Clay's that he uses for dirt biking with his buddy Steve. I will go get it for you Talia, but you'd better grab a warm jacket and gloves."

"Darlene, do you want to come too?" asked Jared.

"No thanks. I'm not interested. I had a close call on the back of one of those things when I was a teenager, and it scared the crap out of me. I'm never getting on one again. Enjoy guys, and please be careful out there."

So, Jared and Ryan, with Talia on the back, went for an hour-long ride around Taos and Jared had found his new passion. He would no longer be lumbering around trying to find something to do, which was good for Darlene, who was fairly self-entertained. She loved gardening, reading, cooking and playing games on her phone. Besides, she really felt like cocooning since her fraud charge. She still felt ashamed of herself and her pride was still healing.

Every second Wednesday, she had to go into town to see her probation officer, who was an overweight Latina named Mrs. Perez. She had to answer an annoyingly repetitive series of questions and bring in a current bank statement each time to show that she wasn't making any large deposits, withdrawals or transfers. This week, she had to show a signed letter from the hair salon owner stating that she had given up her bookkeeping job. The whole thing took about fifteen minutes and was a waste of both their time, but she had to jump through these hoops for a year, regardless.

In late February, Donovan and Shawna had their baby and it was a boy. They named him Toby and Paul and Andrea flew out to New York for a few days to meet him and help out so the new parents could get some rest. He was a healthy, light haired, blue eyed munchkin who, they decided, looked like Paul when he was a baby. They had booked a hotel three blocks from Donovan and Shawna's place so they could pick up coffee and treats and get there early to take over. Paul was a proud grandpa. He cooed and fussed over this little boy who would become his favorite human being on earth. Shawna was successful at getting the baby to latch and nurse, so the night shift was up to her. She was also expressing milk with a pump so that she could sleep in the daytime and let the grandparents give him a bottle. Donovan seemed a little overwhelmed with the idea of going back to work in two weeks, but Paul reassured him that everything would be fine. After all, Shawna's parents lived across town and could drive over in a pinch.

This was the perfect week for Jared and Ryan to take their first little trip. They bought and hooked up electric vests to keep warm and headed southwest towards Phoenix. It was a ten- hour ride and they would split it into two days and then relax in a hot tub for a couple of days at a hotel and casino once they got there. They stopped overnight in Holbrook, Arizona and ate some great Mexican food and shot pool in the bar. Then they carried on riding to Phoenix and checked into their hotel.

The hot tub was pure heaven after such a long ride. They soaked for an hour and then Jared said he would go in and shower first for dinner. When he got to the room, he realized he had left his pass key beside the tub, so he walked back. When he got back outside, a pretty lady had joined Ryan in the tub, and they were chatting. He grabbed his key and gave them a nod.

When Ryan came in for his shower, he asked Jared if it would be okay if Lindsay could join them for dinner. She was on her own, traveling to visit her mother and had nobody to eat with.

"Sure, no problem," said Jared, thinking it seemed friendly enough.

Lindsay was about fifty, but strikingly pretty, with long layered brown hair, hazel eyes, and a thin, muscular physique. She looked like she worked out all the time. It turned out she was an aerobics instructor at a gym in Tucson, where she lived. Her mother lived in Flagstaff and it was her birthday this week. Lindsay hadn't seen her for six months.

After they ate their burgers and fries, Jared said he was tired and was going to crash early. Ryan said he would stay and chat some more and have another beer. He and Lindsay seemed to be really hitting it off. Jared wondered what Talia would think about that.

When Jared woke up at five in the morning, he glanced over at Ryan's bed and it was empty.

"What an asshole," he thought. "Now he has put me in an impossible position. I either have to keep his secret like a scumbag or rat him out to Talia and blow up their relationship." He was furious with Ryan, not so much for cheating as for making him bear the burden of his secret.

When Ryan slunk back in at six o'clock, hoping to find Jared asleep, Jared flicked on the light.

"You're a real asshole, you know that bro. I feel like slugging you in the head right now, you fucking prick. Now I have to either keep a secret from my wife and Talia and everyone else or I have to watch our little community blow up like a bomb. Fuck you Ryan. Fuck you very much!"

"I'm sorry man, I never meant for this to happen. I just had one too many beers and she seduced me."

"Seduced you! Bullshit. It takes two to tango. You were flirting with her all through dinner, telling her how pretty she was and how fit she was. You were asking for it bro. Besides, you're a grown-ass married man. Take some responsibility for your own shit!"

"You're right, you're right, I'm so sorry man. Please can't we just calm down and go get some breakfast and talk about this rationally?" Ryan asked.

"Get your own breakfast. I'm going next door to the Pancake House. I don't want to see your face for the next hour."

Needless to say, it was a long ride home. Jared still wasn't speaking to Ryan whenever they stopped for gas or a coffee. He kept saying he hadn't made up his mind what to do with him yet. When they finally got to Holbrook, Jared said he was ready to talk.

"I have decided it is better for everyone if this stays just between you and me. I'm not even going to tell Darlene, because she would kill you with her bare hands. So, you had better promise me that you will take this to the grave with you. Otherwise, I come out looking like the asshole for not telling them. Understood?"

"Yes, yes, thank you. I totally get it. I feel terrible for putting you in this position Jared. Thank you for having my back. I fucked up big time and I'm sorry. I will never mention a word of it to anyone."

"Not even to me. I don't want to hear about it ever again, are we clear?"

"Totally clear."

"Good, now let's get a room. I'm exhausted."

When they got home the next day, Paul and Andrea were back, and everything had returned to normal. Life went on as though nothing had changed, except that the birth of Toby had been a lovely new addition to their community.

# CHAPTER 27
## PAUL VOLUNTEERS

In late February, since Andrea was always busy with her baby clothes business and it was still too cold for planting, Paul was looking for a project. Andrea encouraged him to do some volunteering. She had seen a notice in the local paper looking for adults to help out with the Boys and Girls Clubs of America after school program in town. She immediately thought of his guitar playing and how good he was with kids. Paul reluctantly agreed to give them a call.

It turned out they specifically wanted someone to work with an older group of boys on career readiness. Paul told them that he had been a self-employed general contractor and they were super keen to have him come and talk about this and maybe do some hands-on projects with the boys. They had access to a full high school shop and perhaps he could teach them how to use some tools to build something rudimentary. Paul was no fool so he immediately asked about their liability insurance and whether he would be covered if some kid hurt himself. They assured him it was taken care of so he agreed to give it a try.

The following week, on Wednesday at two-thirty, he met with Gerry, the coordinator, to plan things out and then at three o'clock, he met the boys. There were nine kids ranging from thirteen to sixteen years old. He was told that they all came from lower income families who qualified for this free after-school programming. Half of them were white; half were Hispanic. He started by telling them his background and then walked around the shop with them explaining the different equipment and safety rules. He suggested they start with bird houses, but they groaned like this was lame. They decided on building a skateboard deck instead. He told them he had no experience with skateboards, but he would check out the specs online and see if he could make it work. Then he would see how expensive the wheels would be to add on and see if Gerry had a budget for this. The boys were excited.

By the third week, he knew them by name and had his favorites. He particularly connected with a boy named Joaquin, who had a sweet smile and was a little shy and withdrawn. Apparently, Joaquin was an only child who lived with his mom and didn't know his father. His mom was a hairdresser in town, and they had a small apartment a few blocks away from the high school. Paul said hello to his mother at pick-up time, which was five o'clock. She was a sweet lady, originally from Albuquerque. They had moved to town just last year when her cousin connected her with a new job.

Paul wanted to do something special for Joaquin, but he didn't know if it would be appropriate to single him out in this way. He asked Gerry if he was allowed to pay him a visit at his home sometime. Gerry said that what he did in his time outside the program was none of his business, but if the other boys found out Joaquin was getting special treatment, he could get face some teasing or jealousy. Paul thought about it and decided he could ask Joaquin to keep it to himself. He arranged with his mother to drop him off at home one evening after boys' club. He told her he would pick up some take-out food and bring them dinner.

He asked Joaquin what his favorite fast-food was and he said KFC, so they drove there and he bought a bucket of chicken, some fries, gravy, coleslaw and pop. When he got to their apartment, his mother, Graciela, greeted them and kissed her son, who looked embarrassed. Paul put him at ease.

"My mom used to kiss me when friends came over too. They just love you so much, they can't help it."

His mother laughed. "Yes, that is right. You are a wise man."

"Wow, could you please tell my wife that? She has no idea."

Graciela laughed. They sat down to eat at their simple, clean kitchen dinette set. It was obvious she had laid it out nicely with placemats and plastic flowers before they arrived. She had some quiet Latino music playing on the radio. She asked Paul if she could say grace and they bowed their heads.

"God, please bless this food and bless this generous man, Paul, for showing us kindness and teaching my son good lessons. Amen."

"Amen."

They ate supper and chatted about their lives and how they both came to be in Taos. Paul asked Joaquin about school to find out which subjects and teachers he liked and hated and how his marks were. Joaquin was totally honest. He said he liked math, but he was failing English because he was a bad reader and writer.

"Hmm, maybe I can help you with that, if you're interested?" Paul offered.

His mother jumped in. "Of course, that would be amazing Joaquin. What were you thinking Mr. Paul?"

"It's just Paul. You can drop the Mister, please. Well, I could meet with his English teacher and get an outline of all the work for the term and ask if we can get it done together at his pace and hand it in one assignment at a time before the end of term. I could come over on Mondays after school for a couple of hours. What do you think, Joaquin?"

"Sure, I guess so, but Mrs. Anderson is mean, so she might say no."

"Well, it can't hurt to try. I will make an appointment with her later this week to ask permission, okay?"

"Sure, I guess so." Joaquin was passive and just followed his lead.

His mother was thrilled. "I don't get home until five-fifteen, but Joaquin has a key, so he can let you in right after school, so like three-fifteen. Is that okay?"

"Perfect, but Joaquin, I think it's best if we don't tell the other boys in the club, okay? I don't want them feeling like you get special treatment."

Joaquin agreed. Paul said good-bye and went home. He felt strangely happy, like he had done something good. He really liked this kid and his mother. When he told Andrea that he was planning on tutoring the boy, she was proud of him.

"You're such a good man, Mr. Paul." She gave him a big hug and a kiss. "I am so proud of you for helping that family. They sound really sweet."

Paul met with Mrs. Anderson on Thursday after school. She was surprised to see a parent she had never met walk in. She was a bit of a hard-ass but she admired what he was doing for Joaquin so she agreed. She gave him the syllabus, some worksheets, and a copy of two novels, The Outsiders and Fahrenheit 911. They had their work cut out for them.

When Paul showed up on Mondays after school, he always brought Joaquin an after-school snack-treat. Paul would read the novels out loud to Joaquin and said to tell him to stop whenever there was a word he didn't know. They would write down these words in his vocabulary notebook and Paul would help him with definitions. He helped him write brief chapter summaries and answer the questions. Then they did the grammar worksheets and creative writing assignments. The two hours went by fast, but they were keeping on schedule. Joaquin was starting to open up more and would talk about the kids at school and situations that were challenging for him. They were forming a tight bond and Paul suddenly realized one day that this kid was really getting attached to him because he had no father figure in his life. He was worried that maybe this commitment was heavier than he had originally thought, but hell, he wasn't going anywhere so what did it matter.

At the beginning of March, Clay and Michelle had their baby. It was a little girl they named Ashley. Karl and Roxanne came to the hospital first, along with Michelle's parents. The new grandparents fell in love with this dark-haired little bundle. Karl was now a great grandpa, which was a term he didn't much care for because it made him feel old. Roxanne had recently rebuilt her trust with her son, by coming by to visit during the pregnancy to reconnect and offer them support. Now she would be welcome to babysit. She was clean and sober.

Once they got home from the hospital, the rest of the Golden Land community gradually swung by in pairs to offer their congratulations and bring them food and small gifts. They all cooed over the baby and said how cute she was. A woman from La Leche League came by to help Michelle with nursing and pumping breast milk, but other than this, they were doing well. Michelle's mother came over frequently to let her daughter take a nap, cook a meal or clean the house.

Clay went back to work on his plumbing jobs a week after the birth. He couldn't afford to take any more time off. Karl offered to help him pro bono whenever he needed a hand with bigger jobs. He remembered what it was like having your first baby and trying to make ends meet and he wanted to support his grandson. Sonya also adored the baby, having never had kids of her own, and wanted to babysit occasionally, so she was a surrogate grandma. It was a happy time for all.

# CHAPTER 28
## DONOVAN MOVES

In March, Donovan announced that he and Shawna and little Toby were ready to make the big move out west. Andrea and Paul started looking around Taos for a place that met their son's specs. They wanted a small traditional adobe house with three bedrooms, two bathrooms and a fenced backyard for Toby to play in with a covered shady porch to keep an eye on him. They had a budget of two hundred and fifty thousand.

They found several places that fit the bill and videotaped a walk-through of each property. Donovan and Shawna picked the one they liked best, sight unseen, and made an offer, which was accepted. They would be moving out the first of June. Andrea and Paul were thrilled. Shawna and the baby would stay in their guest suite for the first week while Donovan and Paul dealt with unloading the moving truck and setting up their new home.

When they arrived, Andrea introduced them to Carmen and Marisol, who had been sewing in the guest suite. Both women were going to take the week off so that Andrea could spend time with her daughter-in-law and the baby. They fussed over Toby and invited Shawna to choose one of their hand-sewn outfits to be embroidered with his name. She chose an adorable little navy and white sailor suit.

Andrea wished them a good vacation week, gave them their paychecks and they all hugged good-bye.

"Those women are lovely," said Shawna. "You are lucky to have such great employees."

"I know right? They have become like family to me. Toby might even grow up calling them Auntie Carmen and Auntie Marisol."

"Well, that's fine by me. I have to sit down and give him lunch now. He has started eating solid food. He loves mashed bananas and Pablum rice cereal."

"I'll feed him," said Andrea. Why don't you go relax and take a shower or have a nap if you want?"

"Are you kidding me? That would be amazing. I want to wash this airplane smell off me. I feel gross."

"Go ahead. I have this fabric baby seat that supports his head, so I don't have to hold him on my lap, and I bought all these plastic baby dishes and bibs and diapers, so you won't need a thing."

"Thank you, Andrea. You're the best grandma in the world." She got out the Pablum, kissed her son and went for a shower.

Then Darlene popped in with the hand mixer Andrea had asked to borrow to mash the baby food. Darlene looked sweaty and worn out because she had been gardening all morning.

"Do you want a cold drink?" Andrea asked. "There's a jug of iced-tea in the fridge. Help yourself."

"Thanks, wow this must be Toby. You weren't kidding, he does look like Paul. I wonder if he will be musical as well?"

"Well Shawna plays piano too, so probably. Will you pass me that cloth over there? I think I need to burp him." She scooped up the baby in her arms but somehow, he wriggled and slipped out of her grip. He fell onto the tiled kitchen floor with a thud and started to scream. Shawna came running in a towel.

"What the hell happened?"

"Oh my god, I'm so sorry! He just wriggled out of my arms when I picked him up."

"Jesus Christ Andrea, how could you be so clumsy," Shawna couldn't help herself. She was freaking out. "Toby are you alright sweetheart?" she held him tightly and examined his head, which had already started to sprout a goose-egg at the crown. She could feel it as she ran her flat hand over his hair. "Oh my god, he's already got a huge bump on his head! I have to get him to a hospital to get checked out! Call Donovan to come get us! I don't even know if there is a hospital in this town!" she was losing her mind.

Darlene tried to calm her down. "Yes of course, there is a really good hospital in Taos only ten minutes away. I will drive you there right now. Andrea, you call Donovan to meet us there."

"I want to come too," said Andrea, "this whole thing is my fault. Please don't make me sit here and wait. The worrying will kill me!"

"Okay fine. Grab Toby's baby bag right there and let's go," Shawna barked at her.

When they got to the hospital, Paul and Donovan were already waiting in the lobby. Toby had stopped crying now and looked really sleepy, but Shawna was trying to keep him awake in case of a concussion. Donovan asked exactly what happened.

"Your stupid mother dropped our baby," Shawna spat out with anger. Andrea started to cry, and Paul hugged and comforted her. Donovan tried to keep the peace.

"It's okay Mom. Accidents happen. Shawna, do you have any idea how many times I came to emergency when I was a kid? I think I broke almost every bone in my body. Let's get him checked in and see what the doctor says." He pulled her away from his parents to the reception counter.

Luckily, it was a quiet afternoon in Emergency, and they were taken right in. Andrea had stopped crying and Paul got her a coffee and some chocolate from the machine in the lobby.

"She is never going to forgive me," Andrea blubbered.

"Yes, she will. She's just a new mom and she is scared. Everything will be fine. Donovan will smooth things over, and we will all move on from this little crisis."

Another hour went by and Andrea had fallen asleep on Paul's shoulder. Donovan and his little family reappeared and said the baby got a mild sedative and an MRI and everything was normal. Toby would probably be sleeping for the next few hours. They could go home and relax. Everyone was so relieved.

Shawna decided to ride with her husband in their rental car back to the house and Paul drove Andrea. They all needed some space to cool down. When they got back, Donovan, Shawna and Toby went for a nap in the guest suite and Paul and Andrea did the same in their house. They all woke up at supper time and Paul texted Donovan to see if they wanted to come over for dinner and they would just order in some pizza. Donovan loved his parents, and he needed his wife to forgive his mother and move on. It took a lot of convincing, but Shawna finally accepted that it was better to bury the hatchet right away than to let feelings fester. If she didn't make peace with her mother-in-law, things would just be really uncomfortable. After all, they were going to be living here now.

When they walked in for dinner, Shawna went over to Andrea and gave her a hug. Andrea started crying again.

"I'm so sorry Shawna. I feel like a terrible grandma. Can you ever forgive me?"

"Of course, I forgive you. Accidents happen. I know Toby can be a very wriggly little guy and you're just not used to him yet. I know you raised Donovan and he turned out fine, so I'm not worried. Let's just move on."

"Oh, thank you so much. You are the best daughter-in-law I could ever ask for. You make Donovan so happy and Toby is just the most beautiful baby I've ever seen."

"Okay, enough you two. Let's eat, I'm starving," said Paul. "You women are so emotional. I can't stand it!" They all laughed. Paul gave everyone a cold beer and poured a glass of red wine for his wife. Then he made a toast.

"Here's to our wonderfully dysfunctional family. We are so glad you guys decided to move out here. The first day has been rough, but now it can only get better from here." They clinked their bottles in agreement and dove into the pizza.

# CHAPTER 29
## TALIA AND JOCELYN

Talia's yoga classes were going really well, and she loved her students. They had become more like a social circle for her. She had been invited to a few of their homes for tea or coffee over the past month and was getting to know them better. Ironically, the person she felt the strongest connection to was Jocelyn, because of their shared background in dance. In fact, they really wanted to incorporate a Kirtan (Indian chanting and drumming) and movement class into their weekly practice, but they needed more space. So, Talia approached Ryan to ask about options.

"Hey honey, do you think it might be possible to build a yoga studio for me beside the cutting shed? Jocelyn and I want to do some movement classes and I just don't have enough space in the guest suite."

"Wow, you and Jocelyn are getting really chummy, aren't you?" Ryan was concerned that his past dalliance with her could be exposed.

"Yah, we get along great. She is really chill, and she was a professional dancer like me."

"That's great sweetheart," he lied. "Well let me talk to the guys about it. You know it will be planting season soon, so we will be busy again, but if we kept it really simple and low budget, then maybe."

"Okay, thanks honey. Let me know what they think."

The guys agreed to build her a large shed with a smooth floor for her class. It would be ready in a couple of months. She agreed to give back all her yoga fees for the next year to pay for the lumber. Ryan could install the heat and lights quite cheaply as her resident electrician. She was thrilled. She drove over to Jocelyn's for coffee one morning to surprise her with the good news.

As they sunk into her oversized couch with their coffee, Talia grabbed Jocelyn by the arm.

"Guess what? Ryan and the guys are going to build us a real yoga studio with a dance floor!"

"Wow, that's amazing! We can have our Kirtan classes now. Maybe we can even do other types of dance classes too?"

"Who knows, we can decide later, but I'm looking forward to throwing parties in thee too. It will be such a fun space to just hang," said Talia.

"I have some great decorating ideas. We could get those big pillows with tassels from the Indian shop in Santa Fe and spread them around on the floor for meditation."

"Oh wow, meditation class, I never even thought of that option. I'd love to get a few more drums. We each have one, but I'd love to get some local Pueblo drums as well. Maybe I can ask Michelle to find me some from out where her grandmother lives in Jemez."

"That's a great idea. We could also have a roll-away Oriental carpet for meditation sessions. That would really warm up the space," said Jocelyn.

"This is so exciting! I can hardly wait to tell the group. I bet they will all be into the meditation idea," said Talia.

"You are adorable when you get so passionate about your work." Suddenly Jocelyn grabbed her by the forearm, pulled her closer and planted a kiss on her lips. Talia pulled back in shock.

"Hey, what was that?" she asked.

"I just got caught up in the excitement of the moment and felt like kissing you. Is that okay?"

"I guess so," said Talia, hesitantly, "but you know I'm happily married to Ryan, right?"

"Oh yah, of course. I totally respect that, but I'm bisexual, so sometimes I let my affection show without warning. I hope I haven't offended you?"

"No, no, it's not a big deal. I really like you too. I have just never gone the other way before, that's all," said Talia.

"Well, you should try it sometime. Women are way sexier and more beautiful than men, if I'm honest. Men are so utilitarian. It's so hard to find that sensitivity in them."

"Well, you could be right about that. It takes years to break through that outer crust and get to the really good gentle man inside. Ryan was a tough nut to crack."

"Well, let me know if you change your mind. I think you're gorgeous Talia, but I'm not going to jeopardize our friendship over it."

"Well, we might be business partners soon as well if we are running classes together. You know that business and sex don't mix well anyhow."

"That doesn't worry me. You are far too honest and decent to let that get in the way. I totally trust you," said Jocelyn. "Are we good?"

Talia gave her a hug. "Of course, we're good. I trust you too and I'm thrilled that we are embarking on this little business venture together. It will be fun."

So, the studio was built over the next few months heading into April and May, in between the planting days. It was a busy time around the property, and everyone felt invigorated by the changing season. The bladderwort mustard flowers covered the front field and made the land golden once again.

Talia and Jocelyn began spreading the word about their upcoming classes around Taos and soon had three sessions a week set up for meditation, Kirtan and yoga. They had their old group of nine, plus about fifteen new members who had heard by word-of-mouth how much fun these women were having together and wanted to join. Sonya and Darlene even signed up for the meditation class, but Andrea was too busy with her sewing.

They drove out to Michelle's grandmother's place with Michelle and the baby one day to purchase some more drums. They bought two large and two small hand drums and had them blessed in a saging ceremony by the shaman who had performed their wedding. Then they had lunch with her grandma, who was delighted to hold and coo over baby Ashley. Then they drove home with the sleeping infant in the back seat.

Talia and Jocelyn met and watched videos about Kirtan and rehearsed leading their upcoming classes with each other until they had a smooth delivery. As they sat on their cushions on the floor drumming and chanting, Talia looked over at Jocelyn and felt a wave of heat pass through her body. She realized that she was sexually aroused.

She leaned over and grabbed Jocelyn's arm. She kissed her deeply, tasting her sweet tongue and lingering there for a long minute. Then they dropped their drums and pressed their bodies together on the rug. Jocelyn put her hand down Talia's loose elastic yoga plants and felt the heat between her legs. She gently massaged her clit over top of her panties for a few minutes until Talia cried out in ecstasy. They held each other tightly for a long time without speaking.

Then Jocelyn pulled back and looked at Talia's face. There were tears running down her flushed cheeks.

"Hey what's the matter? It's all good. You just had an orgasm and there's nothing more natural than that."

"I've never done that before. I've never cheated on Ryan. I mean I feel wonderful, but I also feel guilty."

"I think Ryan would be pretty understanding," said Jocelyn. "He's a pretty open-minded guy, right?" She was careful not to say too much.

"Well maybe, I really don't know. Please don't say anything until I figure this out."

"Don't worry, your secret is safe with me," said Jocelyn.

They tidied up the studio and Jocelyn left in her car. Talia was lost in thought for the rest of the day. She felt a dreamy new connection to Jocelyn that was loaded with potential, but she also worried that she might be pulling away from Ryan. It was all very strange.

# CHAPTER 30
## MARCO RETURNS

It had been a year and a half since Clay got arrested and gave up his cousin Marco for supplying him drugs to sell. His mother, Roxanne, had maintained her sobriety and was having regular visits with the baby. Michelle was thrilled that they could go out for a meal or a movie once in a while and have a second grandma babysit. She even got along with Roxanne quite well and liked her sense of humor, even though she was a little rough around the edges. She looked prematurely old, with too many wrinkles for a woman of sixty. She wore her wispy light brown hair pulled back into a tight ponytail and always had a silver cross necklace on, advertising that she had found Jesus as part of her sobriety.

One day, while Roxanne was babysitting, her cellphone rang. It was her half-sister Janice calling and she considered for a moment whether or not she should answer. The baby was sleeping, but she did not have a great relationship with Janice, and they didn't contact each other very often.

"Hello?"

"Hi Roxanne. I'm just calling to let you know that Marco got out of prison today and he's still pretty pissed at Clay for ratting him out. I think maybe you should warn him."

"Jesus, Roxanne. Clay has a wife and a new baby now. Can't you talk to your son and make him see that things have moved on and he needs to do the same?"

"I tried, believe me, I tried, but you know Marco. He's a hothead. He will nod, like he's listening to me, but then he'll go out and do whatever he damn well pleases. He's a grown-ass man. I can't control him anymore."

"Well why is he out early anyways? He was supposed to be serving three years."

"He ratted out his dealer who was higher up the food chain and had contacts in Juarez, Mexico. You know, some real badass. They were way more interested in him."

"Well, this gives me a bad feeling Janice. How the hell is Clay going to handle this news?"

"Well, maybe Marco won't find him. All he knows is he lives somewhere near Taos. Tell Karl to look out for him, or better yet, tell your son to buy a gun. Obviously, I don't want him to shoot my son, but honestly, it's the only thing that might make him think twice about threatening him ever again."

"Good lord Janice, a gun? Clay can't go buy a gun. He's got a criminal record. If he got caught, he would have to serve time. That's the stupidest idea you've ever had," Roxanne was getting mad.

"Well pardon me all to hell. I was just looking out for your boy. I didn't have to call you in the first place. I could have just let nature take its course, but I thought I'd do the right thing, for once."

"Okay, okay. Let me think about it. I will talk to my dad. He will know what to do," Roxanne calmed down. "I've gotta go, Janice. The baby is crying. I'll talk to yah later."

"Okay, bye."

As Roxanne gently rocked the baby back to sleep, she wondered if she should even tell Clay about the phone call. What if Marco showed up and Clay wasn't prepared for it? That could be scary for the whole family, including sweet little Ashley. She held her closer as if she were shielding her from some imminent danger. She decided to share the bad news when they got back from the movie.

"Clay, Michelle, sit down. I'm afraid I have some bad news."

"What is it?" Michelle looked panicked, "Is Ashley okay? Did something happen to her?"

"No, no, Ashley is fine. She's perfect. She's sleeping like an angel."

"Oh, thank god. You scared the hell out of me," Michelle said.

"What is it Mom?" Clay asked.

"My sister called, and Marco just got out of jail early. Apparently, he ratted out some guy higher up the food chain to get a better deal on his sentence."

"Shit," said Clay. He knew that Marco would be carrying a grudge against him.

"She said that Marco is still pissed at you and was asking where you live."

"What? Janice didn't tell him, did she?"

"No, she just said you were somewhere near Taos. She didn't say where," his mom said.

"She mentioned Taos! Shit! What's wrong with her? Doesn't she know how mean he is?"

"Well, he is her son, so probably not. She did try to talk him out of seeing you though, so she tried at least," said Roxanne.

Michelle spoke up. "I'm scared! What if this guy comes here and threatens you or me or our baby? What are we going to do, Clay?"

"I will look after you honey," he tried to sound reassuring. "I'm not going to let anything happen to you or Ashley."

"Let's call your grandpa and ask him what to do," said Roxanne. "Karl always knows the best way to handle these situations. He's got a cool head."

So, they phoned Karl, even though it was getting late. He advised them to call the police and get a restraining order. He said to do it right now, because the sooner the better. Marco was a hot-head and would probably show up at some point soon.

Clay thanked him and called the cops. He told Michelle to go to bed, but she was too wound up to sleep. A patrol car came by a half hour later. They explained the situation, about his past charge and how his information had landed Marco in prison. The officer believed him but said he would confirm all the details back at the station afterwards. They filled out the forms for a restraining order and he advised them to lock all their doors and call 9-1-1 if they ever saw Marco near the house. They asked where Marco was living now. They said they didn't know but gave Aunt Janice's name and address in Albuquerque as a contact. Finally, they went to bed, exhausted from the commotion.

The next morning, Clay was leaving for work and Michelle was still scared. She asked her cousin Mira to spend the day with her for comfort. Mira also had a baby, and they were very close. Clay reminded her to check the peep hole in the front door before letting Mira in. He kissed his wife and daughter and left for work.

The day went without incident, in fact the next three days were perfectly normal. Then, on the fourth day, Marco showed up at the Golden Land. He surprised Karl, who was changing the oil in his truck out in the yard.

"Hey, old man, how's it hanging?" Marco called out jovially.

It took Karl a moment to recognize who was standing in front of him. He hadn't seen Marco in twenty years.

"Hello Marco. What brings you to this neck of the woods and how did you even know where I lived?"

"My mom told me she had been here for Clay's wedding. So, I hear he has a kid now too?"

"Yes, a little girl. That's my great-grand-daughter. It sounds weird even saying it. "

"Well, congratulations old man. You must be very proud."

"What can I do you for Marco?" the hair on Karl's neck was bristling.

"Well, I wondered where Clay was living now? I wanted to drop off a gift for the baby and see how he's doing."

"Bullshit!" Karl couldn't pretend any longer. "Don't play all nice with me. I wasn't born yesterday. Your mom called us to warn us that you still have a bug up your ass about Clay and you're looking for payback. I'm not going to tell you where he lives, and you can just crawl back into your hole and go back to Santa Fe to start your new life as a free man. You wouldn't want to fuck all that up now anyways because you'll end up right back in prison if you even come near my grandson."

"Is that a threat, old man?"

"I don't have to threaten you. You do a good enough job of that yourself," Karl said.

"Fuck you, old man. I'll find out where Clay lives on my own. I don't need you to tell me shit."

Marco walked off with his familiar tough-guy swagger, got into his old muscle car, and drove off.

Karl phoned his grandson right away to warn him. Clay put a baseball bat beside the bed that night and kept all the curtains drawn. He had a lousy night's sleep, but nothing happened.

The next day he told Michelle to take the baby and spend a few days at her mother's place. She was reluctant to leave him alone, but finally agreed. She bundled up Ashley's baby bag, hugging and kissing Clay for a long time at the door. She reminded him to call the police as soon as he saw Marco.

When Clay got home from work, he took his baseball bat with him and started the barbeque up on the back cement patio. He surveyed the yard and back alley for any signs of Marco but saw nothing. He realized that Michelle needed to come back home soon because they couldn't go on living in fear like this forever. Clay threw a couple of burger patties on the grill and went back into the kitchen to fry up some left-over potatoes. He cracked a beer and turned on the ball game. When he stepped back outside to flip the burgers, he suddenly felt a presence behind him.

"Hello cousin," Marco sneered.

Clay spun around and realized he had left the baseball bat in the kitchen. He reached into his jeans pocket for his cellphone, but before he could dial the cops, Marco's first blow to the head laid him out on the ground and his phone went flying. He started screaming at Marco to stop, but Marco kept pummeling him with blows to the chest, stomach, and face. Clay felt everything fade to black.

Luckily for him, the neighbor in the townhouse two doors down had seen the whole thing from his upstairs window and called the cops, who now appeared with sirens blaring. Marco made a run through the front of Clay's home to the front exit, but another cop car was already waiting for him there. He was arrested and charged with aggravated assault because they found a pistol jammed into the back of his pants.

Clay was taken by ambulance to the hospital and Michelle was called. She left the baby with her mother and came as fast as she could. He was in the x-ray room when she got there and had to wait to see him, so she called Karl and told him what had happened. He called Roxanne and picked her up on his way to the hospital.

Clay was still woozy from some pain meds they had given him, but able to talk. He was already bruised up and looked a mess. The doctor came in and said he had two broken ribs, but thankfully, no concussion. He should rest up for a few days at least before attempting to work and would be in pain for a good few-weeks. They drove him home and said to keep an eye on him for the first twenty-four hours for any worsening of symptoms. Michelle was crying, she was so relieved that he was okay internally and that Marco had been arrested. He would not be able to bother them anymore.

They all drove back to Clay's and his grandpa helped him into bed. He asked if Michelle wanted him to spend the night on the sofa, but she said she could manage. She would call her parents, who lived close by, if she needed anything. Roxanne couldn't resist calling her half-sister to share the news. She stepped outside on the back patio to make the call without upsetting her son.

"Well, your shit-head son came and attacked Clay and now he's going back to prison." Then she hung up on Janice, feeling vindicated. She felt like she had redeemed herself and was no longer the "bad mother" of the family.

# CHAPTER 31
## RYAN EXPOSED

The summer in Taos was upon them and their pot and ginger plants were growing nicely. Darlene spent plenty of time watering her flower garden and growing some vegetables in raised beds that Jared had built for her. Jared was enjoying his motorcycle and used it almost exclusively when he didn't have to pick anything up. As Darlene pulled weeds out of her flower beds, it suddenly occurred to her that Jared hadn't done any riding with Ryan lately. She asked him about it over dinner that night.

"Hey honey, how come you and Ryan don't ride together anymore? I thought that was the whole reason he got a bike. You took that one trip to Phoenix but haven't really spent much time together since."

Jared blurted out without thinking, "Traveling with Ryan is a liability."

"What do you mean? Is he a safe rider?"

Realizing he had already said too much, he tried to backpedal. "No, he's safe enough. I just didn't enjoy the way he stops to chit-chat with everyone he meets. It's exhausting."

This was her brother Jared was talking about and Darlene knew him better than anyone. He was typically a pretty quiet guy around strangers.

"Are we talking about the same Ryan?" Darlene asked. "You do mean my brother, Ryan, right? The one who hardly ever initiates conversation with strangers?"

"Well, he initiates plenty with women, I can tell you that," Jared said.

Now Darlene's Spidey-sense was kicking in. "What are you talking about Jared? Was there a woman he was getting too friendly with on your Phoenix trip?"

"I've already said too much," Jared said, "can we please just drop it?"

"No, I'm not going to drop it because I won't be able to sleep tonight wondering what you mean. Did he cheat on Talia? She's our friend. Jared, we need to look out for her too."

"Yes, I know she's our friend, but he's your brother. He's blood. Shouldn't that come first?"

"No, I don't think so. I've always called him out if he's being a little shit. I've been doing that my whole life. That's what big sisters are for!" She was getting worked up.

"Okay, okay. Yes, there was a woman, and he did spend the night in her room, but I can't tell you what happened. They might have just got too drunk and passed out for all I know."

"The little bugger. I'm going to kill him. You realize that I have to tell Talia now, right?"

"No, why?" implored Jared. "You're just going to blow up their marriage for nothing. It didn't mean a thing. It was a one-night stand. It's not worth it Darlene. Please, just let it go and pretend I never said anything, I'm begging you."

"I'm sorry, honey, but I can't keep this from Talia. If she finds out later that we knew and didn't say anything, she will be furious."

"God damn it, why did I have to open my big mouth," Jared said. "You're going to implode our little community here. It will be a shit show and you know it."

"Not necessarily. Talia is about the most calm, level-headed person on the planet. She might just forgive him. I mean they have been married for thirty-odd years. Do you really think she'd be that petty?"

"I have no idea how women think or react," Jared said with his head in his hands. "You'd think at my age I would know, but I have no idea."

Darlene agreed to wait until Ryan left to get some soil in town the following morning to talk to Talia. She went over to their place and walked into the kitchen, calling her name.

"Hey Darlene, how's it going?"

"Good, good. Do you have a minute to talk?"

"Sure, what's up? Have a seat and I'll get us some coffee." She poured two cups and joined her friend at the kitchen table.

"I'm afraid I have some shitty news, Talia." She looked right into her friend's eyes.

"Okay, I'm not liking the sound of this, but go ahead."

"Well, it seems that when our husbands took their little bike trip to Phoenix in the spring, Ryan hooked up with some woman at the hotel for one night. I'm so sorry Talia."

Talia put her chin down, staring at the backs of her outstretched hands, and got really quiet for a long minute. Then she took a deep breath and said emphatically, "I'm going to kill him."

"That's exactly what I said when Jared told me," said Darlene. "He's my kid brother, so if you want me to beat him up, I'm really good at it."

"No," Talia sighed, "let me deal with it please. I'm not sure how I feel about this yet. Of course, I'm pissed off and upset, but I really need to take some time and let this sink in before I make any rash decisions. I will talk to him when I'm ready. Also, why did Jared wait three months to bring this up?"

"I don't know. Some kind of bro code, I think. He's afraid this will destroy our little community and he doesn't want that to happen and neither do I for that matter. We will respect your choice and support you, whatever happens Talia, even though he is my brother and I love him to bits, the little shit."

"Thank you for telling me Darlene. I know that couldn't have been easy for you." She stood up and gave Darlene a hug. Darlene was surprised that Talia hadn't even jerked a tear. She seemed stoic and resigned to the news.

When Ryan got back from the garden center, he came in to make a sandwich. Talia was in the bathroom with the door locked. She was taking a bath.

"Can I come inside to pee?" Ryan called through the door.

"No, go piss outside," she said abruptly.

"Okay," he hesitated, "is everything okay in there, honey?"

"No, I don't want to talk to you right now," Talia said.

"Can I ask why not?"

"No, you cannot ask why not. Go away and leave me alone." She sounded pissed.

Ryan went outside and pissed on the grass. He was worried and had no idea why his wife was pissed off at him. Then he noticed Darlene over in the garden. He walked over to ask her if she knew anything.

"Hey sis, have you spoken to Talia this morning at all? She is pissed at me and I have no idea why."

"Really? You have no idea why? Think about it bro. Your little trip to Phoenix. Did anything strange happen on that trip?"

Suddenly her brother looked horrified, realizing that it was Jared who had spilled the beans.

"Shit, Jared. Jared told you this. You know it meant nothing right? I'd had too much to drink and she came onto me. It was so stupid, and I've regretted it ever since."

"You should regret it, you little shit. You have the hottest wife who adores you and besides, what about the rest of us? You have jeopardized our group living situation here Ryan. I don't want either of you to bail because of some stupid one-night stand!"

"Well, I don't want that either. Besides, we can't afford to move somewhere else. Surely Talia will realize that too and calm down in a few days."

"You'd better hope so brother, because otherwise I will have to kill you myself," said Darlene.

"God damn it. Can I sleep on your couch tonight if she kicks me out? I have a feeling she's going to. She just made me piss on the grass because she's locked herself in the bathroom. I think she's taking a bath."

"Sure, of course you can. In fact, I would encourage it. Give her some space for as long as she needs. If you're lucky, maybe she'll forgive you and we can get back to normal around here."

"Thanks sis. You're the best. I don't know what I'd do without you, seriously."

Darlene got out of the flower bed and gave her brother a big hug. She could sense that he was really hurting and scared he might lose Talia.

To Ryan's great surprise, Talia didn't kick him out. She packed a small bag and got in the car and left. He had no idea where she was going, and this frightened him even more. He told Darlene what had happened.

"Don't worry, she's probably just staying at one of her yoga friend's places for the night. She needs to let off some steam and talk. I'm sure she'll be home soon."

Talia drove up to Jocelyn's place and knocked on the door.

When she opened it, Talia said, "I need a place to stay for a couple of days. Ryan and I are having a fight." She fell into Jocelyn's arms sobbing.

# CHAPTER 32
## TALIA'S LOVE-LIFE

After Talia stopped crying, she explained to Jocelyn that Ryan had cheated on her on his motorcycle trip. Jocelyn hugged her and told her that it didn't mean anything. He just had a momentary lapse of reason and he still loved her just as much as he always had. She made Talia a nice dinner of prawn pasta with cream sauce and opened a bottle of wine for them to share. Then they settled in to watch a comedy movie to cheer her up.

When the movie was over, Talia asked for a pillow and blanket to sleep on the couch. Jocelyn had other ideas.

"You don't need to sleep on the couch sweetheart. There's plenty of room in my bed, no strings attached. I promise I will leave you alone and let you sleep, unless you want something else."

"No, I think I just want to sleep. It had been an exhausting day," Talia said.

"Sure, of course. I totally understand."

Talia fell asleep two minutes after hitting the pillow and Jocelyn just watched her sleep. She was incredibly beautiful with her long curly dark mane and soft features. She had a tiny, perfect nose that curved upwards, high cheekbones and delicate eyebrows. Her light brown skin looked so delicious that Jocelyn wanted to lick her all over.

However, Jocelyn felt torn. Should she tell Talia about her one afternoon with Ryan a year ago? Would that destroy their friendship and their yoga studio business plans? Talia was already upset about Ryan sleeping with a stranger, so it probably wasn't the best time, but the guilt was killing Jocelyn. If Talia was going to end their friendship, wouldn't it be better if she did it before they got started teaching classes together? She had a hard time falling asleep.

The next morning, Jocelyn woke up to the sound of the shower running. She looked over to see Talia's naked body, as she lathered herself with soap. Jocelyn was getting aroused and decided to take a chance. She opened the shower door and stepped in behind her.

"Hi there gorgeous. Can I wash your back for you?"

"Sure, why not," Talia passed her the soap.

Jocelyn ran the soap slowly over her back while making little circles of lather with her other hand. Then she gradually moved her hand down lower and slipped it between her legs, fingering her from behind. Talia started moaning and spread her legs wider. Jocelyn was kissing her neck and moved her hand to the front to massage her clit. After several minutes of heavy breathing, Talia cried out in orgasmic pleasure.

She turned around and kissed Jocelyn deeply and rubbed her body up against her, grinding their vulvas together. Then she began to reciprocate the sensual touching. She turned Jocelyn's body, so she was standing under the hot water and lowered herself to lick her clit softly. After a few minutes, Jocelyn came with loud, guttural moans.

They got out of the shower, wrapped themselves in towels and fell onto the bed, spent and laughing.

"Well, that was a good way to start the day," Talia laughed. "I've never done that before by the way."

"Wow, well you're a natural," Jocelyn grinned. "Let me make you some coffee to repay you for your kindness."

She also made them fried eggs on toast, which they devoured. Talia decided she didn't want to go home that day.

"Is it okay if I stay here another night?" Talia asked.

"Of course. Stay here as long as you like," said Jocelyn.

"Do you have any clients today for tarot card readings?" Talia asked. This was Jocelyn's way of making money to supplement her pension, since she had quit working at the deli six months ago.

"Nope, I'm totally free today. We can do whatever you like."

"Awesome. Can we go for a hike in the forest? I'd love to try that South Boundary Trail. I've heard it's really pretty."

"Sure, that sounds fun. Maybe we can go out for lunch after. I know a nice place with a great vegetarian menu."

"Awesome, it's a date. Do you have a sunhat I can borrow?"

So off they went for a lovely day together. Talia forgot all about her problems with Ryan for a few hours and enjoyed the fresh air and sunshine. He tried calling her three times, but she ignored his calls. Then they went into town for couscous, chickpeas masala and a cold beer. It was delicious. They looked at a vintage clothing shop beside the restaurant and Talia bought herself a beige suede vest with tassels for twenty dollars. She was thrilled to find such a bargain.

That night, after they watched another movie, Jocelyn decided to come clean. She turned off the tv, turned to face Talia and took her hand.

"There's something I need to tell you Talia. It has been eating away at me ever since I met you and we started to become friends. Now I have developed strong feelings for you, and I would hate to lose you."

"What is going on?" Talia looked worried.

"Well, about a year ago, before I met you, Ryan came into that deli-sandwich shop where I used to work. He was really friendly and started chatting me up. He kept coming back every few days and I got the impression he was hitting on me. Long story short, we slept together, but it was only one time."

"What? You slept together! For fuck's sakes Jocelyn, how could you? Didn't you see he was wearing a wedding ring?"

"Yah, of course I did, and I should have asked more questions, but I didn't. I'm so sorry. It was so quick and afterwards he practically ran away, saying he couldn't do this to his wife. He couldn't do this to you! He loves you, Talia. I know he does, and that's all that really matters. It was a one-off, a mistake. I never meant to hurt you. Can you forgive me Talia? Can you forgive both of us?" Jocelyn pleaded.

"Jesus Christ, what a week I'm having!" Talia was shaking her head. "I don't know Jocelyn. I don't know if I can forgive you or Ryan. This is the second strike for Ryan and he's my husband. I am supposed to be able to trust him. You, I'm not so sure. I'm not sure about anything right now. I need to get away from you both." She started packing her bag.

"Please don't go Talia," Jocelyn followed her around the room. "I promise it will never happen again."

"Oh yah, well it just happened this morning, only now I'm the cheater. My head is about to explode. I need to leave. "

"But what about our plan for the studio classes?" Jocelyn asked.

"I have no idea," said Talia. "I'll let you know when I figure it out. Good-bye Jocelyn."

She got into her car and drove off. Ten minutes down the road, she pulled over and started sobbing. Her whole world was unraveling, and she didn't even know where she was driving to. She couldn't go home. After she calmed down, she called Sonya.

"Can I sleep on your couch tonight Sonya?"

"Sure, of course you can. Are you okay? You sound upset."

"I am upset. I just found out that not only did Ryan sleep with some random stranger on his last bike trip; he also slept with my good friend Jocelyn."

"The one from yoga class?"

"Yes. I am so confused, Sonya. Could you ask Andrea if I can stay in the guest suite for a while? I need my own space. Maybe she can make up the bed in there after she's finished sewing today. Tell her they can still sew in there during the daytime. I will just go out for a few hours."

"Sure, of course. Consider it done. God, Ryan is a dick. I'm so sorry Talia. You don't deserve this. I'm gonna kick his ass."

"No Sonya. Please leave it alone. This is between me and Ryan and I don't want all of you getting involved. Please let us work this out on our own."

"Okay, okay, but it will be hard for me to stay quiet. I'm really pissed at him for treating my best friend like this, but I promise I will back off."

"Thank you, Sonya. I'm just going to grab a few groceries and I'll be home. Tell Ryan to get out of our house in an hour so I can grab my clothes and stuff. You can tell him I'll be staying in the suite, but I want him to leave me alone and stop calling me. Tell him I will talk to him when I'm ready."

"You got it Talia. Please drive carefully. You are upset and it will be hard for you to focus on the road."

"I'm okay now, but thanks. I have calmed down. Thanks Sonya. See you soon."

Talia picked up enough food for a few days, collected some clothes and toiletries from her house and went to the guest suite. Carmen and Marisol were just leaving, and Andrea gave her a big hug.

"Sonya told me everything. I'm so sorry sweetheart. Don't worry about us either, we can sew in the crop drying shed for a few days. I'll ask Paul and Jared to move the machines over there this afternoon. You need your space right now. I love you, Talia."

"I love you too." She hugged Andrea again and flopped into bed for a long nap.

# CHAPTER 33
## ACCIDENT AT PAUL'S SHOP CLASS

In June, things were winding down at the high school towards the year's end. Paul had really enjoyed teaching the after-school program for the Boy's Club and they were in the process of attaching the wheels to the rudimentary skateboard decks they had all built. Paul managed to buy some cheap wheels in bulk from a supplier, with the help of Coordinator Jerry, who agreed to fund the project.

Joaquin's tutoring at home was also going well. Paul had helped him keep his assignments up to date and taught him how to write a chapter summary. He got him some plastic covers and colorful bindings and had taught him how to make proper headings, underline them, and make his work look nice before handing it in. The boy seemed to be gaining more confidence in his abilities.

He had also put together a small ramp for them to try out because there were a few of them who had a lot of skateboarding experience. It was only about six inches high, but they were psyched, nonetheless. He let two of them spray paint the ramp bright red with a black skull stencil, so it looked pretty cool. They had also spray painted their boards with the same logo, so they felt like a true skateboard club of nine members. This was Paul's way of creating a bond in the group and making Joaquin feel more like he had friends.

With their boards assembled, they were all eager to try out the ramp. Paul insisted that the boys skate around the playground a few times so he could see who the beginners were and who was more advanced. Clearly Joaquin was a total beginner, as well as three other boys. He forbade them from going on the ramp until they had a lot more practice under their belts. They watched in awe as the more experienced boys tried it out and there was one boy who could do a half-turn as he landed, which they all thought was super cool.

Paul realized it was five o'clock, so a few mothers started to pick up the boys. He said good-bye to the older ones who walked home and told Joaquin to wait for him while he went inside to lock up the shop. Then he would lock the ramp in the outside metal storage container owned by the Boy's and Girl's Club.

Paul strolled inside, locked the spray paint in the top cupboard, shut off the computer and the

lights and finally, locked the double doors. Walking back to meet Joaquin, he heard a funny moaning sound. Looking up, he saw Joaquin lying on the ground by the ramp holding his ankle. He ran towards him in a panic.

"What happened Joaquin? Are you okay?"

"No, it hurts real bad. I'm sorry, but I tried to go over the ramp."

Paul could see the ankle was already swelling up.

"Shit Joaquin, I told you to stay away from the ramp," he couldn't help sounding angry.

"I'm sorry. I didn't mean to," was the boy's inadequate response. He was obviously in a lot of pain.

Paul looked across to where his car was parked and then looked back at Joaquin, wondering how heavy he was, and decided he could manage it. He got his key fob ready in his hand to unlock the car.

"I'm going to pick you up now Joaquin and carry you to my car so I can take you to the hospital for an x-ray. I want you to relax and trust me to carry you and don't wriggle or squirm, or I might drop you. Do you understand?"

"Yes," he said, whimpering.

Paul lifted the boy and carried him under the bum, with his body flopped over his shoulder like a sack of potatoes. He unlocked the car and gently plopped him onto the back seat and told him to slide his bum over and keep his foot elevated across the seat. Then he drove quickly to Emergency. He asked the nursing team to bring a stretcher outside so he wouldn't have to carry him again. It was a strain on his back for sure. They took him into the trauma examination room immediately.

Paul sat down to fill out the intake form and then realized he hadn't called Joaquin's mother yet.

Graciela was already home from work and had been slightly worried when they didn't show up on time. She rushed to the hospital to meet them and signed the admissions form. They took her right in to see her son and talk to the doctor.

"What happened, mi amor?" She kissed him and then noticed his swollen, discolored ankle. "Aye, dios mio Joaquin, que paso?" Joaquin started crying again as soon as he saw his mother. He had been bravely holding himself together for Paul, but now he crumbled. The doctor explained.

"We did an x-ray and I'm afraid your son will need surgery right away to reset the bone. We are going to prep him now, but first I need to know if you have any insurance."

Now it was Graciela who started crying. "No, we don't. My work doesn't offer any and it's too expensive. How much is the operation?"

"I'm afraid it will cost about nine thousand dollars ma'am."

"Nine thousand dollars! My God! I don't have that kind of money! What are we going to do?" Now she was really crying.

"Listen, you can work out a payment schedule with the cashier's office, but we need to get going on this surgery right away. It has to be done or your son's mobility could be affected for the rest of his life. Could you please sign this consent for surgery form?"

Feeling completely helpless, she signed. She kissed Joaquin and told him not to worry about anything; she would be here when he woke up. They got an IV going and rolled him away.

Graciela came back into the waiting room crying and sat down heavily beside Paul.

"What's wrong Graciela?" Paul asked.

"He has to have an operation. They are taking him right now. It's going to cost nine thousand dollars and we don't have any insurance."

"Oh my god," Paul wrapped his arms around her, and she put her head on his shoulder. "Don't worry, Graciela, let me see what I can do. Let me talk to the Boys' Club director, Jerry. I believe they have some kind of blanket insurance for the group. I will call him and find out."

"Oh, thank you Mr. Paul. You are a lifesaver."

Paul walked outside to get some air and call Jerry without her hearing the conversation. Apparently, they have third party liability insurance and accident insurance, so Joaquin would be fully covered. What a relief! Paul just had to fill out a batch of forms giving the details of the accident and stating that it happened on school property, so that was easy.

Paul went back in to tell Graciela the good news. She jumped up and embraced him and just kept thanking him over and over again.

"You are the best thing that ever happened to us!" she said.

"Well not really. If it hadn't been for my skateboard ramp project, this would never have happened."

"But Joaquin loves you Mr. Paul, don't you see? You are like the father he never had."

"Okay, okay, thank you Graciela. He is a terrific boy. I am just happy that he will be okay. So how about we go and get something to eat? He won't be awake for a few hours and I'm starving."

"Are you sure? Okay, but not too far away please. I want to make sure I can get back quickly if they need me." She sounded nervous.

"No problem. Let's just grab a burger around the corner at the Burger Hut. They have wraps and burritos too if you don't like burgers."

So, they left the hospital and Paul called Andrea to tell her what was going on. She told him to wish the boy's mother well and take his time. She was just relieved that her husband would not be found liable for the accident.

Joaquin's surgery went fine, and he was released the following morning. Paul visited him several times over the next few weeks because his mother still had to work, so the boy was home alone. Paul even went to his school and picked up his remaining assignments. The school year was wrapping up in a week and he was a little behind on his final Social Studies project. Paul helped him learn about the Civil War and make a timeline. They also completed a few math sheets and one quiz and he dropped the package back to the school. When the last day came, Paul went and picked up his report card from the office.

When Joaquin opened it, he got a B in English and a C+ in Math. He and his mother were thrilled. She insisted on cooking a special meal for Paul to thank him for tutoring her son. So a week later Paul picked up a bottle of red wine on the way and drove back to their small apartment. He also had a gift for Joaquin, which was a used game system and a couple of games for him to play on while he was laid up with his cast. Joaquin was over the moon.

Graciela had pulled out all the stops. There were beef enchiladas with mole sauce, chicken tamales, refried beans with sour cream and tortilla chips with homemade salsa. Everything was delicious. They drank the wine and she told him about growing up in Albuquerque and how much she missed her family there.

He helped her clear the table and brought the dishes into the kitchen where she was making coffee. As he was placing the dirty dishes beside the sink, she turned quickly and bumped into him. She looked up into his eyes and planted a quick kiss on his lips. Then immediately, she got embarrassed.

"Oh, perdoname," she blurted out in Spanish, "I'm so sorry Paul, I didn't mean to do that. I just get so lonely sometimes and you got too close to me. I'm so ashamed. I'm so sorry."

"It's okay, Graciela, I forgive you. I think you just had a little too much wine. It's okay. Please don't worry about it."

Paul had set up the game for Joaquin, who had immediately started playing it and was oblivious to the drama unfolding in the kitchen. Paul went back to check play against him and had a cup of coffee, just to be polite, but he felt uncomfortable now. He wanted to get out of there as soon as possible.

When he said good night at the door, Graciela apologized again.

"Really, it's nothing." Paul was being a total gentleman, because it didn't feel like nothing.

He drove home, wondering if he should tell Andrea or leave it alone.

Paul never told Andrea about the kiss. She decided there wasn't any point because it would only make things more awkward. Instead, he decided to ask his wife to help this kind, lonely woman to meet some Hispanic friends in the community.

"Hey sweetheart, I think Joaquin's mother, Graciela, is really lonely here. They came here a year ago for a job and she hasn't met any Latina friends to socialize with. Do you think Carmen and Marisol might be able to connect with her?"

"Sure, I can ask them. They both have large families here and I'm sure they could invite her to some sort of party or maybe to their church."

"That would be awesome. I will give you Graciela's number to give to them."

The plan worked perfectly. The following Sunday, Graciela was invited to their church's pot-luck dinner, where she met many of the Mexican expats in town, some who were second or third generation Americans. She had a wonderful time and pretty soon, had met a widower who asked her over for coffee. She wouldn't need to be kissing Paul unexpectedly anymore.

# CHAPTER 34
## BREAKING THE SILENCE

In the summer, Andrea would take her baby clothes to the farmer's market in Taos every Saturday. She would load up her bins, a folding table, and two collapsible chairs into their truck and head into town to set up early. She loved meeting people and a busy day could net her over a thousand dollars in sales. Usually, either Marisol or Carmen would come and help her, but this Saturday she invited Talia to help take her mind off her marital problems.

Back at home, Jared and Paul took this opportunity to check in on Ryan, who was moping around at home. They walked in to find him drinking coffee in his underwear and watching college football. They poured themselves a cup and sat down.

"How are you doing bud?" asked Paul.

"Shitty. What do you think? Talia won't even talk to me. I think I've really lost her this time."

"Give her some time," said Jared, "she will come around. She just needs some space to figure it out for a little while."

"How long is a little while? I'm losing my mind over here!" said Ryan.

"Be patient. She's had a bit of a week, from what Andrea told me," said Paul. "You slept with Jocelyn? Don't you know that sleeping with your wife's friends is off limits, man?"

"They weren't even friends when it happened. They hadn't even met yet. It was a pure fluke that she showed up here for yoga class. I almost shit myself when I saw her parking her Jeep here that first day," said Ryan.

"Well, we're rooting for yah buddy. I can't even imagine life around here without you two being together. It would be so strange," said Jared. "Hell, I'm married to your sister. She will be a wreck if you guys don't fix this."

"I know, believe me, I know. Darlene already threatened to kill me if I don't make this right. I just don't know how."

"Well why don't you take this opportunity, now that Talia's gone into town, and do something nice to surprise her when she gets back?" said Jared.

"Like what? I'm fresh out of ideas at this point."

"Well, I'm sure between the three other women here you could gather enough bath products to make her a little gift basket and leave it on her doorstep with an apology card telling her how much you love her and miss her," said Paul. "We can help you right now, if you put some pants on, that is."

"Okay, I'm game to try anything. Where will I get a basket?"

"We have a wicker picnic basket I can get for you," said Paul. "Let me text Sonya. She will go around and gather some things. I will choose something out of Andrea's beauty products and come back here in ten minutes. I'll bring you a nice card. Andrea has thousands of them."

"Thanks man, you guys are the best."

So, with a little coaching on what to say in the card, Ryan got it together and left the gift on her doorstep at the guest suite. He felt a little better just doing something pro-active to win his wife back. He even put a photo of Lucy in the basket to remind her that she missed her dog. Then he waited and watched for Andrea's car to pull up the drive, back from the market.

He peeked out the side window in their bedroom, where he had a view of the guest suite porch. He saw Talia walk up, pick up the basket and pull the card off the top. She opened it and began to read as she closed the door behind her.

Ten minutes later, he got a text. All it said was, "Thank you for the card and gift basket." Nothing else. Ryan felt disappointed. He has hoped she would invite him over to talk. He would have to wait a little longer.

Two days passed and nothing. Then on the third day he got the text he's been waiting for.

"Can I come over at six tonight to talk?"

He said yes right away and went to shower and shave so he would look good. Then he waited anxiously for her to arrive, mentally rehearsing what he wanted to say to her.

She knocked and walked in right at six. She sat down in the armchair facing him and began to talk.

"Look Ryan, after almost thirty-five years together, you know I love you. I will always love you; that's not even a question. But now I find out that you have cheated on me, not once, but twice; and I'm guessing there have been a whole lot more times that I don't know anything about, and I really don't want to know. I think at this stage in our lives, it's time to be real with each other. I don't expect us to be monogamous anymore. If you want to have sex with someone, go ahead, and I will do the same. Life is too short, and we should find pleasure wherever we can."

Ryan's mouth was agog like he was in shock. He hadn't expected this reaction from his wife.

"But I don't want to see other people anymore. I just want you back," he said. "I feel terrible about my mistakes and I want to prove that I can be faithful to you and make this right."

"I'm afraid it's too late for that," she said. "Besides, I have a confession to make too. I have also slept with somebody else."

"What? Who? When did this happen?"

"It's not what you think," said Talia. "It's a woman. I have been sleeping with Jocelyn."

"Jocelyn? You mean our Jocelyn? The one I slept with?" he looked amazed.

"Yes. We are becoming really close, and I want to continue sleeping with her. I don't know how you feel about that?"

"Well, I'm totally shocked. When did this start?"

"Just in the past couple of weeks, and you know she is the first woman I've ever had sex with, so it's a totally new experience for me."

"Wow. This is wild." He was at a loss for words, just processing this new information.

"So, what do you think?" Talia asked.

"I don't know what to think," said Ryan. "Do you still want to sleep with me?"

"I'm not sure at this point. I think I want to stay in the guest suite for a while and see how I feel.

I think we need to take a little break and see where we're at. I don't want to do anything to jeopardize our group lifestyle here. I love you and we will always be close, but I don't know if I can get back to sexual intimacy with you anymore. If it happens, it happens. We are three feet away from each other, so if we end up falling into bed together some night, great."

"Ryan started to tear up. He couldn't believe this was happening. He had expected to apologize and win her back, but it wasn't turning out that way at all. He put his head in his hands and started to cry.

Talia came over and sat beside him on the sofa. She pulled him into her lap and ran her fingers through his hair and kissed his cheek.

"Don't cry sweetheart. You know I will always love you and I'm not going anywhere. I'm just loosening my death-grip on you a tiny bit."

"I know, but I love you. You're my wife. I don't want to lose you and I don't even want to share you," he sobbed. "Fucking Jocelyn. She has ruined our lives."

"Well, I don't think that's really fair. It's not entirely her fault that we were both attracted to her. She's a good person and you know it. She really never wanted to hurt either of us."

"She's evil," he couldn't let it go. "If she never came along, none of this would be happening."

"Okay honey, I hear you, but you did sleep with that other woman on your bike trip, so it wasn't just Jocelyn. Ryan stopped crying, pulled himself together and sat up.

"So how long are you going to stay in the guest suite?" he asked.

"I'm not sure. If I decide to come back and live with you then I will talk to you first and see if that's what you want."

"That is what I want," he said emphatically.

"Well, your feelings could change. I'm not going to take that for granted," said Talia.

"What about when we have visitors. April and Krishna will need to stay in the suite sometimes," he reminded her.

"Then I can stay on Darlene or Sonya's couch for a week." She didn't want to say she could stay at Jocelyn's because that would just upset him again.

"So how are we going to tell the group?" Ryan asked.

"Let's do it together tomorrow morning. I will invite everyone for coffee, and I can do the talking, if it's too emotional for you. Does that sound okay?"

"Sure, fine. Are you going to tell them about Jocelyn too?"

"No, I think we'll keep that between us for now. I might tell them gradually when it feels right. Is that okay?"

"Yes. I prefer to leave her out of it," said Ryan. "It's too weird. I need more time to get used to all this. Are you still planning on running classes with her? I wish you wouldn't. I don't really feel like seeing her around here all the time."

"It won't be all the time. It will only be a couple of hours a week and I can ask her to just come and go from the studio without any visiting for now, if that would make you more comfortable."

"Yes please. God, this is all so weird. I'm sorry Talia. I'm sorry for everything. I never wanted to hurt you."

"I'm sorry too. I don't want to hurt you either. We've been through so many good times together. I'm not throwing that away. You will always be part of my life."

They hugged and agreed to meet the next morning.

The other six came to the guest suite for coffee at ten o'clock. Talia told everyone that she and Ryan were taking a break. Nobody was terribly shocked because they had all heard about his recent cheating.

They figured it was a natural reaction and agreed to let her stay in the guest suite for as long as she needed. There were hugs all around and Ryan choked up again, but at least he felt loved and supported. Everyone was relieved that they were working it out civilly and nobody was moving away.

# CHAPTER 35
## DONOVAN'S WEDDING

In June, Paul had helped his son to find an office to rent with a therapy room, but when they crunched the numbers, it made more sense to join an already established physio practice. In July, Donovan and Shawna began to finally feel settled in their new home and routine. Every morning he made breakfast for Shawna and made silly faces at Toby while he ate his Cheerios in a highchair. Then he would take the big ten-minute walk to work so that Shawna could have the car. They were comfortable and happy with their decision to leave the "Big Apple".

Donovan and Shawna still weren't married, and they had been engaged for over a year. Paul and Andrea offered to host their wedding in August, and they agreed, as long as it was small and low-key. They didn't want a lot of fuss. They would just invite Shawna's immediate family to fly out, as well as April and Krishna, and also include his new work colleagues. Then there were Clay and Michelle and baby Ashley, and a neighbor Shawna had befriended at her townhouse. They just wanted a BBQ and salads and a simple sheet cake. They asked Paul to play guitar and get everyone singing around the firepit afterwards. They hired a local Justice of the Peace to perform the ceremony.

The crop was in full bloom, so they tarped over the greenhouse for the day because they were afraid Donovan's new work colleagues would spread the word around town about their weed. If anybody asked, they would once again say it was a new building under construction. Shawna said her family was cool about weed, so they already knew, and it wasn't an issue.

On the day of the wedding, Clay and Michelle's daughter Ashley was sick with an ear infection, so Michelle stayed home with the baby. Clay came by himself and promised to be home by ten and keep his phone on in case the baby got worse. They already had some antibiotics for her, so he wasn't too worried.

April and Krishna agreed to bunk at Paul and Andrea's on an air mattress so that Shawna's family could have the guest suite. She had her parents and younger sister, Jade, who had just finished nursing college. Her dad, Tom, and her sister were both tall and slender with ginger hair, while her mom, Carrie, was short, blonde and curvaceous. Talia moved in with Sonya and Karl for the long weekend and slept on the couch. It was a cozy affair with everyone on-site.

The bride and groom kept it casual because it was very hot. They had a canopy set up for shade and Shawna wore a pretty knee-length pink floral sundress. Her red hair had grown mid-length and she had two little French braids swooping down her temples and joined at the back. Donovan wore a short-sleeved shirt, dress pants and a pink bow tie to match her dress. They looked comfortable and lovely.

Paul played "Here Comes the Sun" on his guitar as they walked down the grass and they exchanged simple vows and gold bands. Everyone cheered as they kissed and then milled around drinking champagne. Sonya and Talia took photos on the grass while Jared, Ryan and Karl fired up three barbecues to cook steak and prawns for everyone.

Clay couldn't help noticing how gorgeous Shawna's sister was, with her long red hair and blue eyes. Karl caught him staring.

"I see you boy. You'd better put your tongue back in your head and think about your lovely wife and baby girl back home."

"Just because I'm married, doesn't mean I can't look. I'm not dead yet, Grandpa."

"Fair enough, as long as it's only looking," said Karl, and he walked away.

The problem was, she was looking back at him with those sideways glances and smirks that tell you the feeling is mutual. He got the distinct feeling that she was game for anything.

After a delicious barbecue dinner, they cut the wedding cake and the bride and groom smeared icing on each other's noses to make everyone laugh. After dessert, everyone pitched in to clear the dishes into their four home dishwashers and fold up the tables. As the sun went down, Paul called the guests over to the firepit and took out his guitar.

Jade came over to chat with Clay by the fire pit.

"So, who are you connected with here?" she asked.

"I'm that tall, lanky guy's grandson. I used to live here, but now I live in town." He failed to mention his wife and child. "So, you live in New York, right?"

"Yah, I just finished nursing school. I will be starting my first full-time job in September. I'm super stoked to finally start making my own money."

"No doubt. Nursing school sounds hard. I'm a plumber. I did an apprenticeship with my grandpa over there. It's actually a good job. I'm pretty happy with it."

"Great, great. Do you wanna go smoke a joint out back?" Jade asked.

"Sure, why not?" Clay followed her around the side of Ryan's place to a quiet spot. She pulled out a spliff and lit it up. He watched her pursed lips draw the smoke in and thought she was beautiful.

After they passed it back and forth a few times, she moved to face him and pressed him up against the house with her body. She kissed him deeply and rolled her tongue around his mouth seductively. He couldn't resist her because he was so turned on. He felt his erection digging into her groin.

"Is there somewhere more private we can go?" she asked.

"Come on" said Clay, and he pulled her inside Ryan's place and shut the door. He took her into Ryan's bedroom, and she pushed him down onto the bed and started undoing his belt. Then she straddled him, took him inside her, and began to grind rhythmically up and down, moaning with pleasure.

Clay suddenly panicked. "Are you on the pill or something? I should be wearing a condom."

"Relax, we're protected. I use the ring. Just fuck me, you idiot."

Clay wasn't sure what the ring was, but he figured if she was a nurse, she must know what she was doing. He stopped worrying and let the pleasure flow over him and finally came hard inside her. She climbed off him and they both fell onto the bed beside each other.

"When do you think you might be ready to go again?" she asked.

"Go again? Nah, I think we'd better get back to the party before anyone misses us. I can't risk getting caught in here."

"Why not? You're a grown-ass man?" she asked.

He blurted it out, "Because I'm married!"

"What? Why didn't you say so, you jerk! I'm not a homewrecker. Jesus, where is your wife?"

"She's at home with our baby," he said.

"Baby? Oh, it gets even better. Okay, I'm outta here. Catch yah later dude. You never saw me here and I never saw you, okay?"

"Perfect," said Clay, and he watched her quickly get dressed and head for the door.

As she got to the door, Ryan suddenly walked in and gave her a surprised look.

"Oh, hey Jade, can I get you something?"

"No, I'm good thanks. I just needed to use your bathroom. See yah back out there."

"Yah, see yah," Ryan came in and went to the fridge to get a beer. Suddenly he heard a noise and got a feeling that he wasn't alone. He turned around to see Clay coming out of his bedroom, looking disheveled.

"Clay, what are you doing in my bedroom, man?" Then suddenly Ryan put two and two together.

"Aw shit man, you didn't? You just fucked that girl in my bed, didn't you? Jesus man, you're married. Shit, now I'm going to have to keep your secret, aren't I?" said Ryan.

"Would you please? I can't have my grandpa finding out about this. He would kill me."

"Your grandpa, what about your wife? I would be more concerned about her, buddy. I should know, I've been there. Talia just moved out because I cheated on her. It's no joke pal."

"I know, I know. She just came on to me so hard. I couldn't get her off me!" said Clay.

"Oh dude, that is not going to work as an explanation. That is so weak, your wife would just laugh in your face if you told her that. Don't even go there. Did you at least use protection?"

"Yah, she told me she's on the ring, whatever that is, but she's a nurse. She must know what she's doing right?"

"What about STDs though? The ring doesn't protect you from those."

"Shit, I forgot about that, but a nurse wouldn't have sex with me if she had something nasty right?"

"Nurses are just people dude. Besides, some STDs don't even show symptoms right away. She could carry something and not even know it."

"God damn it, you're freaking me out right now Ryan. What time is it? I've got to get home by ten."

"It's nine-forty."

"Shit, I gotta go. You promise me you won't tell anyone about this? Please Ryan."

"Yah, you've got my word buddy, but go get yourself checked out at the doctor's just to be safe okay?"

"Ok, I will. See yah later." Clay left in a hurry, cursing himself for being so stupid.

When he got home, he crawled into bed and kissed Michelle, who was already sleeping. Two days later, he made up an excuse to go to the doctor, telling her he had a pain in his ear and maybe he caught something off the baby. The doctor tested him for S.T.D.s and he told Michelle he just had sinus congestion and that's why his ears hurt.

Then came the bed news. He had chlamydia and needed antibiotics. He lied and told Michelle they had done a throat swab and it came back as strep. Luckily, she believed him, and it also gave him an excuse to avoid sex for five days by saying he didn't feel well. He even stayed home from work for two days and slept on the couch for the full effect.

The most awkward thing was the doctor telling him that he should let his recent partners know to go get tested. He had to think of a way to get Jade's number without looking suspicious. He called Shawna and said that her sister wanted some info about a music festival in Vermont they were talking about. He would call her and fill her in on the details. Shawna seemed to buy it.

Clay dreaded making the call, but he bit the bullet when his wife went to the store.

"Hello, is this Jade?"

"Yes, who's this?" She recognized the New Mexico prefix, but not the number.

"It's Clay from the wedding. I have to tell you something."

"Okay, what is it?"

"You gave me chlamydia. I mean, you have chlamydia."

"What? You're kidding. Is this some kind of sick joke?"

"Hell no. I've been on antibiotics for the past week because of you. Shit, you're a nurse. You should have known better."

"Don't put this on me. How do you know it was me who gave it to you?"

"Who else could it be? I've only been with my wife for the past four years."

"Well maybe she has been whoring around on you then," Jade said.

"Fuck you Jade, you slut. Don't you ever talk about my wife like that! Fuck you. I don't care what you do. You can either go get tested or let your pussy rot for all I care." He hung up on her and started to cry. He felt terrible for all his deceit. He knew he had the best wife in the world and the most beautiful daughter. How could he have done this awful thing to her?

After five minutes of wallowing in his misery, he realized that Michelle would be home soon and pulled himself together. He went into the bathroom and splashed cold water on his face. Then he drank a coffee and put on some heavy metal music to pull him out of his funk. When she got home, she didn't suspect a thing. In fact, she was happy to see him up and about and feeling better.

# CHAPTER 36
## KARL'S HEALTH CRISIS

After Donovan's wedding, everyone left, and life returned to normal. Michelle never found out about Clay's adultery and he was lucky that Jade never said anything to her sister Shawna. Talia went back to living in the guest suite, although she did sleep at Jocelyn's occasionally. She and Jocelyn were planning to start running two classes each in the fall, Talia would continue with yoga and Jocelyn would run the Kirtan group. Ryan quit moping around Talia and started getting used to living on his own. It helped that the group was super busy preparing for the pot harvest once again.

At the beginning of September, Karl was turning sixty-three. They had a small dinner party at a local restaurant for his birthday and Sonya got him what he wanted: a weed-whacker. She thought it was the most ridiculously unromantic birthday present ever, but that's what he wanted.

Karl's birthday always reminded him to go to see his doctor for his annual physical and blood test. He always dreaded getting a finger stuck up his butt, but he knew that was just part of the drill for all men his age. He wasn't expecting his doctor 's reaction though.

"Okay, I'm feeling something that may be of concern, but we will wait for your PSA blood test results to come back before we get excited about this."

Karl was alarmed. "What are you feeling doc?"

"I'm feeling a small area that is harder than the rest, like a small bump, but I can't be certain. If your PSA is elevated, then we will need to do some follow-up screening. I will call you in a couple of days when the results come back."

Karl told Sonya about his appointment and they waited anxiously for the phone call.

"I'm afraid that your PSA is quite elevated, so I'd like you to go for an MRI at the hospital's medical imaging department. I've sent in the referral and they should be calling you in the next few days. If you don't hear from them by Friday, call me back."

"Okay doc, thank you I guess," said Karl grimly.

Sonya looked worried. She insisted on going with him, even though it was just a scan. Then she thought about their medical insurance.

"God forbid, but I don't even know if our insurance covers prostate cancer. We have pretty basic coverage. I'd better download the policy and read the fine print. Can you make us a cup of tea honey?"

Fifteen minutes later, after reading through about ten pages online, Karl brought her the tea.

"Holy shit Karl, you are covered for the MRI, but not for any cancer treatment. How the hell did I miss this? What are we going to do?"

"Slow down Sonya. We don't even know if I have cancer yet. Please don't get all doom and gloom on me. I'm trying to think positive about this."

"I know, me too, but this policy was just renewed in June. They're not going to let me change it until the renewal date next year. They certainly won't give us cancer coverage if your doctor has already booked screenings. That's a red flag for a pre-existing condition."

"Okay Sonya, I understand what you're saying, and I really need you to stop telling me this right now because you're freaking me out. If there's nothing I can do about our coverage anyhow, then I'm not going to worry about it until I have to."

"Shit, I'm sorry sweetheart. I feel bad that I didn't pay more attention to the details."

"That's okay. I love you and I'm not going anywhere. I promise, said Karl, wrapping his arms around her.

The next Monday, he went for the MRI and had to meet with his doctor again on Thursday. Sonya went into the room with him for support.

"I have good news and bad news," said the doctor. "The bad news is you do have a lump that is cancerous. The good news is we caught it early, so treatment has a very high chance of being effective."

Sonya started to cry, and the doctor passed her a box of tissues. She blurted out, "But we don't have any coverage for cancer treatment!"

"Oh dear. That is unfortunate. Treatment can be quite expensive."

"How much is quite expensive?" asked Karl.

"Well, it depends, but usually in the range of fifteen thousand dollars. You had better tell the oncologist about your financial concerns and see what he can do to give you treatment that is the most cost effective."

"Jesus Christ," said Karl, I can't believe after working my whole god damn life, it has come down to this."

"I'm sorry Karl. I have already booked an appointment with the oncologist, Dr. Nieman, at the hospital on Tuesday at one o'clock. He will outline the best course of treatment and set up a series of appointments for you."

They left the office and sat in the car for about ten minutes in shock.

"We are not skimping on your treatment. We can take out a bank loan if we have to. You're getting the best treatment they have, and I don't want any arguments from you. We can use the house as collateral," said Sonya.

"Sure honey, whatever you say, but the property is in Darlene and Paul's names, so they would have to sign for the loan."

"Okay, well I'm sure they won't have a problem with that. We will talk to them tonight after supper. Let's go home and take a nap. I'm exhausted."

After dinner, they called the group over for coffee and Bailey's and gave them the news. Everyone said how sorry they were for Karl's troubles and Darlene said she would look at their finances and figure out how to best raise the money needed to help him. Karl was humbled by this outpouring of support from this adoptive family he had found. They had only known him for a few years, yet they treated him like a brother.

"You guys are amazing," he said, "I don't know what I would do without you." Everyone hugged and said good night.

Dr. Nieman was all business when they arrived at the hospital. He recommended five weeks of external beam radiation. Karl would have to go into the hospital every day for that period. The first few sessions would be used to situate a few marker "seeds" in position and test for exact placement and body positioning. Then he would start getting zapped by the beam for a few minutes at each session. He was told to expect more frequent urination and possibly pain in his abdomen, fatigue, difficulty passing bowel movements or erectile dysfunction in the weeks and months ahead.

"Terrific," said Karl sardonically, "and what about the fees? We don't have coverage for cancer treatment in our policy."

"I see," said Dr, Nieman. "Well, the total cost will be around fifteen thousand. You should go down to the cashier's office and set up a schedule of affordable payments for yourselves. Our finance department will work that out for you."

"Okay doctor, thank you. See you on Wednesday."

They went downstairs and Sonya said she would bring Darlene with her to the cashier's office to work out the finances. She told him not to worry about a thing and to just focus on attending all the treatments and getting better. She offered to drive him every time, but he said maybe just for the first few sessions to see how it went.

Darlene met with the group without Karl present and told them that it would be best if they used the money coming in from their marijuana and ginger sales this year to pay for Karl's treatment rather than pulling out any of their investments, which were making good interest and were locked in for a few years. After initially complaining and feeling bummed out, everyone reconciled to her idea that this was the best course of action. They would all work hard on the harvest and they would do it knowing it would save Karl's life.

Sonya took Darlene to the Finance office at the hospital, and they worked out a payment schedule spread over two years. Sonya thanked her profusely for co-signing the paperwork.

They went home and Sonya told Karl that everything was in order and he didn't have to worry any more. It was all taken care of. He hugged her tightly and thanked her, with tears welling up in his eyes.

Thankfully, the pot harvest went even better than in the previous year because they had grown more plants. They ended up banking eleven thousand dollars but would have to wait until December to work on the ginger. Sonya and Karl wanted to express their gratitude for everyone's hard work, so Sonya baked all of them a batch of fruit pies and made cards to deliver to every house. She got Karl to sign them when he was feeling up to it. He was tired a lot, but generally tolerating the radiation treatment well. The doctor was hopeful that he would beat it and be able to live a long and healthy life.

# CHAPTER 37
## RYAN'S BACK

Talia was spending a couple of nights a week over at Jocelyn's place. The sex was fantastic, but she couldn't help feeling that she wanted to get out of there as soon as morning came. She was finding that more and more of Jocelyn's little habits irritated her. She hated the fast upbeat jazz Jocelyn put on every morning and longed for her own quiet, Zen music to wake up gradually. Jocelyn would zip around the kitchen talking loudly and making food, whereas Talia preferred to just sit and drink her green tea in peace for the first hour and eat later on. Then there were the cats. Talia was a dog person, so she didn't like how the cats would jump up on the table when they were eating and beg for scraps. Jocelyn would feed them bits of egg and cheese to encourage this and then pet them so their fur would shed onto the eating table. This grossed Talia out. In the bathroom, Jocelyn would leave wet towels all over the place and her garbage pail was overflowing. She just wasn't a particularly tidy person. Talia began making excuses for why she had to leave as soon as she woke up.

"I have to run and take Lucy for her morning walk. Ryan had to go into town to get a new pipe for the kitchen sink," she lied.

"Okay sweet cheeks, I'll see yah later for Kirtan. Will you be joining the group today?"

"Maybe, I haven't decided yet. I have to see what needs doing in the greenhouse when I get back. If you don't see me, that's where I'll be." Talia gave her a kiss and left.

When she got back to the guest suite, she felt like she could breathe again. She loved having her own space to be alone and relax. She would curl up and read a book or write in her journal or cook a nice meal for herself. It was heaven.

As she sat there reading some poetry, she got a text. It was Ryan. He had taken a bath and he couldn't stand up. His old back injury from his car accident years ago had flared up again. He wanted her to come and help him out of the bath and onto the couch. She didn't really want to grab his wet, naked body at this moment, but she couldn't refuse. He needed her.

She ran over and Lucy met her at the door, flipping her tail and whining, obviously agitated about Ryan's safety. She comforted the dog with a quick petting and went into the bathroom. She grabbed the biggest towel and wrapped it around his torso to get a good grip and hauled him up with all her strength. He yelled out, swearing in pain. He leaned on her hard with his arm across her shoulder and walked slowly to the couch, butt naked. She quickly threw a blanket over him and propped up his head with pillows.

"Get me my pills from the bathroom cabinet. The two prescription bottles."

She got them and fetched a glass of water. He took one muscle relaxant and one pain killer.

"Thank you so much Talia. I'm sorry to impose on you like this but thank god you were home."

"No problem Ryan. God, how many times have we done this over the years?" she said. "This has been part of the drill pretty much annually since your accident thirty years ago, right? I just wish they would fix your back issues surgically once and for all. It just sucks for you that it keeps flaring up like this."

"I know. I wish they could have made me the bionic man and put some steel rods in my spine, but they said it would be too risky. I'm thinking now that it might have been worth the risk. I feel like I have been a burden on you all these years."

"No Ryan, I have never felt that way. You have helped me so many times. Remember when I fell during that video shoot and sprained my ankle and you had to leave a meeting and drive into L.A. to come get me. So, it goes both ways; it always has. Now what can I get you? Are you hungry?"

"Sure, maybe just some toast and peanut butter and a coffee please. That would be great. Oh, and that magazine over there and the TV remote please."

"Okay, I'm on it. Has Lucy had a walk yet today?"

"No, just a piddle outside."

"Ok, I will take her after I get your toast."

"Thanks Talia. You're the best. I love you." Ryan let it slip out without filtering and suddenly realized what he had said. "Sorry, I guess you don't want to hear that."

"I don't mind hearing that Ryan. I love you too. "She carried on making the coffee without missing a beat, but she started reflecting on how easy it felt to fall back into this old life. She had only been here fifteen minutes, but it felt like she had never left. Here she was in her own kitchen making food for her husband and caring for him as if nothing had changed. It was weird. Did she prefer this to being with Jocelyn? Did she prefer this to being on her own?

She grabbed Lucy's leash and ball and whistled for her. They headed off down the front drive and out onto the road. It was a beautiful September day, and everything was tinder dry. She saw a small lizard skittle off into the underbrush. She threw Lucy's ball as far as she could to get her running. Then she'd ruffle the scruff of her neck hard until she dropped it each time. She felt so happy to be with her dog again. She missed Lucy every time she stayed at Jocelyn's place. At Ryan's, the dog normally slept at the foot of their bed and followed her around every morning. She was a constant reassuring companion. Talia suddenly felt she had given up too much. She missed her dog, her home and yes, even her husband. She missed his warm arms around her and his scruffy beard when he hadn't shaved. She missed his stupid expressions like, "You're the cream in my coffee girl," and "Don't forget to kiss your good luck charm," whenever she left the house. She felt so conflicted all of a sudden and couldn't fight back the tears. What the hell was she doing? She felt so confused. She decided, in that moment, that she would take care of him for the next few days until he was fully mobile again and then reassess her feelings.

When she got back, Ryan was trying to pull himself up by grabbing onto the edge of the couch, but he was struggling.

"What's going on?" Talia rushed to assist him.

"I need to go to the bathroom," he said.

"Okay, let me help you." She slid under his arm, guided him to the toilet, helped him sit down and shut the door quickly. "Call me when you're done," she called through the door.

Ten minutes later, there was a repeat performance back to the couch.

"Wow, you are seeing me at my absolute finest hour," Ryan said, obviously a little embarrassed.

"It's nothing I haven't seen before," she said. They both laughed.

"Yah, I guess that's true," said Ryan.

"So, I've decided that I'm going to stay here for the next few days and take care of you until you're moving again and no arguments," said Talia. "I know you would do the same for me in a heartbeat if the tables were turned."

"Wow, okay Talia, if you're sure it won't interfere with your life and your studio classes. I can always ask my sister or one of the guys to step up if you're busy."

"We'll see. Maybe Darlene can come over while I teach my class tomorrow, or at least be on call. I'll let everyone know your situation so the guys can come visit you and watch a game or hang out. I'll ask Darlene to keep her phone with her."

"Great, well maybe I should actually put some clothes on. What do you think?"

She suddenly realized he was still naked under the blanket. They both started laughing.

"Yah, I'll get you some loose sweatpants and a t-shirt and help you get dressed. You can skip the underwear for today. It's just one less thing to deal with when you have to go."

She fetched the clothes and helped slide them gently onto his body. She couldn't help noticing what great shape he was in. He was still muscular and didn't even have a belly. At fifty-nine years old, he was the baby of their group, still not showing any grey hair at all. He looked great for his age and she was seeing him with fresh eyes, after being separated for two months.

Everyone rallied around Ryan for the next few days. Paul and Jared came over to watch Monday night football and brought a pizza over that evening. Darlene stepped in while Talia taught her yoga class the next day. Andrea brought him some fresh baked chocolate chip cookies. Sonya was too busy taking care of Karl, but she dropped off a half-sack of beer for him. He felt like a king with servants.

Talia called Jocelyn and explained the situation and why she couldn't see her for the rest of the week. When Talia hung up the phone, she realized her own sense of relief in not having to go sleep there. It was a real moment of clarity for her. Was she just using Jocelyn for sex? She suddenly felt ashamed of herself. She knew Jocelyn was a good friend and she respected her as a dance instructor, but beyond that she realized the attraction was purely physical. There was no deep soul connection like she felt with Ryan. She knew she had to end her physical relationship with Jocelyn, but she wasn't looking forward to it.

That night, after Paul and Jared left, the awkward question loomed of where Talia would sleep. Ryan must have sensed this because he offered to stay on the couch, telling her that it was easier than walking to the bedroom.

"Nonsense," said Talia, "you need to be close to the washroom and you need to sleep on the good mattress. I will help you get into bed."

She got him up and slowly helped him across the room and into bed. She gave him a peck on the forehead and said good night. He looked lovingly into her eyes.

"Thank you, Talia. You know, I would be lost without you. I mean it, thank you for everything."

"You're welcome sweetie. You can call me during the night if you need to pee, now get some rest." She kissed him again, but this time on the lips. He grabbed her arm to keep her mouth there longer.

"I love you Talia."

"I love you too Ryan." She grabbed a blanket and curled up on the sofa with Lucy lying on the floor beside her. She felt like she was home.

# CHAPTER 38
## TALIA'S DECISION

After two weeks of radiation treatment, Karl was pretty wiped out with fatigue and abdominal discomfort. He spent much of the day watching sports on TV or videos on YouTube of home projects that he didn't have the energy to try. Sonya took excellent care of him and Clay and Michelle came by with the baby to try and cheer him up, but he wasn't a happy camper. He didn't know how he was going to handle another three weeks of treatment.

Talia made a big batch of tabouli salad and brought a bowl over to give to Sonya and Karl. Darlene was visiting her brother so she could get away for an hour. Sonya served up some tabouli for herself and Karl and invited Talia to sit down at the kitchen table. It felt like they hadn't really connected for a while, since she had started hanging out with Jocelyn so much.

"So, how have you been girl?" asked Sonya. "It feels like we never get to spend quality time together these days."

"I know right? We are both looking after these invalid men." She winked at Karl and both women laughed.

"So how are you and Ryan getting along these days?" Sonya asked.

"Well, a lot better now that he is completely helpless. What does that say about me?" Sonya laughed.

"Yah, maybe you like to be in control," said Sonya.

"But isn't that true of most women?" asked Talia.

"Yah, you're probably right. Men do all the work, but women tend to call the shots, I think. Maybe nature intended it to be that way because otherwise the children would never get fed or bathed. I'm talking out of my ass at this point, obviously."

"Obviously, since neither one of us has ever had kids." They both smiled.

"So, are you and Jocelyn still a thing?" Sonya asked.

"I honestly don't know at this point. Truth be told, since I've been staying with Ryan, I have been doing a lot of thinking. I think I was drawn to Jocelyn more for a new experience more than anything. I think it was just exciting and pulled me out of my everyday existence. Do you know what I mean?"

"Totally," said Sonya. "What woman hasn't fantasized about running off with someone twenty years younger or, in your case, trying out a different gender. I think you finding out about Ryan's cheating was just the catalyst. Otherwise, you would have probably never jumped ship."

"You're right, Sonya. Exactly. There was nothing wrong with our relationship. We were both happy and now I think I'm ready to recommit to that. The only problem is, how do I let Jocelyn down easy? I think she really wanted this to grow into something more. I don't want to hurt her, especially since we are running classes together in the studio now. "

"Well, just be honest Talia. That's all you can do. It's early enough in the game that she must have at least wondered if you'd change your mind and go back home. It doesn't have to be awkward if she accepts your decision like a mature adult. Surely, she can understand that a thirty-five-year marriage trumps a two-month fling."

"Yah, I guess you're right. I just hope she doesn't get mad and walk out on our joint venture, but it's a risk I'll have to take. Life will go on regardless. I mean, I was running my own classes before she came along so I will just continue without her. Thanks for the good advice Sonya. I should have talked to you sooner. I forget sometimes how well you read me." She got up and gave her a hug.

"It's good to catch up with you finally," said Sonya. "Let's do this more often."

"For sure, I promise, and let me know if this old coot gives you any trouble." She squeezed Karl's shoulder on her way out.

Talia arranged to meet Jocelyn after her Kirtan class the next day. She sat down on the studio floor on a cushion and asked Jocelyn to come and sit with her. Then she laid it out.

"Hey, Jocelyn, I need to tell you what I've been thinking," she reached for her hand and held it.

"Oh, that doesn't sound good. What's going on?"

"Well, ever since Ryan threw his back out, I've been taking care of him, as you know. I've been doing a lot of soul searching and I don't think I can keep seeing you. I really feel like Ryan is my home. We have invested most of our lives into each other and it's hard to just throw that away. I have loved our time together and I think you are wonderful, sexy, beautiful and really the whole package for somebody; it just can't be me. I hope you don't feel like you were being misled. I truly never meant to hurt you or give you false hopes. Can you forgive me?" Jocelyn pulled her hand away.

"God damn it Talia, to tell you the truth, I'm kind of mad. I really thought we were great together and I was hoping you would move in with me. It has been hard living alone for so long and I feel like I have been playing second fiddle to Ryan this whole time. I just sensed that you weren't completely with me. I was just hoping I was wrong."

"Can we move past this and still be friends and work in the studio together?" Talia asked.

"I don't think so Talia. I just want to get out of your way. It's not so much that I'm mad, I am just hurt. I feel rejected by you and by Ryan. To be honest, I think you are both just a couple of players fooling around at my expense. You can either continue the Kirtan class yourself or I will call everyone and cancel the sessions."

"Can I let you know tomorrow? I need to think about our ginger harvest and everything else that's going on before I commit to two more classes a week."

"Sure, just leave a message on my cell. I don't want to talk to you anymore. Good-bye Talia. I hope you and Ryan get your shit sorted out. Good luck with all that." She got up and walked out of the studio unceremoniously. Talia could hear her start her Jeep and drive off.

Talia sat there for a few long minutes in the silence and felt a huge wave of relief wash over her. Now she could focus on getting back on track with Ryan and her closest friends. She wouldn't have to feel like she was cut in half anymore. She took a deep breath, got up, and went home.

# CHAPTER 39
## KARL'S RECOVERY

The last three weeks of Karl's treatment really dragged his energy down. He was sleeping a good part of the day and eating less than usual. He had to take laxatives and pain killers for the abdominal cramps. Everyone could sense that Sonya was getting tired of being stuck in the house, so they took turns spelling her off. They tried to encourage Karl to sit outside for some fresh air every day, but the weather was getting cooler. Occasionally, he would come out for the campfire after dark, wrapped in a blanket. He looked like he'd aged ten years in a matter of weeks.

Finally, one morning, Sonya came over and confided in Talia.

"I'm so worried about Karl. He just seems to have given up. I can't even get a chuckle out of him. He just sleeps all the time. He doesn't even get excited when Clay brings Ashley over to visit. I'm just at a loss Talia." She shook her head and started to tear up a little, wiping her eyes with her sleeve.

"I'm sure it will get easier once the radiation gradually leaves his body," Talia tried to sound knowledgeable. "He has just been on the worst ride for the past 5 weeks and he's drained. Give it a little time."

"Yah, you're right, I just have to be more patient," Sonya lifted her head up and took a sip of her coffee. "Can I just sound awfully selfish with you for a second?" Sonya asked.

"Of course. Vent! That's what I'm here for. You need to get this shit out or it will wear you down girl."

"I'm scared we will never have sex again," Sonya blurred out. "It's been six months since we made love Talia and Mama's got needs! God, that sounds awful. I know what he's going though is so much bigger and more important than sex. I'm ashamed of myself for even saying something."

"Nonsense. You need to tell someone how you're really feeling. Caregiving is hard work. It can burn you out, both mentally and physically. Have you asked about joining the cancer caregivers' support group at the hospital?"

"No, I thought I'd be fine and didn't need help, but maybe you're right. It would be good to hear from others that this is normal," Sonya said.

"Well good, let's set that up for you. Now that Ryan's back is feeling better, I can take over for you whenever there's a meeting."

"Thank you, Talia, that would be amazing. It's only once a week I think," said Sonya, "but only if it doesn't conflict with your studio times."

"Okay, let's call the hospital right now and see what day it's on." Talia made the call. It was all set for Monday morning.

When Sonya arrived at the group session in one of the conference rooms near the hospital gift shop, there were about ten other people who welcomed her. They were all parents or spouses or children of cancer patients. She introduced herself and listened for the first half hour as they went around the circle telling their own personal stories and most recent challenges. Sonya was blown away by the outpouring of frustration and small triumphs of their past week. These people were really in the trenches of caregiving and many were struggling way more than she was.

Finally, her turn came to speak. She felt a little embarrassed of her outburst at Sonya's place. She wasn't ready to tell these strangers about her sex life. It would sound too self-involved in a first session. She decided to focus on Karl instead.

"Well, my spouse just finished his first round of radiation for prostate cancer and he's really despondent and has no energy. I feel like I'm already living with a man who has given up and I don't know how to turn his mood around," she said.

The others nodded and the facilitator encouraged her to continue.

"I can't get him out of bed. He sleeps most of the day and he's eating less than before. He seems to want soup and soda crackers all the time and he's really off meat. He won't even come sit on the balcony for a little while, even on sunny days. He barely has interest in watching television, even his favorite shows, and I have to remind him to take a shower. He just seems depressed."

Everyone nodded some more and then one woman spoke up. She reassured Sonya that everything about Karl's behavior matched her own husband. She said to ask Dr. Nieman to talk to Karl on the phone about taking some anti-depressants and to get him to phone in a prescription to the pharmacy. She said to just be patient and let Karl sleep as much as he wanted. She said as long as he was eating something, not to fret. He would put the weight back on eventually.

Sonya left feeling much better and she called Dr. Nieman's office right away from her car for the anti-depressants. They called back to say she could pick up some Prozac for him at the pharmacy in an hour. Sonya went to get lunch at Baker's grill. She would say hi to Michelle, who had just gone back at work after her maternity leave. She was leaving baby Ashley with her mother every time she had a shift.

She sat at in a booth for two and ordered a burger. She waved to Michelle across the restaurant and she came over.

"Hey Sonya," they hugged, "what brings you to town today."

"I've just gone to my first caregivers' support meeting."

"How's Karl doing?"

"Honestly, not great, but maybe you should sugar-coat it a little for Clay. I don't want him worrying. Karl just sleeps all day and I just picked up some anti-depressants for him."

"Wow, that sounds a little rough, Sonya. I'm sorry."

"We'll get through it," Sonya wanted to sound strong for Clay's sake. "So how are you adjusting to coming back to work?"

"I was a wreck the first day, leaving Ashley, but it's getting easier.

My mom is excellent with her and they adore each other, so I know she's in good hands. Actually, it's nice to get out and talk to people again. Having a baby can be isolating."

"Well, you look fantastic, Michelle. You've lost all the baby weight and got your shape back. Careful these customers will be hitting on you again." They both smiled.

"I gotta get back to work. Give my love to Karl."

"Okay sweetie. Talk to yah soon."

Sonya ate her burger and picked up the Prozac. When she got home, Dr. Nieman had already spoken to Karl and he didn't make too much of a fuss about taking the new pills. He even apologized to Sonya for being such a burden.

After he swallowed his first pill, she ran her fingers through his hair and told him she loved him. She told him about the support group and how the woman had said it would get easier over time. She reassured him that his fatigue was normal, and his energy and his mood would improve gradually. She felt relieved and he seemed to appreciate how she was struggling.

"You're a fucking saint, woman," said Karl in his gruff way. "I don't know what I'd do without you. I'm sorry I've been such a pain in the ass lately."

"Don't apologize to me for being sick, honey. I know you'd do the same for me in a heartbeat if the tables were turned." She kissed him and hugged him close.

The next few weeks got easier, as Karl's energy did improve, and he started spending parts of the day out of bed and would venture outside more often for some fresh air. Sonya decided to surprise him with an uplifting gift. She went to the local SPCA and chose a rescue dog for him. It was a female golden lab named Willow. She was 4 years old and had a lovely, sweet demeanor. Karl was thrilled and they became instant companions for life. She followed him around the house, and he pet her constantly and gave her too many treats. He didn't have the energy to walk her yet, but that became his ultimate goal. Sonya was thrilled seeing how much he loved her. His face would light up whenever she came close and rubbed up against his leg.

Meanwhile, Talia and Ryan seemed to be having a second honeymoon of sorts. The sex had never been better, as he had become more attentive to her needs. It seemed they were no longer taking each other for granted. Everything felt new and exciting, having been apart for a couple of months. It seems like the right time to make a fresh commitment to each other. They decided to renew their vows at Christmas.

# CHAPTER 40
## LESS GINGER FOR CHRISTMAS

December came and there was fresh snow on the mountains around Taos. It was time to cultivate the ginger. It was all hands-on deck, except of course Karl, who was still recuperating. They moved the sewing machines to the back of the shed and set up the peeling tables, chairs, food processors, the dehydrator, capsule filler, bottles and labeling machine. The plants looked in good shape when, so they moved into the greenhouse and started pulling them out of the soil.

After removing the leaves and washing and drying the roots, they took a coffee break. Then they went back to start peeling and chopping them into chunks for the food processor. Suddenly Sonya stopped working.

She blurted out, "Oh no! What's this?"

Everyone came over to look. There were black spots in the center of the root when she cut it in half. Paul, the botanist, spoke up.

"This black shit right here, it's called bacterial wilt. Any root that looks like this has to be thrown away and this doesn't bode well for the rest of our crop. We either got a bad batch of soil or we didn't aerate the containers enough. I am just wondering how many plants will be affected." Everyone looked devastated.

"Well let's just keep cutting and find out," said Jared, "there's no use worrying about it. What's done is done, I'm afraid."

As they continued working through the roots, they realized that it was the two troughs at the back of the greenhouse that were the culprit because they had reused the soil from last year. They learned the hard way to replace the soil every year. The final batch of capsules was a big disappointment because they had lost a third of their roots. They would only end up earning about three thousand dollars.

Sonya lamented, "I'm so sorry guys. I know this money was slated to pay off Karl's hospital bills."

"It's not your fault," said Andrea, "this was a group effort. We will be okay because Darlene spread out the hospital payments over two years anyhow, so we have time to make it up."

"Thanks Andrea. You're a sweetheart. Maybe we can go to the summer market with you and sell some of our vegetables to make a little extra. We always have way too many cucumbers, zucchini, and apples."

"That's a great idea," said Darlene. "I will help with that, since I'm the one who usually plants the garden in the spring."

"Thank you, Darlene, and all of you. I don't know where Karl and I would be without you. You have really saved his life you know." Sonya started to cry, so they all came over and gave her hugs.

After taking the ginger to market, they were all exhausted. They took a couple of days to rest before setting up to receive Christmas guests. They put up some lights and reindeer at the gate and in front of their four homes. Then they put fresh sheets and decorations in the suite for April's new family, including her new boyfriend Nick and their two children would be flying out in a few days. April and Nick had moved in together at April's house and Nick had sold his home. Krishna was now eight years old and Nick's son, Taylor, was six. The two children got along well, according to April. The kids both spent the weekdays with April and Nick and the weekends with their other respective parents.

When April's family arrived on December twenty-second, Paul and Andrea met them with two vehicles. Everyone hugged and the two men shook hands. Andrea made a fuss over Krishna's new little stepbrother.

"So, you must be Taylor? Krishna has told me so much about you. I hear you like Lego and Captain America, right?"

"Yah, I sent a letter to Santa asking for a Lego space cruiser," Taylor said.

"Wow, that's so exciting. Well, I can't wait to show you our Christmas tree," said Andrea.

"Krishna said we get to sleep in bunk beds. Is that true?"

"Absolutely, did you two already decide who gets to sleep up top?" Andrea asked.

"I am," shouted Taylor. Krishna nodded at her grandma.

"Well, you are very brave," said Andrea. "I hope you like climbing ladders then?"

"I'm not scared," said Taylor.

Andrea drove the kids and Paul took April and Nick back to the house in his truck. Donovan's family was already there to meet them, and he greeted his sister with a big hug, shook Nick's hand, and introduced his wife and baby. April had never met Krishna's new cousin Toby. Clay and Michelle also came by with Ashley. Krishna fussed over Toby, who was now just starting to walk. She wanted to keep picking him up, which made Shawna nervous, especially after Andrea's incident of dropping him and going to Emergency. April had to tell Krishna and Taylor they were not allowed to pick up Toby or Ashley, but they could make funny faces and hold them on their laps sitting down, which the babies loved. They were also excited by the two dogs, Lucy and Willow. There just seemed to be a constant pile of kids and dogs rolling on the carpet throughout the day.

For Christmas Eve dinner, the community also invited Carmen, Marisol, Joaquin and his mother, Graciela and her new boyfriend. They set up two long folding tables in Andrea and Paul's living room and dining room to serve buffet style. All four households pitched in to cook part of the meal in their separate kitchens. Andrea and Paul did the turkey and stuffing. Talia and Ryan did the Brussel sprouts and yams. Darlene and Jared were on mashed potatoes and gravy and Sonya was baking dessert. They had organized a small gift exchange for the adults, but everyone was encouraged to bring a gift for the children.

Everything went according to plan, except that Paul had planned to make a speech before they broke bread and Nick ended up stealing his thunder. Nick stood up and spoke about how grateful he and Taylor were to be welcomed into this new family. He made gushing remarks about how happy he was with April and how excited Taylor was to have a stepsister. Then he invited everyone to toast the chefs and Paul had to hold his tongue, or the food would have gone cold.

Later that night, as the children got tired and grouchy, Nick seemed to be the one disciplining them and telling them to clean up their toys for bed. Andrea couldn't help noticing that he sounded a bit harsh and impatient. She was concerned that her granddaughter was on the receiving end of this man's gruff style of parenting. April didn't seem to mind; she just went along with whatever he said. Andrea was surprised to see her daughter, who had previously dominated Sim with her headstrong ways, now quiet and passive with this new partner. Andrea debated whether or not to say anything or let it go.

When they got into bed that night, she asked Paul about it.

"Honey, have you noticed the way Nick bosses the kids around? He seems kind of harsh to me."

"Yah, I did notice he's a lot more assertive than Sim used to be, that's for sure," said Paul.

"Doesn't it surprise you that Andrea lets him take charge like this? She used to wear the pants in her marriage."

"Well, as long as they have found their own balance and she's happy, I don't really care. It's not like he's laid a hand on Krishna or anything. He is just being a firm disciplinarian, and that's fine by me. That's the kind of father Jared had, and he turned out all right. I'll bet you his bark is worse than his bite."

Andrea felt better upon hearing Paul's perception and decided to let it go. "I guess you're right honey," she said and kissed him goodnight.

Christmas day was quiet. The kids played with their new toys while the adults cleaned up the dinner from the night before. Then they put on The Polar Express movie for the kids and all sat around

Paul and Andrea's living room on couches and cushions. Some of the grown-ups fell asleep during the movie.

Sonya had thawed a batch of chili from her freezer and heated it up in a crock pot with some buns for a simple dinner. Then Jared went out and got the fire pit going for the kids so they could roast marshmallows. Paul played guitar and led them in singing Christmas carols. Even Karl joined them and seemed to be feeling a bit more energetic.

Andrea asked her daughter if she could keep Krishna overnight for some extra Grandma time and Paul offered to sleep on the couch so they could cuddle up together in the big bed. April agreed to this, so Andrea took Krishna to get her toothbrush and nighty and favorite stuffie to sleep with. She asked her to pick a stuffie for Grandma too.

"You can have this tiger. His name is Zuzu."

"Oh, thank you," said Andrea. "That's a great name. How did you come up with it?"

"That's the sound he makes when he purrs," said Krishna, matter-of-factly.

"Oh, I see. He won't bite or scratch me with his big claws while I'm sleeping, will he?"

"No Grandma. He's not really alive, he's a stuffed animal, silly."

Andrea realized that Krishna was growing up fast. As they got ready for bed, Krishna called out to her,

"Grandma, I'm stuck!"

Andrea came running into the bedroom to find her head stuck in her sweater hole, so she pulled it up over her ears gently. As Krishna was lifting her arms, Andrea noticed a mark on her back. It looked like a bruise.

"What happened to your back here darling?"

"Oh, Nick poked me with the corner of my math textbook when I left it on the kitchen table at dinner time."

"Oh, why did he do that?" Andrea asked innocently.

"Because I was supposed to clean off the dinner table and I accidentally left it there. He wanted me to put it away."

All kinds of little alarm bells were going off in Andrea's brain. She decided to push a little harder.

"Does Nick ever spank you?" she asked sweetly.

"Sometimes, if he gets really mad. He did one time when I spilled white glue on my bedroom carpet."

"Did he spank you with his hand?" Andrea asked.

"Yah, it really hurt actually, but he spanks Taylor too, so I guess it's only fair," said Krishna.

"Was mommy home when you got the spanking?"

"No, mommy was at work," she said.

Andrea decided she couldn't ignore this. It was unacceptable. She had to talk to her daughter. She pretended everything was fine for the time being so she could enjoy her sleep-over with her grand-daughter. She read her two bedtime stories, wrapped her arms around her in a protective hug and Krishna fell asleep. As Andrea drifted off, her little brother Michael appeared once again, standing in the doorway staring at her, dragging his blanket behind him.

The next morning, while Krishna was in the bathroom, she told Paul what was on her mind. Now, Paul was also alarmed. He did not like the sound of this grown man spanking his granddaughter any more than his wife did. Andrea would drop Krishna off back at the guest suite and ask to speak with April. Andrea pretended that Paul had a little surprise for her.

"What is dad up to this time?" April asked as they walked back over to her parents' house.

"Oh, nothing much. You'll see dear. I had a lovely time with Krishna last night. She is such a sweetheart. I just adore her."

"I know you do Mom. She adores you too."

They walked in and Paul gave his daughter a hug. They poured her a coffee with Baileys and sat down at the kitchen table.

"So, what's this surprise Dad?" April asked.

"Well honey, your mother and I need to talk to you about something."

"That doesn't sound good," April said.

Andrea took the floor. "Well honey, I noticed a bruise on Krishna's back last night when she was getting changed and she told me that Nick poked her with her math textbook. Then she told me that Nick spanked her while you were at work for spilling glue on her bedroom carpet. Were you aware of all this?"

"You're kidding me, right? No. She told me she got in trouble for the glue thing, but she never mentioned any spanking. What bruise? I never noticed any bruising." Andrea seemed to be in the dark.

"It's on her left side, just under her rib cage. Apparently, he poked her with the textbook to get her to clear the dining table. Look Andrea, all my warning bells are going off at this point. I'm sorry to say this, but Nick sounds like a real asshole to me!"

"He's not an asshole Mom!" She sounded defensive. Paul decided to wade in before the two women got really mad at each other.

"Look April, we know you love this man and you've just moved in together. We are just saying that he should not be laying a hand on Krishna for any reason. It's not okay, in this day and age, to spank your kids anymore. I'm also worried that he might lay a hand on you at some point. I'm your father and I need to protect you."

"It's okay Dad. He would never lay a hand on me. He loves me. I will talk to him about the kids. I know his father was pretty harsh with him growing up, so maybe he's never learned any other way. I will teach him how to set boundaries with the kids without getting physical. We can do time-outs or take away their electronics or TV privileges. I will teach him how to discipline the kids properly."

"Well, I hope it works," said Andrea, "but it's pretty hard to change a cat's stripes this late in the game. If he ever lays a hand on you or Krishna again, you should seriously walk out immediately and call the cops. There are no second chances here, April. You have to be crystal clear in your expectations."

"Maybe counseling would help?" said Paul. "I would feel better about that because then I would know that you have a witness in your corner."

"Oh my god, you guys are blowing this way out of proportion," April was getting frustrated.

"I don't think we are," Paul said firmly. "We are just looking out for your best interests, sweetheart. You know that, right?"

"Yes, I know, but it doesn't make this any easier for me. Shit, he just sold his fucking house so we could be together." She started to cry.

Paul comforted her with a hug, but Andrea kept talking.

"I know you've invested everything into this new relationship, but if it doesn't work out honey, it's better to cut your losses and walk away now than to have it drag on for years. We will support you no matter what."

"Okay Mom, I know you love me, but I will have to work this out for myself. Please, promise me you won't say anything to Nick, or anyone else for that matter. Give us a little time to work through this."

"We promise honey. This will just stay between us three. We won't even tell Donovan."

"Oh god, please don't tell Donovan. He would lose his mind and punch Nick in the head. Please keep this from him, I'm begging you."

"We won't honey, we promise."

"I've gotta get back. We'll see you this afternoon and please act normal. I'm taking this packet of sugar cookies so I can tell my family that this was the surprise. See you later," and Andrea left.

# CHAPTER 41
## RYAN AND TALIA RENEW THEIR VOWS

On Boxing Day, Talia and Ryan's had scheduled their re-commitment ceremony for the afternoon. Everyone gathered in their home at three o'clock for the event.

A local shaman from the Taos Pueblo came to officiate. He started by saging their home and lighting a candle. Then he played a hand drum and blessed their reunion with a prayer in his native Tiwa language. Afterwards, they began reading their vows to each other.

Ryan spoke first.

"Talia, we have been down a long road together and you have always been by my side. You helped me through the darkest year of my car accident. When I lost all hope, you were the one who pulled me out of the darkness. We grew up and sewed our wild oats together and you worked so hard on your dance career until you became widely respected as one of the best videographers in L.A. I always admired your drive and independence. Even though we couldn't have children because of your brother's schizophrenia, you never let it get you down. You always supported me in my work, even when long hours kept me away on building projects. Recently, I have strayed from our marriage and you forgave me and took me back in. I am so grateful for your love in my life. You are the most beautiful woman I have ever met, both outwards and inwards. You make me feel calm and I need your warm presence around me. I want to devote the rest of my life to making you happy."

Everyone smiled and took a deep breath in admiration, as Talia pulled a little folded note from her pocket to read.

"Ryan, you were a little feral and withdrawn when we met. Getting you to open up and talk about your feelings was like getting blood from a stone. It took you a long while to trust in what we had. I felt like I robbed you of having children and when you couldn't adopt Carlos, I could see that you were devastated. I felt guilty about this for a long time, but you always reassured me that it wasn't my fault. I appreciate how you encouraged me in my career and made me feel like your equal partner. We balanced each other out and we loved each other's friends and family and dogs. Recently, I too have strayed from our marriage and learned a lot about myself. We are only on this earth for a short time and you are the one I want to spend the rest of that time with. I want to recommit myself to you today in mind, body, and spirit and move forward with unbreakable trust and unconditional love for each other.

The shaman invited them each to drink, from the same gourd, a sip of water he had brought from the sacred Blue Lake of his pueblo. They decided to exchange handmade beaded necklaces instead of rings, so they placed the necklaces around each other's necks and kissed. Everyone cheered and hugged them in turn and they cracked open the bottle of champagne for a toast.

"To Ryan and Talia!" shouted Jared.

"To Ryan and Talia," they all responded, and drank their champagne. Even the dogs were excited, after coming back inside for the celebration. Their tails were wagging as they sensed the happy mood.

Talia and Ryan thanked the shaman, paid his fee, and offered him a food basket to take home to his family. Then they walked over to Paul and Andrea's place to eat the leftovers from Christmas Eve's turkey dinner.

"Well, you two, we are all really relieved that you decided to stay together. We were worried we would lose one of you to the outside world," said Sonya.

"Yah, and I wouldn't want my brother to leave," said Darlene. "No offense, Talia. You know I love you too."

"None taken." She smiled. "I know that blood is thicker than water."

"So, am I allowed to ask if Jocelyn will still be teaching in your studio?" said Andrea.

"No, she's pretty much done with both of us. She thinks we're manipulative and pathetic and that we have just settled for staying together out of laziness," said Talia.

"Well, that's pretty dismissive," said Paul. "I guess she doesn't understand what all goes into a thirty-five-year marriage."

"Nope, her loss," said Ryan and he kissed Talia on the cheek while she chewed her food.

"Well, I'm glad she's out of the picture, to be honest," said Karl. "I never really liked that woman anyhow."

Sonya laughed. "You're funny, old man. You barely even knew her."

"Well, I know what I like," he winked at her, "and she's not it."

They all laughed. It felt good to release the tension of the past few months, when everyone had been left to wonder what Ryan and Talia were up to. It was an acknowledgement that they had all been walking on eggshells for a while.

"So, is there going to be a honeymoon?" Paul asked.

"Yah, we thought we'd take a motorcycle ride up to Colorado when the weather warms up, just the two of us. We'll find a little log cabin to rent for a long weekend in the spring. There's no rush."

"That sounds lovely," said Andrea. "It will do you good to get away from us for a few days and get some alone time."

"Who is driving April's family to the airport tomorrow?" asked Darlene.

"Both of us," said Paul. "They can't all fit in my car with their bags and besides, Andrea wants to see them off too."

"Well April, you sure have created a nice little family there," said Sonya. Andrea felt like kicking her under the table.

"Yah, it's great that the kids have each other because growing up as an only child sucks," said April. The holidays are so boring without a playmate."

Nick chimed in. "We have thoroughly enjoyed spending this holiday with you all. Thank you so much for your hospitality. This is probably the last time we'll see you all together like this. Children, can you say thank you to our hosts?"

Krishna and Taylor spoke up from the carpet, where they were petting the dogs. "Thank you!"

"You're welcome guys. We are your family, so you're always welcome here, any time," said Jared.

Little did he know that this would be the last time Nick and Taylor would be spending the holidays in Taos.

# CHAPTER 42
## JARED'S MISADVENTURE

After Christmas, Paul took some soil and discarded ginger samples from the ginger crop to a local lab for analysis. They confirmed the problem was bacterial wilt and a local horticulture expert at the garden shop gave him some good advice for next year. He would use some very loamy organic soil and mix in some manure to keep the PH level optimized. He went back home and drilled a bunch more holes in the bottom of the containers for improved drainage. He felt confident that there would be no more black spots next time around.

Andrea decided to call her daughter more often to get updates on how things were going with Nick. She was worried about her granddaughter's safety, but April reassured her that everything was fine. She loved Nick and their life together was happy. Andrea had a hard time feeling relaxed about the situation and her guard was still up. She didn't like the idea of Krishna being alone with Nick, so she told April to make sure that Krishna knew her mother's cell phone number by heart in case she ever needed to call her.

Jared was really enjoying his motorcycle, but it felt too small for him, now that he had been riding for a while. He really wanted a Harley Davidson, so he talked to Darlene about the cost. They agreed that he could probably sell his current bike for a bit of money and get a used Harley fairly reasonably. They asked the group's permission to spend four thousand dollars, and everyone agreed that since Jared had never asked for anything, it was his turn for a perk. He found a local older guy who couldn't ride any more due to back pain and got a great deal. He came home on his new black 2006 1450cc Fat-boy, excited as a kid in a candy store.

When spring came, he decided to go on a day trip down to Santa Fe for his first longer ride. He also agreed to pick up some special fabric for Andrea's baby clothes from a shop there, since he had large enough saddle bags to fit this in. He rigged up an electric vest to keep toasty warm and set out on his ride.

The air was crisp and clean and most of the snow had melted on the local mountains. It very quickly got warmer as he headed south. And he shut off the electric vest in Espanola, where he stopped for lunch at a local tavern called Mile's End Saloon. The place had a lot of character from the outside, with a gunslinger sign that looked a bit like Yosemite Sam above the front door.

He walked in and sat at the counter. The bartender gave him a strange sideways look and said hello.

"Are you new around here or just passing through?"

"Just passing through on my way to Santa Fe. I'll take a clubhouse sandwich with fries and a pint of whatever you have on tap."

"Coming right up," said the bartender and he took his menu and poured him a beer in a frosty mug.

The music on the stereo was Jimmy Buffet and he was practically the only customer in there, except for two old-timers nursing beer with tomato juice who looked like they lived in the place.

Jared was reading the kitchy paper placemat with a local tourist map on it, when three men walked in wearing leather jackets with biker club patches on them that said Vagos Motorcycle Club. He had heard about this gang recently on the news; some story about a shooting involving the rival with the Bandidos gang.

One of the men, who was a large, bald, Mexican American, walked towards him, posturing with attitude. He looked at Jared's bike helmet and leather gloves on the counter.

"You're parked in my spot," he said, looking down his nose at Jared.

"I didn't see any reserved sign out there. It's a free country buddy," said Jared coolly. His past military training gave him the nerve not to just cave to this kind of idiotic bullying.

"It's only free here if you're a member," he said.

"A member of what?" Jared asked.

"You're not Vagos so you're in my spot. Move your bike or I'll move it for you."

"Be my guest," said Jared. "It weighs close to seven hundred pounds so you might need a little help from one of your buddies there."

That was enough to incite this man. Without a moment's hesitation, he punched Jared in the face. He fell off his bar stool and onto the floor.

"Fuck man, what is wrong with you?" Jared said, clutching his now bloody nose in pain. "Fuck, okay, I'll move my bike you maniac."

"I thought you might," said his attacker, who then went to sit down at a table with his friends.

The bartender passed him a handful of napkins to wipe his nose with as Jared slowly got up off the floor. He went outside and thought about what to do next. He had a bad headache and wondered if his nose might be broken. He called Darlene.

"Hi Darlene, I need your help."

"What's wrong Jared? Your voice sounds funny."

"Don't panic, please, but I need you to Google medical clinics in Espanola."

"Why? What's wrong? Are you okay?"

"This asshole Mexican biker just punched me in the face for no damn reason. I think my nose might be broken."

"Oh my god, that's awful. Why don't you call the cops?" said Darlene.

"Are you kidding me? Do you know what kind of repercussions that would have for me, for us Darlene? Think about it. I don't need that in my life right now. I just want to get my nose looked at as soon as possible."

"Okay, okay, hang on, I'm searching...hang on. Okay, there's a Rio

Health Center in town with two doctors available today. They accept walk-in patients. I'm texting you the address right now."

"Thanks honey. I'll call you after I see the doctor."

"Are you sure you're okay to ride over there. Maybe you should call a taxi."

"No, I'll be okay. The bleeding has pretty much stopped now, but I have to get going. Talk to yah soon."

"Okay honey, take care and ride slowly."

He rode slowly over to the clinic and the receptionist took pity on him, so he was seen after just a five-minute wait.

A tall thin male doctor in his fifties came in and seemed very nice. He took one look at Jared and asked what happened. Jared told him he got in a fight. The doctor sensed that this was not a man who was going to overshare, so he got on with the examination. He touched Jared's face and nose and asked him for a pain level between one and ten. He asked how bad his headache was and if his vision or hearing felt impaired. He asked him how long he had been bleeding for. Then he rendered a diagnosis.

"Well, your nose is not bent, and your nasal septum seems to be intact and the bleeding stopped by itself fairly quickly so I'm going to say that it isn't broken. However, we really need to wait a few days for the swelling to go down and then take another look. In the meantime, you need to ice it at least four times a day for fifteen minutes and sleep with extra pillows to stay propped up in case there's any more bleeding or sinus drainage. You will probably get some black bruising around your nose and eyes. Don't be alarmed by that; it's normal. Can you come back and see me on Thursday?"

"Sorry Doc. I live in Taos and I'm heading home as soon as possible. I can go see my regular GP though for a follow-up."

"Okay, here's a prescription for some Tylenol 3's in case the pain gets worse. Just wait here a moment and I'll get you an ice pack and a couple of sample packs of ibuprofen to get you started. Keep taking it every four hours until the swelling goes down."

He left the office and came back with the necessities. Jared put the ice pack on his face and took two of the pills.

"I see your helmet there. Are you riding a motorcycle?"

"Yes Doc."

"Well, I don't think you should be driving anything for twenty-four hours, especially not a motorcycle. You need to rest and ice and stay close to medical treatment to make sure there are no repercussions for the next couple of days. Can you call someone to pick you up?"

Jared felt discouraged. "Yah, I guess so, but it's an hour's drive for them to get here and then what do I do with the bike?" he thought out loud.

"Well, you could book a hotel room here in town, but I'd prefer it if you weren't alone overnight," said the doctor.

"Ok Doc, I'll call the wife and get the ball rolling on that. Is it okay if I sit in your waiting room until she gets here?"

"Sure, that's no problem. In fact, it's a good idea because my nurse at reception can keep an eye on you and freshen up that ice pack when it gets warm."

"Thanks Doc."

Jared went outside for a private conversation with Darlene. They decided that Ryan would come with Paul in the truck and bring some boards to brace the front wheel and tie-downs for the bike. The two of them could load the bike into the box of the truck and bring him home. Jared reminded them to tell Andrea to get her fabric delivered by FedEx.

Jared sat and nursed his wounds and got loads of sympathy and attention from the nurse, who was a real talker. He just wanted to close his eyes and sleep in the chair, but she wouldn't shut up.

Finally, he was thrilled to see his friends arrive. He asked them if they could get him something to eat before heading back because he was starving. They went to a drive-through hamburger joint and ate in the truck on the drive home. Paul and Ryan asked him how he got messed up with a motorcycle gang and Jared just kept saying that he did nothing to provoke the guy. He was simply in the wrong place at the wrong time. They felt really sorry for him and imagined that his ego was hurt, since he had done military service and was a pretty tough guy in his own right. Jared kept insisting that he was coldcocked and there was nothing he could have done differently. He said that any retaliation would have just made things ten times worse, especially since he was with two other men from an organized gang.

"I do not have a death wish," were his final words before he fell asleep on Ryan's shoulder on the ride home.

# CHAPTER 43
## ANDREA'S HUNCH

In March, Jared's nose had healed up nicely and the yellow flowers were starting to bloom across the Golden Land once again. Sonya was helping Darlene plan out their vegetable garden for market purposes. Darlene had saved a lot of seeds from last year's crop, but they needed to drive into the nursery for a few others. They decided to try a different kind of cucumber that doesn't need peeling and Darlene felt confident that her tomatoes were big enough to sell if they planted more of them. They asked Jared and Ryan to build them a dedicated tomato trough along the sunniest side of Darlene's house. Then they asked Paul to hammer in a lightweight six-foot trellis for runner beans and then they hung some netting diagonally over the beds to keep the rabbits out.

Andrea was sewing in the shed with Carmen and Marisol when she got a call from April.

"Hi sweetheart. What a nice surprise. How are you doing?"

"Bad," said April, "I'm having a really shitty day Mom."

"Why? What's going on honey? Are you okay?"

"No, I'm not okay. You were right about Nick. He's an asshole and I don't know what to do right now."

"Why, what's happened?" Andrea asked.

"I just got home from work and the babysitter left. I told Taylor to get changed for baseball practice and when he took off his shirt, he was covered in bruises all over his back. When I asked him what happened, he said his dad got mad at him for scratching the back of his car with his bike. I took a few photos of the bruises. I told him it was just to make sure they healed up properly. I am freaking out right now. What should I do?"

"Oh my god, I'm so sorry honey, but you need to call the police and report him."

"I'm scared Mom," she started to cry, "what will happen to him if I call?"

"Well, I hope they will arrest him!" said Andrea. "He's beating your children. You can't stand by this man anymore, April. He's a monster!"

"Okay, okay, I know you're right. It's just all happening so fast. The kids are in the other room and I have to explain to them what is happening right now if we're not going to baseball. What should I say?"

"Tell them you just got a call and baseball has been canceled because the coach is sick. Then you need to get them out of the house, in case he comes home. Take them anywhere, like to McDonald's for dinner and ask the cop to meet you in the parking lot there discreetly while the kids are eating. You can pretend the cop is an old friend of yours from high school if the kids ask. Then you can wait for the cops to tell you he's been picked up before you go back home."

"Ok, thanks Mom, that's a good plan. I'm going to do that now. I'll call you later when it's all done."

"Good luck honey. Stay strong. Those kids need you right now. Talk to you soon."

She hung up and explained to Carmen and Marisol what was happening. The two women each gave Andrea a big hug and told her what a good mother she was. They said she was brave and reassured her that she had given April the best advice. Then they left because it was the end of their workday.

Andrea went to tell Paul what was going on. She was a nervous wreck. Paul was furious.

"I'm gonna kill that bastard the next time I see him!"

"I don't think we will ever see him again dear," said Andrea. "This should be the end of it."

"It had better be the end of it, or I will fly out there and drag April and Krishna out of that house myself if I have to."

"It's her house, Paul. He's the one who needs to leave. Oh my god, I forgot to tell April to call Taylor's mom. I guess she will figure that out after Nick's arrested."

Paul nuked some left-overs for dinner, but they couldn't really eat. They were too anxious.

Finally, the phone rang and Andrea answered it.

"Hello April? What's happening?"

"Well, I did it. They arrested Paul right in the driveway in front of the neighbors, apparently. I haven't really had time to explain to the kids what's going on. I just told Taylor that I wasn't feeling well, so his mom took them for the night and she's going to drop them off at school tomorrow. We had a quick conversation on the phone, and she had no idea this abuse was happening and she's in shock right now. I told her we would talk to the kids together after we see what the cops say. I have to go down to the station right now and fill out a form. Then Child Protection Services are coming over to talk to me at the house first thing tomorrow morning."

"Good job April. I'm proud of you. That took a lot of guts, but you did the right thing."

"Do you think so Mom?" she was crying again, "It feels so awful. What if he goes to jail?"

"Well, that's out of your hands now. You need to focus on taking care of yourself and the kids right now and that's the only thing that's important. Hang on April, your dad wants to talk to you."

"Hi honey, are you okay?"

"Yah Dad, I'm fine, just a little shaky. I'm going to drink a glass of wine and eat something to calm down. "

"Good idea. Look April, you have absolutely done the right thing here. Do not feel guilty about this. He's an asshole and he doesn't deserve you. He doesn't deserve to even see his son, probably not for a long time, until he gets his shit together," said Paul.

"Yah, I know Dad. Child Protection Services is coming tomorrow morning. They will guide me through the process. Don't worry Dad, I know it was the right thing to do. I can't live my life in fear for Krishna and Taylor's safety."

"He would have probably ended up hitting you too sweetheart. It was just a matter of time," said Paul.

"I know Dad, you're right. Look, I'm exhausted. I'll call you guys tomorrow when I know more, okay?"

"Okay sweetie, go and have a good rest. We love you."

"I love you guys too. Good night."

The next morning, a very efficient and neatly dressed black woman named Celia Tucker came to the house. She was surprised the children were not present when she arrived.

"They slept at his ex-wife's house. I didn't want to expose them to this conversation until we came up with a plan on the best way to tell them what's going on."

"Okay, I totally understand. We will arrange to have someone from our counseling department to be present and assist you with that. Here is their card. You can call them to set up an appointment with the children as soon as I leave. They guarantee a short wait time of no more than three days. In the meantime, can you tell the children that daddy has gone on a business trip?"

"I suppose so. Can his ex-wife come to the appointment as well? We all need to be on the same page."

"Of course. That is absolutely the best way to go. Most families don't get along well enough to make that happen, so kudos to you," said Celia.

"What about their teachers? Should I tell the school what's going on?"

"Yes, that is a good idea because there's sure to be some emotional fallout for a while and the children may not perform in their usual manner. If you wish, the counselor can talk to the school on your behalf. It's completely up to you."

"I think I'd rather tell them myself because Donna and I, that's his ex, need to work out a schedule first. Do you think it's better if the two kids stay with their own moms right now or should the kids stay together to support each other?"

"Those are questions for the counselor. I suggest you start writing these thoughts in a notebook because your mind will be racing for a few days and you might forget things. Usually there's an emotional letdown after the first couple of days and you will feel exhausted. See if you can book time off work at the end of the week for this."

Celia guided April through all the steps, including changing the locks on the house and arranging with her office a supervised time for Nick to collect his stuff once he got released on bail. Suddenly, everything started sinking in for April. There would be nothing normal about this break-up. There would be no conversation with Nick about what went wrong or what was fair in dividing up their assets. It would be police and lawyers all the way through. She would never feel his kiss, or his hard body pressed against her ever again. It was over.

After Celia left, Andrea got a call from her daughter. She could hear the sadness and finality in her voice and felt bad for her.

"I'm sorry about all this April. This is not your fault, and this is not the happy ending you deserve," said Andrea.

"Thanks Mom. It's just awful. I feel like such an idiot for not believing you when Krishna had that bruise back at Christmas time. I feel like a bad mother. What if Krishna doesn't trust me any more to confide in? I feel like I let her down big time," she started to cry.

"She'll be fine. Kids are resilient. You are doing everything correctly right now to make sure the kids feel safe and protected. The counselor will help you make sure the kids get back on track. Try not to worry darling."

"Okay Mom, I will try. I've gotta go pick them up from school. I'll talk to yah later."

"Bye sweetheart. Call us any time, day or night," said Andrea.

Nick was given a thirty-day sentence, one year's probation and a restraining order to stay away from April, Krishna, Donna and Taylor during that year. He would be allowed weekly supervised visits with his son in a public space during that time, but his relationship with April and Krishna was officially over. Paul and Andrea were so relieved.

# CHAPTER 44
## THE TRIP

In the spring, good things started to happen to the Golden Land community. The marijuana and vegetable plants were starting to sprout, Talia's yoga and Kirtan classes were going well, even though Jocelyn had poached a few members who were friends of hers. Clay and Michelle announced they were pregnant with their second child. Ryan and Talia were together again and seemed really happy. Karl's energy had improved, and he was up and about. The doctor announced that his cancer was in remission and they threw a dinner party to celebrate.

At the end of April, they decided to take a little trip as a group now that everyone was healthy. Darlene found a great deal for a week in Turks and Caicos. They left Clay in charge of the property and the dogs and flew out via Miami. They booked four adjacent rooms for the four couples at an all-inclusive resort and planned on relaxing and drinking cocktails by the pool.

When they arrived, the beach was even more spectacular than they thought. The water was crystal blue, and the sand was soft and white. They made a beeline for the loungers that were shaded by palm trees and brought down a pitcher of margaritas to share. They all slathered their white skin in fifty SPF sunscreen, except for Talia, who was naturally brown. They lamented their old, wrinkled bodies for the first few minutes and then quickly realized that almost everyone there was retired and looked just as saggy as they did.

They ate delicious fresh seafood at the buffet, went on a boat ride and snorkeling excursion, danced to salsa music, made love and napped whenever they felt like it, and generally had the most wonderful vacation. The worst thing that happened all week is that Sonya got a jellyfish sting on her foot. The hotel doctor rinsed it with vinegar and gave her a Benadryl tablet and some topical cream to stop the itching and pain. It felt better already the next morning.

When they got home, there was more good news. Donovan and Shawna were also pregnant with their second child and Paul and Andrea were over the moon. Andrea secretly hoped it would be a girl so she could dress her up in the little outfits she made and spoil her rotten. Shawna announced that her parents and sister Jade would fly out again after the baby was born and this sent Clay into a secret panic. What if Jade told Michelle about their one-time sexual encounter? It would destroy her. He would be stuck worrying about this for the next nine months.

One morning, out of the blue, Andrea got an email from Kid Design magazine. They wanted to feature her baby clothes in their publication. She was thrilled and called them right away to sort out the details. Two weeks later, a photographer and journalist came out to the property to shoot the article. They had asked for two babies to model the clothing, one boy and one girl so naturally Andrea asked Michelle and Shawna to bring over Toby and Ashley. The two moms were excited to see their babies as models in a national magazine. Aside from one ten-minute crying jag, they got the photos they needed. The article would be featured in the June issue.

This extra attention brought in multiple orders that summer and left Andrea feeling quite overwhelmed. She asked Carmen and Marisol if they knew another seamstress and they brought in their cousin Liliana to help sew. Andrea had to buy a fourth sewing machine to make this work, but the investment proved worthwhile. She also received a ton of positive feedback via email and Twitter. It was an exciting time.

Paul, Darlene and Jared helped with the packaging, labeling and shipping of the clothing. There was good money coming into Andrea's business PayPal account and she was looking forward to helping her son so he could take some time off to spend with the new baby in the fall. That was her plan, until Darlene approached her to help pay off the rest of Karl's hospital bills. This created some tension between them, but Andrea finally agreed that this was more important for the community in the long run. Donovan would have to return to work after his usual two-week parental leave.

April was doing better, and her lawyer had settled her separation from Nick quite quickly, since they had kept their bank accounts and home ownership separate. She was relieved to be moving on with her life. Krishna had adjusted fairly easily to their former version of normal, which was living in her own house with mommy and visiting Sim on weekends. April had arranged with Donna to have a playdate with Taylor occasionally, but that soon fizzled out because Krishna was getting older and didn't really want to spend time with a younger boy anymore. April was relieved because she really didn't want to hear about Nick from Taylor's mom either.

Sonya had stepped in to help out Talia with her Kirtan classes by playing the drum rhythmically while Talia led the movements and chanting. The group was still mostly older women, but they had recruited a younger couple from down the road and a man named Hal from the seniors center who had traveled through Nepal and India when he was younger. The group was really friendly and would organize a pot-luck lunch after class once a month. One time, Hal brought his old clunky slide projector from the seventies and showed them slides from his travels. It was great fun to see him so young and handsome, hiking and visiting temples.

Jared and Ryan continued riding their motorcycles and Talia and Sonya would join them occasionally on the back. They would take day trips around Taos and up to southern Colorado, have lunch in a pub and ride back. They met other nice motorcyclists along the way at rest stops and gas stations and would occasionally ride with them to the next town and share a beer. It was always a fun diversion.

The pot crop was growing tall, as they cruised through the summer.

One night the alarm sounded on the greenhouse door and Paul and Jared ran outside in their bathrobes to see what the commotion was. They found a bear had dumped over the garbage containers against the door, which had triggered the alarm. He had his head inside there because Clay had dumped some fast-food containers when he visited that day. They shooed off the bear and Karl had to read Clay the riot act about tying up his garbage.

The big news came when Andrea received a phone call one morning from a large retail box store. They were interested in buying out her business, with all her designs and patterns, and mass producing her line of baby clothes. They offered her fifty thousand dollars. She had no idea how to respond. She called the group together at her place after dinner to discuss the offer.

"Wow, how exciting to be recognized on this scale!" said Darlene. "That magazine really got you some big exposure."

"Yah, I mean I'm flattered and all, but I love my little business and I'm not sure I want to give it up," said Andrea.

"You have been complaining that your hands are aching at the end of the day," said Paul. "Maybe it's time?"

"Yah, that's true," said Andrea, "but what about Carmen and Marisol? They rely on this income to help support their families."

"You can't think about that," said Jared, "it's your business and you have to make the decision that's right for you."

"How much does your business bring in per year?" asked Karl.

"About fifteen thousand," said Andrea.

"Wow, that's not chicken scratch. Darlene, do you think we will be okay without this money coming in?"

"Yes, we should be fine. I knew Andrea couldn't do this forever because it's a physically demanding activity, so I always budgeted accordingly."

Paul and Jared had taken over signing their accounts for the year Dalene was on probation, but she was always the brains behind the operation, advising them how to invest their money. Now she was back to having full signing authority. She gave her final verdict to Andrea.

"I think it's a good offer and you should take it. This money may never come again. They are offering you a little more than three years profit, which is typical for a small business buyout, and you don't have to do any of the work. They don't want your equipment, so if you want to do something nice for Carmen and Marisol, you can give them your two sewing machines as a gift to use as they see fit, but they need to sign a nondisclosure agreement not to use your patterns."

"That's a good idea," said Andrea, "then they could make and sell their own clothes to make extra money. Maybe Liliana can stay on and help them to continue."

"Okay, so it's settled then?" asked Andrea.

Karl spoke up. "You will need to hire a lawyer to represent you in signing the deal. He or she will read over the terms and confirm that everything is legit. I know a guy in town who is great."

"Right, thanks Karl. I forgot about the lawyer part. Well, I guess it's decided then. Should I call them back right now and accept the offer?"

"Just tell them that tentatively it's a yes, but you need your lawyer to read the terms first. They can fax it over to him," said Jared.

"Wow, this is exciting honey! We should celebrate tonight. Let's go to Marshall's Steakhouse for dinner, my treat," said Paul.

"No Paul, I need a day to talk to Carmen and Marisol. I'm worried they might get upset. Besides, if we are going out for supper, they have to be included anyhow. I will let you know what day works for them later this week."

"Okay sweetheart. That sounds good." He gave her a big hug. "Congratulations, you are officially retired for the second time."

"Thanks honey and thank you everyone for helping me with this decision. It's not easy, but I know it's good timing. I appreciate all your support." said Andrea.

"Well thank you Andrea, for working so hard to bring in extra income for us these past few years. You are really a creative genius," said Sonya.

They all gave her hugs and she started to cry. Her tears marked the ending of a special part of her life.

# CHAPTER 45
## ANDREA FORGETS

One morning, at the end of August, Paul came running into Jared and Darlene's place, where Andrea was having coffee.

"The plants are fucked! The leaves have this white coating on them. Our whole crop is fucked!"

They all went out to take a look. Sure enough, the leaves had turned white with some kind of residue.

"What is it?" Jared asked.

Paul recognized the issue from his horticultural research.

"It's called powdery mildew. We either overwatered them or the dehumidifier stopped working and it got too humid in here. Either way, we have lost our crop, god damn it!"

Darlene tried to comfort him. "Well, it's a good thing Andrea just sold her business. That money will more than make up for this loss."

"I'm so sorry honey," Andrea gave him a hug.

Jared was checking the dehumidifier. "Here's the problem, he said. The filter light is on, so it needs changing and the settings are all out of whack because of it. I thought you put in a new filter at the start of the season?"

Paul took responsibility. "I must have forgotten. This is totally my fault."

"It doesn't matter whose fault it is bro," said Jared, "this is a team effort. I should have double checked it myself."

"Well let's go tell the others. Jared and Paul, you go to Ryan and Talia's place and Andrea and I will tell Karl and Sonya," said Darlene. "We'll see you for lunch in thirty."

They all went and shared the news, and everyone felt dejected for the rest of the day. It felt like a real failure and loss. That night they gathered at the fire pit to drown their sorrows and commiserate. They all slept in late the following day.

When Paul woke up, he went into the kitchen and was surprised to find that Andrea had pulled out her files from the bottom drawer of her desk and was sitting on the living room floor going through them. He poured himself a cup of coffee.

"What'cha doing there, honey?" he asked his wife.

"I'm looking for a photo of Krishna and Sim together. I thought I might paint a portrait of them as a Christmas gift for April."

"Really? Do you really think that's something April would want?"

"Why not? I would love to have a picture of you and April together," she said.

"But we're not divorced," said Paul.

"Oh right. Never mind," she started putting the folders away.

Paul thought this whole conversation was really odd, but he put it out of his mind.

Two days later, Andrea was hunting around for her car keys.

"They're right here on the hook by the door where they always are sweetheart," he said, handing them to her.

"Oh right. Thanks sweetheart," she said, and she kissed him goodbye to go get some groceries.

When she got to the store, she had forgotten her list, so she phoned Paul.

"I think I left my shopping list on the counter. Can you read it to me please?"

"Sure honey, I see it now. It says: bread, milk, eggs, cheese, pork chops, salsa and bananas."

"Ok thanks. Gotta go." She hung up.

An hour later, she came home with only three items: bread, milk and cheese.

Paul was getting concerned. He started noticing a pattern of dishes left around the house, whereas the wife he knew was extremely tidy and would always put his plates in the dishwasher. He also found laundry that had been sitting in the washer, but never dried. He found the coffee cream left out on the counter and the lid left off the toothpaste. One time, she said she was going to Sonya's but then Sonya texted him asking where she was. They found her in the shed, sorting through her old bolts of fabric.

He confided in Darlene and Jared.

"There's something wrong with Andrea's memory. I'm really getting worried. What if it's Alzheimer's like her mother had?"

"God, she's only sixty-three," said Darlene, "I really doubt it. Maybe it's just the change of routine with her not working anymore? Or it could be a hormone imbalance. That affects a lot of women our age," she tried to reassure him.

Jared spoke calmly," You need to take her for a physical and tell the doctor what you have noticed. Maybe you can talk to the doctor ahead of time, so you don't have to tell him in front of Andrea."

"That's a good idea," said Paul, "but how do I get her to agree to go in the first place?"

"Tell her the doctor's office called you to remind you that she's due for her annual physical. If her memory isn't good, then she won't remember the last time she had one," said Darlene.

"Okay, that's smart. I like that idea. Thanks guys. I'll let you know how it goes."

Paul went outside and called the doctor's office. The doctor phoned him back and Paul explained what he had been noticing.

"Well, I can give her the Folstein test, which is a questionnaire. If she scores low on this, I will refer her to the neurologist at the hospital. He will send her for a CT scan, which could show a loss of brain mass associated with Alzheimer's, but it could also rule out tumors, stroke or any brain bleed that might have the same symptoms."

"Ok Doc, can you please do that 30 question test you mentioned, but please don't tell Andrea why you're doing it. I don't want to upset her."

"That's fine Paul, I'll just say it's a routine part of my physical for anyone over sixty."

"Thanks Doc, you're the best."

When Andrea did the doctor's test the following week, she scored twenty-two out of thirty, which indicates mild dementia. He told her he was a little concerned that she may have suffered a mild stroke. She was shocked and wondered how she could have missed such an event. The doctor told her that it may have happened in her sleep and she wouldn't have even noticed. He just wanted to make sure her brain was healthy, so he referred her for the scan.

As Andrea lay on the CT scanner bed, her little brother Michael appeared to her with his big-eyed stare. She felt safe whenever he showed up. She smiled and focused on him and this helped her to stay very still through the procedure.

Unfortunately, the scan was inconclusive, but the brain measurements would be compared a year later to see if there was any change. They asked Paul to keep a journal of everything he noticed as a memory lapse. He wondered how he was going to do this without Andrea noticing, and decided to keep it in his phone. He was also worried she might wander off, lose her way driving, or leave the stove on. He had to be extra vigilant, so he called on everyone in the group to help him and to be discrete about it.

He also faced the unpleasant task of telling his children. He stopped by Donovan's place to deliver a toy for Toby and broke the news as gently as he could. Donovan took it really hard and started to cry. Shawna comforted him and thankfully Toby was oblivious, playing with his new Tonka truck.

They realized that the hardest part was going to be running interference between Grandma Andrea and this new baby that was coming. She would want to babysit, and he couldn't let her do this alone. He decided that he would always babysit with her, by telling her that he wanted to spend time playing with Toby while she cuddled the new baby. He would keep an eye on all of them. This whole scenario worried Shawna, but she agreed and said she would make up excuses to keep their babysitting to a minimum. She might even hire a sitter if necessary. Paul thanked her for understanding, hugged his son, and left.

When he phoned April, she was more stoic. She offered to take time off and fly out to help with her mom, but Paul said he was fine for the moment. He would let her know if it came to that. She said she would bring Krishna out a Christmas again to spend time with Grandma while she was still healthy enough to remember everything. This idea upset Paul and he had to end the call. April could hear his voice breaking as he said good-bye.

The next few months were really hard for Paul, but he was grateful to have his six best friends there to support him. They would text him whenever they noticed something Andrea did that seemed out of the ordinary and he would add it to his log. He would go with her whenever she drove someplace or would ask one of the others to accompany her. Andrea seemed none the wiser to all their secret efforts. She was happily oblivious to her own unraveling.

# CHAPTER 46
## BEGINNINGS AND ENDINGS

In the fall of that year, Clay and Michelle gave birth to their second daughter, a baby called Isabelle. Karl was a great-grandpa once again and there was much good cheer and gift giving all around. Andrea gave her some left-over inventory of little outfits she had made. Karl built her a cedar blanket box and Michelle's family bought them a deep freeze for their groceries. Clay's plumbing business was going well, so they moved into a larger townhouse to accommodate the extra little person in their lives.

Andrea was doing fairly well, all things considered. Her memory lapses were still quite benign, such as losing her cell phone or putting the milk in the cupboard instead of the fridge. Her friends kept a watchful eye on her to make sure nothing bad happened. Paul did everything in his power to protect her from feeling inadequate. He loved her more than life itself, so that was simply a labor of love for him. In his eyes, she was as beautiful as the first day they met. Even though her long blonde hair had turned completely white and she'd naturally gained a few pounds and a few wrinkles, she still moved as gracefully as when they worked side by side on the pot farm in northern California.

In November, the second addition to their community was born early. Donovan and Shawna had a second boy called Dylan. Paul was relieved that it was a boy because he didn't want Andrea to get overly involved with a baby girl while her memory was slipping. Paul looked forward to having these two little buddies to pull around the yard in a trailer behind his ATV. He wanted to get them little dirt bikes and fishing rods and teach them how to camp out and live off the land. Of course, he would need Donovan to come too because realistically, he wouldn't have the energy at sixty-four to run after them all day, but he liked to think he did.

When Shawna's family flew out to see the baby, there was no mention of Clay's infidelity three years back, or at least he never heard anything. He was so relieved. Life carried on as normal and he and Michelle truly loved each other. He had learned his lesson the hard way to never be so irresponsible again. He had been terrified of losing her for the past three years.

In December, the ginger crop was harvested again, and it was healthy this year. They made close to five thousand dollars from it and felt relieved. At Christmas, there was a pile of babies and toddlers around and April and Krishna also flew out. Their big cousin Krishna helped out a lot by playing with the babies and feeding them. She loved taking on the role of babysitter while she visited, even though she was only ten, and got loads of praise from the two young mothers.

April was doing better. She was still single, by choice, having sworn off men after her bad experience with Nick. She was focused on her career and her daughter and they were very happy. She had received a promotion at work and was now a project manager at Cisco, earning great money. She wanted to do something nice for her parents while her mom was still able to enjoy it. She bought them two tickets to Barbados for the month of February. They were shocked and thrilled.

"Wow honey, are you sure you can afford such a lavish gift?"

"Yes Mom, it's no big deal. You guys totally deserve it. I want you to go and have the time of your lives." She gave her mother a big hug.

"Well thank you, darling. You are the best daughter in the world. We are so lucky to have you."

Donovan chimed in, "Way to go sis. You're making me look like a real chump over here." They both laughed.

After all the business of Christmas visitors, everyone was tired. It took a few days to recuperate from all the entertaining and clean up the mess. A week later, everyone was back to normal, except for Karl, who was still sleeping in late every day. Sonya started to worry about him. She confided in Talia.

"I'm worried about Karl. He is sleeping really late every morning. It's not like him. He is usually up bright and early. Do you think I should take him to the doctor? I'm scared what the results might be."

"Well, why don't you just ask him how he's feeling and see where the conversation goes. He will probably admit that he is worried himself. Then you can reassure him that he might just be iron-deficient or something simple like that and not to jump to conclusions. That's what I would say to you too, by the way," Talia said.

"Yah, I guess you're right. It could be something as simple as a virus I suppose, but you can't blame me for thinking the worst. It's only natural, given what he's been through right?" asked Sonya.

"Of course. I totally understand that. If Ryan had cancer, I would be worried all the time too." Talia gave her a hug, "Let's try to stay positive, for Karl's sake."

So, Sonya went back home to bring Karl a cup of coffee and gently wake him up. She sat on the edge of the bed and looked at the deep lines in his face. His long grey hair was pulled back in a neat ponytail and even his moustache was totally grey now. He had definitely aged in the last couple of years.

"Hey sweetheart, I brought you a coffee. It's almost eleven o'clock. You've had quite a sleep." She kissed his face and he yawned and stretched.

"Eleven o'clock? Holy shit, I don't know what's wrong with me lately. I'm just so tired all the time." He sat up and sipped the coffee.

"Well, maybe we should go see the doc again. You could just be iron deficient or something simple like that."

"Yah, I suppose you're right. I have thought about it lately, but honestly Sonya, I'm scared. I don't think I could handle that radiation treatment again. It was awful."

"I know honey, I know. I'm scared too but putting off the check-up could be dangerous. We don't want to wait if you do need some kind of treatment again. It doesn't necessarily have to be radiation. It could just be a surgery," she said.

"Or it could be worse. It could be chemotherapy," said Karl.

"I have been reading about chemo lately," said Sonya. "There are plenty of people who don't get the terrible side-effects like nausea and hair loss. They have more effective anti-nausea drugs now than they used to."

"It's okay sweetie, you don't need to put lipstick on this pig. I'm a big boy and I can handle the truth. I will make an appointment today. I don't want you worrying either," said Karl.

"We will figure this out together," said Sonya, giving him a hug. "I will be right there beside you the whole way."

"Thanks, I know you've got my back," he kissed her, "now get out of my way woman, I've got to pee."

They went to the doctor's and he did the dreaded finger exam and blood work first. His PSA score was high again, so the doc sent back to the urologist at the hospital for another core biopsy. The results did show some cancerous cells, but not too many, so the oncologist recommended a surgery called laser ablation to remove only the affected cells. Karl was so relieved that he wouldn't have to go through radiation again or the dreaded chemo, but he would have to go to the bigger hospital in Albuquerque for the surgery with a laser specialist. He was scheduled in for four weeks later.

Sonya and Karl explained the surgery to their community, and everyone offered to help out. Ryan and Talia would take Willow for the week because she and Lucy were best fur friends anyhow. Andrea would step in to play the drum for Sonya at Kirtan class. Darlene and Jared would take over Karl and Sonya's duties in the greenhouse and Paul would water their house plants and get their mail.

In the meantime, Paul and Andrea took their trip to Barbados. They stayed in a small chalet on the beach with an incredible ocean view and personalized room service. A lovely man named Tino brought them cocktails on the veranda and plates of ceviche whenever they called. April had included a couple's massage in the gift, and they were spoiled by two women rubbing scented oils on the bodies to the sound of the waves gently rolling into the shore. It was the most decadent thing they had ever done. They tried out a two-seater kayak and went on a snorkeling excursion to a small island offshore. The boat staff made them a fresh fish lunch afterwards and they danced on the deck to salsa music with the ten other guests. They made love to candlelight in the evening breeze with the chalet windows wide open. It was a magical holiday that felt like a second honeymoon.

Back at home, when the time came for Karl's surgery, Sonya booked a hotel room and drove him to Albuquerque. They checked in and he began fasting for the surgery the following morning. A catheter would be inserted to help with urinary function afterwards and he would stay overnight to monitor this. Then he could go home and rest for a few weeks, avoiding sex or any strenuous activity. Sonya kissed him goodbye as they took him in and promised she would see him soon in the recovery room.

She went and grabbed something to eat because she was starving, after not wanting to eat in front of him that morning. She found the cafeteria downstairs, which was bustling with doctors and nurses having their morning coffee break. She admired the casual routine of these extraordinary humans, who saved people's lives every day. She wished she had that kind of wisdom and strength.

She thought about her own work, which was acting, dancing and comedy. It suddenly felt so trivial to her and she longed to accomplish something more useful, but what was she good at?

She reflected on the community and how wonderful it had been living these past few years with her group of friends. Why didn't more people do this? The benefits were so obvious to her.

She realized, in that moment, that she wanted to share their story with the world. Then maybe others could see the value in what they had created. She thought about Karl and their current circumstance and how much easier it was to leave home knowing that everything would be taken care of while they were gone. She thought of Andrea, with her memory problems, and how they all looked out for her to make sure she was safe and supported. None of this would be possible without their communal living arrangement.

She decided she wanted to write the story of their lives together, but she wondered if she was a good enough writer. She enjoyed journaling and she had had boxes of journals stowed away that she had written throughout her life. She could always pay an editor to read her work and make corrections for her before approaching a publisher. In fact, she knew that self-publishing was an option nowadays, so she really didn't need anyone else's approval to tell her story. The more she thought about it, the more she became determined to undertake the project. She wanted the world to know how wonderful their lives could be if they shared their space with other people.

She looked at her watch and realized that Karl would be in the recovery room by now. She went quickly upstairs and found him, groggy but okay. She kissed him, took his hand and told him she loved him. He smiled and fell back asleep. They moved him upstairs to his overnight room and she placed his small bag of belongings in the locker provided. She asked the nurse to tell him that his cell phone was in there and to call her when he woke up and she would come back.

She went for a long walk outside to get some air. It was a beautiful, yet cold day in Albuquerque. As she walked, she planned out the story she would tell in her mind, beginning with their migration from California, building their homes and settling in. She never expected to meet the love of her life so quickly, but there he was. He was literally part of the new scenery, hooking up their well as they moved in. She appreciated how lucky she was to find him.

She remembered her initial connection to Clay and how she felt like the surrogate mother he never had. She recalled how young and tentative he was, meeting his first girlfriend and learning his career. Then she recalled all the wonderful gatherings they had created over many holidays and life changing events, with children, grandchildren and great-grand-children. Sure, there had been a few bumps along the road, like Ryan's infidelity and Karl's cancer, but overall, they were happy years. Even their small business endeavors had brought them joy, working with their hands in the soil to produce something worthwhile. Yes, she would write their story because it was unique. She thought of Andrea and was determined to tell her part, knowing that soon, she wouldn't be able to speak for herself.

Suddenly, Sonya's phone rang and startled her back to the present. It was Karl and he was fully awake and wanted a coffee and a danish. She said she'd walk back and pick one up along the way. She turned and strolled back towards the hospital, excited to tell him about her new writing project. It would become the book that would tell the story of their lives together.

# ABOUT THE AUTHOR

Naomi P Lane was born in England but grew up in the suburbs of Vancouver Canada. She's married to a wonderful man named Chris and they have two very nice adult children and one very spoiled rescue cat. She was a French Immersion and Special Education teacher for thirty years. Now, recently retired, she devotes most of her time to writing. She enjoys nature walks, yoga, playing guitar, listening to world music, and collaborating with several writers' groups. She also has a weekly blog called The Friday Blog, which you can follow at: naomiplane.com where all her social media links can be found.

Her first book is called The Ultimate Cat: A Baby-Boomer's Guide to Retirement. It's a humorous autobiographical account of when she and her husband were transitioning from working life and elder care into retirement, when we suddenly look at each other in disbelief. She wrote the book to help others who are approaching retirement with the many hurdles of this monumental transition.

Her second book, a novel called The Ordinary Life of Nadia Lewis, was recently released by Olympia Publishing of London. It tells the story of Nadia Lewis and her closest female friend Susan, from childhood through all the stages of their lives. In adulthood, an incident of harm between the women's children rocks their social circle to the core. As she gets older, Nadia wishes to rebuild her broken friendships. She revisits past emotional wounds and works towards mutual understanding of what transpired all those years before and how it affected all the players.

*Both titles are available in hardcopy and e-book format.

CPSIA information can be obtained
at www.ICGtesting.com
Printed in the USA
LVHW110115230621
690870LV00004B/214

9 781777 660208